559-7032

MAJA HADERLAP

ANGEL OF OBLIVION

Translated from the German by Tess Lewis

archipelago books

First published as *Engel des Vergessens*, 2012 Wallstein Verlag

Archipelago Books
232 Third Street # A111
Brooklyn, NY 11215
www.archipelagobooks.org

Library of Congress Cataloging-in-Publication Data
Haderlap, Maja, 1961- author. | Lewis, Tess, translator.
Angel of oblivion / Maja Haderlap ; translated by Tess Lewis.
Other titles: Engel des Vergessens. English
First Archipelago Books edition. | Brooklyn, NY : Archipelago, 2016.
LCCN 2016017961 (print) | LCCN 2016019684 (ebook) |
ISBN 9780914671466 (paperback) | ISBN 9780914671473 (E-book)

Distributed by Penguin Random House
www.penguinrandomhouse.com

Cover art: *The Angel Troubling the Pool* by Joseph Mallord William Turner

Archipelago Books is grateful for the generous support of the Lannan Foundation,
the Austrian Cultural Forum New York, the Austrian Federal Ministry for the Arts and Culture,
the National Endowment for the Arts, the New York City Department of Cultural Affairs,
and the New York State Council on the Arts, a state agency.

BUNDESKANZLERAMT ÖSTERREICH

PRINTED IN THE UNITED STATES OF AMERICA

ANGEL OF OBLIVION

GRANDMOTHER signals with her hand, she wants me to follow.

We pass through the smoke kitchen into the larder. Old smoke clings to the vaulted ceiling like dark, greasy resin. It smells of smoked meat and freshly baked bread. An acrid vapor hovers over the feed tub, in which we collect scraps of food for the pigs. The mud floor shines as if polished in the most heavily trafficked areas.

In the larder, Grandmother scoops pork schmaltz from a jar and spreads it around the roasting pan, then with a spoon she scrapes a thin layer of whitish mold off the apple jam and flings it onto the scraps. *Malada* is written on the labels she has glued onto the jars with a paste made of flour, milk, and spit.

She places a handful of eggs in my skirt, which I hold out for her. Flakes of soot loosened by the draft through the smoke kitchen settle onto the loaves of bread stored on their sides on wooden shelves. Under the mouth of the oven near the entrance, ashes have been swept into a small pile.

Grandmother works in the kitchen. The dishes she prepares all taste like the smoke kitchen, like the dark, badly lit grotto we pass through several times each day. It seems to me that everything we eat absorbs the color and smell of the smoke kitchen. The ham and the buckwheat flour, the lard and the jam, even the eggs smell like earth, smoke, and yeasty air.

When she cooks, Grandmother assigns the food specific characteristics. Her dishes have secret powers, they can connect the here and now with the hereafter, heal visible and invisible wounds, they can make you ill.

I drink barley coffee from the bottle she keeps hidden for me on the bottom shelf of the sideboard. You're too big for a bottle, she says, but as long as you want one, I'll make one for you. I stretch out on the kitchen bench to keep out of sight and suck down the coffee substitute. Much too big, Grandmother repeats. If anyone comes in, put the bottle on the floor immediately.

Grandmother says my mother doesn't know enough to work in the kitchen. She has no idea how to cook and whatever those nuns taught her in school has no place in our house. She also has no idea that there's food for the living and food for the dead and that you can heal people or destroy them with specially prepared dishes. But she simply refuses to believe Grandmother.

I, on the other hand, believe every word Grandmother says and enthusiastically turn the crank when she roasts barley for the coffee. I listen as she recounts how many people she used to cook for, back when there were farmhands and farm-maids and lots and lots of children. She tells me she also stole food for herself and the others, she kept an eye out for every single potato peel, for anything that looked edible, back then, when she washed the cauldrons, it was great luck, she says, that she ended up in the kitchen, in the camp. I know.

After washing up she sets the small enamel bowls and pots to dry on the windowsill. She empties the metal tub of dishwater outside, her long reddened fingers purple from the water. They look like the claws of some bird of prey. Now and then she raps me on the head with them. With a poker, she lifts a cast iron lid the size of a plate off the top of the wood stove and spreads the embers so they will cool faster.

As soon as she starts moving, I follow her. She is my queen bee and I am her drone. The scent of her clothes reaches my nose, they smell of milk and smoke with a hint of the bitter herbs hung from her apron. She performs the waggle dance and I prance after her, matching my short steps to her trudging pace. I buzz a gentle melody of questions and she plays the bass.

We go to the sitting room to check on the milk centrifuge behind the door. We spin it a few times a week to separate the cream from the milk. We open the windows in the small adjacent room and air the beds we sleep in, loosen the straw mattresses filled with corn leaves, check and turn the herbs drying on the windowsill or hung on hooks, climb the stairs to the attic, which I find eerie, and look in the garret where ghosts took refuge years ago and chased away all who had slept there, according to Grandmother.

Grandmother continues her dance out the door and binds the yellow kerria to the plum tree in front of the barn. She talks to the elder bush next to the manure pile so it will bloom more quickly. Then she comes back to get me. We cross the courtyard for fodder in the lower basement and the storehouse. She opens flour sacks, chests, and wooden tubs and fills her apron pockets with fresh or dried fruit. She scatters grains of wheat and corn for the chickens. Her forehead is as wrinkled as the shingled roof of the grain silo. She hurries on ahead of me, wants to check the drying kiln near the stream and the frames on which we dry plums and pears in the fall.

Twice a week, she inspects the hen roosts in the tool shed and the barn. If, at the end of the week, there are no eggs in a particular nest, she will look for the bird she suspects is dallying instead of laying. When that hen strays within reach, she pounces on the screeching fowl and sticks her index and middle finger in its behind. If there's a flash of white between her fingers, she says, the egg will come tomorrow or the day after, the shell is still soft.

Once, to my delight, she pulls an egg out of the chicken and it dissolves in her hands. I have to laugh. Egg-girl, Grandmother calls me. Grandfather gave me the name, she tells me, when he was lying sick on the bench by the stove and had to watch over me. I was a toddler, not much more than a year old, and had discovered the eggs in the bottom drawer of the sideboard. I let them roll one after another across the wooden floor, and as each yolk burst from the shell, I cried, *sonči gre*, the little sun has come out! Grandfather watched me and was so charmed he let me take all the bowls off the shelves and wouldn't let Grandmother scold me. As she wiped the scrambled eggs off the floor, he told her she should take pity on me and on him. He died soon after, even though I had kept him entertained.

Only when it comes to kneading does Grandmother appreciate Mother's help. Then she watches Mother as she stirs the flour. The dough squeaks and squelches in the kneading-trough. Beads of sweat form on Mother's forehead and drop into the nascent bread. She stands up and wipes the sweat from her face with her upper arm. Her cheeks are flushed, the sleeves of her blouse rolled up, and I can see her undershirt beneath her neckline. She asks about the proportion of rye to wheat flour and of sourdough to water, she'd like to know how many kilos of flour to use. Grandmother says, when the flour covers this notch in the side of the trough, it's good. Then Mother bends over the dough again. When it begins to loosen from her fingers and no longer squeaks, her work is done. Grandmother cuts a cross into the dough, covers it, and leaves it to rise.

Two hours after Grandmother has fed the two light gray, floury paunches into the oven's maw, the oven returns the bread. She pulls the piping hot loaves from the oven, wipes them with a cloth, makes the sign of the cross over them, and places them in my apron. I carry the bread into the sitting room to cool and slide it onto the table or the wide bench.

The smell of freshly baked bread wafts through the house. Grandmother paces through all the rooms as if to make sure that the plumes of sourdough have reached every corner.

We only had this much bread to eat in the camp, that's it, Grandmother separates her thumb and index finger slightly to show how thin the pieces of bread allotted to the prisoners were. It had to last for a day, sometimes two. Later, we didn't even get that much, she says, and so we had to imagine the bread. I look at her. She says, as she always does, *je bilo čudno*. It was strange, she says although she means it was terrible, but the word *grozno* doesn't occur to her.

She stores crumbs and old crusts of bread in her apron pockets. When she crosses the courtyard and goes into the barn, she divides the bread among the animals. She scatters the crumbs in a wide arc for the chickens and stuffs the crusts right in the cows' and pigs' mouths. When you've got bread you have to remember the animals, Grandmother says, because the bread you share comes back to you.

On All Souls' Day, she places a loaf of bread and a pitcher of milk on the table for the dead. So they'll have something to eat when they come at night and will leave us in peace, she says.

I picture the dead eating with invisible hands, but the next morning, nothing seems to have been touched. The knife lies next to the loaf of bread, the milk is still on the table as if undisturbed by even the faintest breeze. Did they come? I ask. Yes, Grandmother answers. She must know, I think, she's on close terms with Death. After all, she saw him back when he appeared every day and every hour.

MOTHER works outside. At breakfast I can see her working in the barn. A wicker basket on her back, she hurries over to the threshing floor and then back to the stalls. Her feet firmly planted, she leans over the feeding trough, from which steam rises, and mixes handfuls of cut and sifted hay into the pig slop. When she passes the house carrying tools, she usually comes up to the kitchen window to look for me. She knocks on the windowpane and calls out, where is my *kokica*, my little chick. Sometimes she just winks and leaves without a word.

She wears brighter aprons than Grandmother and loves to sing while she works.

Following the direction her singing comes from, I can figure out where she is at any given time. If she's in a cheerful mood, she lures me outdoors with pet names she also uses for the animals and gives me a chore to do or hugs me tightly. Her caresses are rough. She reaches for me the way Grandmother grabs at the chickens and pulls me close. She tickles and bites me when I try to get away. Whenever she's feeling dejected, she won't let me near her. Her sorrow has a magnetic attraction for me. In such moments, I want to climb over her like a cat in a tree and look down, from the top of her head, into her eyes, to lick her cheeks, to rub her nose a bit and sink my claws into her back should she ever try to shake me off. Mother certainly has no sympathy for my desires. As soon as I touch her hip, she pushes me away like a mother animal her young and asks when I might be planning to do the chore she assigned me. Now, I say, hoping Grandmother has heard everything and will take over my duties, which she gladly does, if only to annoy Mother.

Sometimes I find Mother crying in her and my father's bedroom. At those times she sits on the bed with her rubber boots still on her feet. She doesn't like it when I surprise her in this state. What are you looking for, she asks. You, I answer, you! Her despair must be very great because her rubber boots and her stained apron don't go at all with the light linen coverlet embroidered with colorful flowers spread over the marriage bed.

On mild evenings she sits in the meadow behind the house and looks at the sky or leans against the wooden balcony on the south side of the outbuilding where no one can see her. One day she is kneeling in the entrance hall in front of a refrigerator that has just been delivered. What's the point of that gadget, Grandmother rails in the kitchen, it only costs money. Mother wipes the refrigerator with a soft rag she keeps dipping into a washbowl of hot water and wringing out again. Every household needs a refrigerator like this nowadays, she answers stubbornly.

Nonsense, Grandmother replies, she's never owned a refrigerator, no one needs such a gadget.

One evening Mother hangs two small, framed pictures of angels over my bed in the room I share with Grandmother. After my brother came, I stopped sleeping in the outbuilding with my parents and moved into Grandmother's room, which I'm happy about because she is the pillar of my childhood. As she hammers two small nails into the wall for the pictures, Mother says she's brought me two guardian angels to watch over me. This young man with curly blond hair and wings growing out of his back is supposed to protect me. He's a careless young man, I decide, since he wears impractical open-toed sandals as he leads two children over a suspension bridge. A deep mountain canyon yawns below. Mother recites the prayer *sveti angel varuh moj, bodi vedno ti z menoj, stoj mi dan in noč ob strani, vsega hudega me brani, amen* with me and tells me that angels can see into a person's soul and read their most secret thoughts.

I look skeptically at the well-fed, chubby-cheeked beings because I don't believe my thoughts are there to be spied on and because I'm worried the angels are too naive and inexperienced to protect me. Their dreamy, misty-eyed gaze is directed at the heavens and, while half-naked, the few clothes they do wear seem expensive. They play the strangest instruments and are at home in the clouds, not on earth. I ask myself if these winged creatures really want to know everything and see all I'd rather keep secret. Although I do like the singing girlish boys and would like to see swarms of them perching on church altars and frescos like swallows on electric lines in late summer, they make me uneasy.

One morning when I get up, it strikes me that my father must have fallen from heaven or from a bridge. He's lying on the kitchen floor, his face covered with blood. Grandmother slides a pillow under his head and covers him with a woolen blanket. Mother has placed a washbasin filled with cold water next to him. She wants to wipe the blood off his cheeks but he raises his hand defensively.

We can't just leave him lying here, Mother says in a strained voice.

Leave him alone, if that's what he wants, Grandmother orders and pushes Mother aside.

When Father notices me huddled against the stove in distress, he smiles. A small stream of blood gushes from his mouth and rolls down his cheek and seeps into his light shirt collar.

He's lost his teeth, Mother wails and bolts out of the kitchen. She stops outside the door and plucks at the flowers that are just beginning to bloom in the window boxes. What happened, I want to know. Father fell off his motorcycle, Mother sobs, we have to call the doctor. Then she runs off.

Father is driven to the doctor that afternoon. A neighbor picks him up in his car.

He's had lots of guardian angels, Mother says. Did the angels cushion the motorcycle's fall, I wonder, or did they wake the neighbor who found him lying in the field and helped him get up? I need to rethink the whole angel situation, I decide, maybe they're not as useless as I thought.

FATHER likes wearing corduroy knickerbockers best. When he walks, the clasps swing against his calves because in his hurry he forgets to fasten them. He has a purposeful gait and always seems to need to rub his hands with impatience or delight. In summer, he leaps barefoot into the wooden clogs set out by the front door. In winter, he shoves his stocking feet so impatiently into the leather lining of his wooden shoes that bulges of wool form around the most frequently darned spots. Everything is set in motion when he hurries across the courtyard. The dog Piko runs back and forth on his chain, the cats come up to the barn door, the sows in their pens make piercing noises. Mother rushes into the barn carrying buckets sloshing with pig swill.

Father has already set the cows loose from the rope and herds them towards the water trough. He doesn't have time to grab the hazelnut switch kept near the barn door and guides the stumbling animals with his hand and yells. Sometimes it sounds like he's cheering.

The cows are too slow for his pace. They've barely returned to their places before he has lost patience and begun cursing and flailing his arms, as if shooing away bothersome flies. When he carries hay into the stalls and, from the threshold, shouts the name of the cow that should move to make room for him, that particular cow actually moves aside so he can stuff their fodder into the crib. His movements are sweeping and rhythmic. Cleaning the pigsty has to run like a well-oiled machine, the muckrake has to dig into a pile of straw with one thrust, the shovel must scrape the floor of the stall in a steady cadence. The steaming cowpats are only waiting to be lifted from the manure gutter and conveyed to the dung heap. You can read Father's mood from the cowpats' flight. If he tosses the manure in a high arc to the back of the heap, he's feeling confident. If he flings the cowpats hard against the front of the manure pile, he's irate.

The pigs throng against the pivoting gate to the trough. Mother shoves the gate back with her boot and urges the animals' patience. You can all wait just a bit longer, she says and pours the swill in a wide arc into the trough. As soon as the gate swings back, the pigs huddle, slurping, over the mash.

Mother begins milking. She wipes the first cow's udder with a cloth, then squats on the stool and braces her head against the animal's flank. Her grip on the teats draws a powerful stream of milk that crashes against the bottom of the pail. On this signal, everything calms down. The pigs slurp more quietly, the hens draw in their heads, the cats gather silently around their drinking bowl, the milk foams in the pail. When she has finished milking the first cow, Mother gives the cats milk to drink. She pours the milk into a bowl Father carved from a piece of wood. Pink cat tongues flap against the white liquid, the cats' jaws are wet with milk. Their tongues lick the milk from their fur.

I stand, snug in a veil of haze and cast a glance over the dirty walls. My hands smell of the pigs that press their massive bodies against the gate when they're done eating in the hope that I'll scratch their backs. The dog Piko has wiped his morning's sweat on my dress. Cat hairs, damp with milk, are already stuck to my cheeks. I ask Mother when the next calf will come because I love feeding animals with a bottle. The way they butt with their heads as they nurse always makes me laugh. After I feed the calves, I always let them lick my hands until I become afraid my whole arm might disappear into the warm gullets behind their nubbly tongues. You'll have to wait a bit longer, Mother says. Father stands outside the barn door and looks at the sky. Fine weather is coming, he says, we'll have to get a move on tomorrow, fine weather is coming!

On warm spring weekends, Father sits on the bench next to the beehive and watches the bees' flight. He has one arm draped over the back of the bench and acts as if he wouldn't mind my sitting next to him. He looks at the alighting boards in front of the hives' entrance holes where the foragers land and perform their waggle dances. There will be a good harvest this year, he'll say, or, I'm worried about the second hive. In late winter, when the thaw sets in, he shovels the snow in front of the apiary so the sun will warm the area in front of the hives more quickly. He has made wooden hive frames, stretched wires across them and pressed sheets of wax onto the wires. He brought the honeycomb into the apiary and swept the piles of dead bees from the apiary floor. On the last day in January, he sent me into the bee-house to listen to the hives, to hear if the colonies were giving any signs of life. When I told him there was a mysterious humming, he looked like a weight had fallen from his shoulders. Now he asks if I'd be willing to help him do the spring check and smoke the hives. I nod and immediately sense that I've made a mistake, but it's too late to retreat.

The apiary is filled with semi-darkness. A milky light shines through a small, smudged window onto the wooden building's far wall. Next to the window stand two wardrobes in which Grandmother keeps her clothes. Beehives tower along the front like a broad buzzing wall. In spring, woolen blankets are still draped over the hives. In a separate back room is the honey extractor and fresh sheets of beeswax are piled on a small table near the door.

Father is glad when I go into the apiary with him. He says he doesn't like to work alone and presses the smoker into my hands. With a gentle grip, he opens the first hive and I reach the smoker inside the case. I run back outside right away. One by one, Father pulls the honeycombs out of the hive. With an eagle feather, he brushes away the bees hanging onto the frame and takes each honeycomb outside to check it. I wait at a suitable distance until Father comes out carrying a honeycomb crowded with bees and summons me with a nod of his head so that I can get a look at the seething mass. The first to find the queen bee gets to cheer. Stretching my neck, I bend over the colony and call out *matica, matica,* as soon as I've spotted the queen. Father sighs and looks for the queen cells with the tip of his feather. Sometimes he sweeps a colony, made weak by winter, as he says, away from the entrance of another hive and hopes that the weakened bees will be taken in by a neighboring colony. He tells me to stay calm and not make any sudden movements. He says he chose the right day, the bees have flown out and I don't need to worry, no one will get stung on a day like this. I don't entirely trust his confidence because I've often seen him swollen with beestings. Father likes to blow his cigarette smoke on the bees' backs. They especially like that, he says, his tobacco can tame the fiercest creatures. He smiles when he sees me draw my head in, afraid an angry worker bee will attack me.

Grandmother usually comes into the apiary to ask about the state of the bee colonies. She takes a small brown notebook with yellowed pages from a drawer in the wardrobe and notes down the size of the colonies and the number of queens. The cover of the notebook is emblazoned with the German Imperial Eagle. Under the insignia is written Employ-ment Record Book, Name and Location, Nationality: *Deutsches Reich*. This notebook belonged to your grandfather, she says, though he never used it. He took over the farm on February 1st, 1927 and married on February 27th, 1927, that's recorded in the notebook, Grandmother tells me. She kept a record of all the rest on the inside of the wardrobe door, where the dates of marriages and deaths are listed in pencil.

Grandmother can't bear to throw anything away, Father says, she even uses the old Hitler stuff until it completely falls apart. Nonsense, Grandmother retorts, the winter coat, the one she keeps in this closet, for example, she only wore it once and won't ever put it on again. She opens the wardrobe and points at a dark gray-green wool coat folded up on the floor. She "organized" it in Ravensbrück and from then on didn't let it out of her sight, she says. She wore the coat on the day the camp was evacuated. It remained her best coat. Yeah, yeah, Father says and turns back to the bees. I cast a curious look at the coat before Grandmother closes the wardrobe door again and goes to get a jar of honey from the back room with the extractor. I'm surprised she used the word "organized," which I'd never heard from her lips before. It must have something to do with the secret activity that kept her alive in the camp, I think.

As soon as summer is palpable and you can't go into the fields because grass has grown high, the bees call attention to themselves again after a brief rain shower. On such days you can hear the hum of a swarm flying to a branch that protrudes near the house or hanging from a tree at some distance from the farm like a seething cluster of grapes. Father is called from all corners of the farm, he must bring the escapees back to the old queen.

He rushes to the suspiciously buzzing trees armed with a wooden box and a ladder. This time he has pulled a white hat with a veil over his head and his pleas for help bringing the swarm back home are roundly ignored.

One time, Mother, trying to help fasten the wooden frame under the swarm of bees, faints after being stung several times. My younger brother and I stand there petrified next to Mother lying on the ground. Father has put a damp cloth on her forehead and raises her gently until she regains consciousness and vomits. From that day on Mother is terrified of bees and I, too, can barely master my distrust of them.

You have to bear what you've provoked, Mother says after I cavalierly cross the bee's flight paths.

This time I'm helping Father pull the honey. He brought all the honeycombs with caps into the extraction room and started to remove the top layer of wax from the combs with a broad capping fork. He scrapes the gathered wax off onto the edge of an earthenware bowl painted with flowers that is only used for harvesting honey. I put a few pieces of honeycomb in my mouth and chew them until I've sucked out all the honey. If a small piece of honeycomb breaks off the frame during the uncapping, Father hands it to me, and I put the dripping comb in my mouth. The honey streams over my gums like a sticky pap and fills me with delight.

Father puts the unsealed cells, in which the honey, now visible, sticks like liquid resin, into the extractor and starts to turn the crank. As soon as the honey begins to flow and Father starts praising its color, Grandmother comes back into the apiary. She pulls out her little notebook and starts estimating and writing down the number of liters per hive.

After the extraction, I return to the front section of the bee-house where a few worker bees are flying about wildly. My fingers are sticky and damp. The bees suddenly attack me and as I'm trying to brush them out of my hair, I feel the stings on my scalp, which tightens from the pain as from a hard blow. I start screaming and hope I won't faint. Father and

Grandmother rush over to me and talk to me, but the pain that is now flooding over my entire body is stronger than any imploring words.

My eyelids are swollen from tears and beestings when I finally stop crying. My scalp is covered with painful bulges that are visible under my hair. Grandmother puts a bottle of chocolate milk on the table to comfort me and lays cold poultices on my forehead and temples. As I lift the bottle to my mouth, my father's cousin Michi walks in the kitchen. Such a big girl drinking out of a bottle, it can't be true, he says reproachfully. Since there is as much astonishment as reproach in his comment, I understand, despite my predicament, that at my age, I really should start using a cup. Leave her alone, Grandmother says, she got stung by the bees. She shows Michi the stings, separating my hair in one section after another as if she were filing index cards. Michi sits with us on the kitchen bench and consolingly strokes my burning cheeks.

MOTHER helps me practice the Slovenian poetry I'm supposed to learn by heart for school. She says, we'll do it together, I'll memorize them with you! While she irons the clothes, I read from my poetry books and schoolbooks. Together we let the flowers grow. We crow with the roosters and peal with the church bells. We croak with the frogs and sing *tra-la-la* and *hop-sa-sa* for their weddings. We laugh with the ravens at the scarecrows, let soap bubbles rise like the sun, earth, and moon that turn without wheels and fly without wings. We load springtime with its garlands of flowers onto a boat and sail into the distance. We sit for hours in meadows of language and speak in the rhythm of rhymes. We realize that nature must be adorned with verse and the flowers woven into wreaths. With rhymes we can leap from stanza to stanza like butterflies from one blossom to another without fear of falling. They bring everything to a good conclusion, they turn tears into laughter and silence into celebration. What was dried out will bloom again, what had stiffened will be able to dance again. We believe that every rejected child like Videk in the fairy tale will be given a warm shirt by the forest animals and will find food in the wild garden. Mother loves poems where winter threatens to take away all lazy children and birds promise parents they will raise their children.

In spring, Mother puts dandelion flowers in my hair and tells me I must be content with simple things. All she needs to be happy is nature, songs, and the Catholic Church. She says there is only one way to live in grace, through industriousness and observing God's commands. She says, you must observe all the Catholic holidays, attend mass, and say your morning and evening prayers. You have to stop at the wooden crosses on roadsides and at the edges of meadows and cross yourself before the altar. Mother's ideal room is a church sanctuary. She has to have pictures of saints on the wall above her bed. She insists on having little clouds and divine embellishments decorate the area around the crucifix in our prayer corner. She reads pamphlets and books about martyrs mutilated or killed for their faith or about those who renounced all pleasure in their lives in order to ascend to heaven while still alive. She says that the Virgin Mary may appear to those who work hard and are pure of heart. She sends me and my younger brother to church regularly and thinks nothing of the fact that we have to walk seven kilometers to Eisenkappel. The way to God is always difficult, Mother says.

I, however, believe that she summons songs and miracles to fight Grandmother's influence on me. Come, Grandmother says, if you do as I say and finish your homework, you can go watch television at Michi's house.

I make myself useful and sometimes in the evening I take my brother across the field and through a small wood to our friendly neighbors who let us sit on their couch and watch television. We often hope in vain to make out human forms in the black and white ripples on the screen.

On some days Michi tries, with Father's help, to get better reception. The men walk around the perimeter of the house holding the antenna, which looks like a bare Christmas tree, and we call out the window, *now! now!*, when the forms on the screen start to emerge more clearly. The mountain shepherd Kekec will soon be able to trill his song to the sun again and play his wondrous flute, putting men and animals under his spell and chasing dark forces away from his mountain village.

Reception of Slovenian television is unreliable and is certainly not officially sanctioned. Politics won't ever want it set up for Carinthian Slovenes, Michi says to Father. That would be the Eighth Wonder of the world. We have no choice but to make do with the shadow television and to feel like pirates in fog.

GRANDMOTHER has her own understanding with nature. She believes the fields and forests must be propitiated, not adorned with verses. A poem means nothing to nature, she says, we must always be humble before it.

In the attic, she has gathered willow branches that she pulls from the palm bundles blessed in church every year on Palm Sunday. She makes small crosses from the willow branches, crosses we bring out to the fields in spring and stick in the plowed earth to keep the potato fields fertile and the wheat plentiful. When a thunderstorm is brewing, she places pieces of willow on glowing embers and carries them through the house in a cast iron skillet. The bitter smoke is meant to clear the air and appease the atmospheric forces. You must carry your belief in God in your heart, Grandmother says, it's not enough to put it on show in church. You can't rely on the Church, according to her, the Church cannot be trusted.

Grandmother only trusts abnormal signs in the heavens, and she can read them. She believes in the Ember days and the 8th of May, on which she goes to mass every year to give thanks for the end of the Nazi era. She believes in speech that is directed inward to one's own will, not to the human ear. She says that words are very powerful, that they can cast spells on things and heal people, that bread over which a spell has been uttered along with a plea for intercession can help in sickness and need. Her oldest son was bitten by a snake, she recounts. The wound refused to heal, and the doctors had no idea how to help him. She went to old Rastočnik so that he could put a spell against the snake venom in the bread. But old Rastočnik refused because he was afraid of intensifying the dangerous poison. So then she walked over to see Želodec, who blessed the bread for her. Poisonous animal, take your venom back from this man, Želodec pleaded of the snake's spirit. I don't exorcise his flesh, I don't exorcise his blood, I exorcise the terrible cramp, were the words with which she had consecrated Grandmother's bread. After Grandmother's son had eaten a bite of the bread every day and recited the Lord's Prayer without saying amen at the end, he was healed. The venom had seeped out of him. And the word became bread and dwelt within him as often as he had insalivated the healing word. The bread spoken, the word consumed.

Grandmother can pray away the occasional sty in my eye. I must answer her intercession with *ne verujem* – I don't believe – and must have faith in the healing, she says. She recites her incantation and, with her hand, mimics a reaping motion. *Ječmen žanjem*, she says, *Ječmen žanjem*, while I repeat that I don't believe she's slicing the sty. Because I admit my doubt, I'm telling the truth and the spell works, at least I believe it does, but I don't know for sure.

Grandmother confides to me that her mother gave her a house blessing as a dowry, as a roof of words over her head. She only has to recite it in times of need or nail it onto the door for the house to be protected from lightning and hail and all harm. She keeps the blessing in an envelope that no one is allowed to open without being asked. The prayer could be rubbed or read right off the page. In any case, it's better if it's learned by heart because the power lies in the spoken word, not in writing.

I picture the words rising from the envelope, through my eyes, into my head and from there to unknown heights. I also imagine how the words, untouched, could work their effect from the envelope; how, with the speaker's voice, they could spread a wing of words over the conjuror.

Old lady Keberin also gave my grandfather a blessing, wrapped in a velvet cloth, before he went off to join the partisans to protect him from sudden death, from betrayal, and from evil deeds, Grandmother tells me. He had to say five Our Fathers and five Hail Marys each day. He prayed every day and he survived as a partisan. He came back from the forest. Just like the man who survived the war, the man Romana from Remschenig could remember, Grandmother says. Back then, when Romana was arrested, she was barely ten years old. She was interrogated in the Klagenfurt prison, and they yanked her hair when a partisan was brought into the room whom she didn't know and on whom they had found the holy shield, the *ščit božji* as he called it. The Gestapo asked the partisan what good it was and he answered, I am under God's protection. At that, they beat him until he collapsed, covered with blood, under their blows. The girl was forced to watch it all, but the partisan survived and was carried unconscious from the room. He was protected by the word, Grandmother says.

This terrifies me. I beg the holy shield to keep me from thinking about what it might be able to prevent from happening to me. Don't brood on it, Grandmother says, you've heard too much and believed too much. She smiles her thin, restrained smile and pushes me out of the room and into the courtyard.

Barking, Piko runs back and forth on his chain. Clucking loudly, the chickens scurry down the sloping meadow behind our house. They spread their wings and try to fly.

There must be hawk, Grandmother says, now it's hunting right outside our door! She will tell the hunters about the incident so they'll shoot the bird of prey. Mother comes out from behind the house, a rooster bleeding in her arms. It fought the hawk, she had to tear the rooster out of its claws, the hawk had sunk them so deeply into the rooster's wings, she explains and lays the wounded fowl on the ground. The rooster shakes itself and spreads its bloodied wings. Limping and crowing, it hops towards the henhouse.

Will you bandage its wounds, I ask Mother.

It will heal on its own, she says, bandages won't help.

Once we're alone, I want to know what a partisan is. Mother is surprised. Grandmother has been telling her stories again? Partisans lived in dugouts and hid from the Germans, she answers. That was a long time ago and you shouldn't worry about it. Grandmother says that Grandfather was one, too, I say.

Mother goes into the house without a word. Grandmother comes outside immediately. I'm not going to let you tell me how to treat the girl, certainly not you, she says reproachfully and sits on the water well near the front door. Mother stays on the doorstep. I turn my face towards her, keeping Grandmother in sight. The low roof seems to extend imperceptibly towards the ground. For several minutes, the water in the well plashes in our silence.

GRANDMOTHER decides to take over my upbringing. Enough of this singing falderal and useless stories, she declares. She is suspicious of my rapture for the books I bring home from school. What are you doing with that drivel, she asks when she catches me reading, a girl has to be able to do more than read. Dancing, for example, is just as important. After they were liberated from the camp, she taught the young women how to dance. Whenever anyone played music, she grabbed a woman and they spun in circles. It was a laugh and a joy after we escaped the devil, Grandmother says.

When the radio at home plays a polka or a waltz, she takes me by the hand and shows me the steps while leading me in a circle. I hold onto to her forearms and watch her slippered feet move to the rhythm of the music. Before long, I've learned how to dance the polka and the waltz. On holidays, when Father plays his accordion, a *steirische harmonica*, Grandmother, beaming with pride, invites me to dance. The neighbors, who always come to our house on such occasions, are also delighted.

How wonderful there's dancing in this room again, they exclaim, we've missed dancing here for so long!

While Grandmother turns me in circles, I try to picture what the dances in our sitting room, which they all claim they remember, must have looked like. There were so many who danced back when the girls still lived at home, girls scattered to the four winds, two of whom were sent back to our valleys only as ashes, so the stories go. I love the exhilarated atmosphere in our sitting room, which makes you feel like you are connected to the past, and I'm happy to see Grandmother smile.

Her second lesson is how to play cards. As soon as I get home from school and find her darning socks or spinning wool, she says, come, let's play a hand! She calls her favorite card game "Business, High Card Wins." We play as farmers betting their farms and line up the farms in our valley, one next to the other, choosing candidates from among them, and among the farms in the next valley over, the properties left idle and abandoned. Grandmother plays on behalf of the homeless or for the farmers with the most land in the area. I play on behalf of the smallholder whose children go to school with me and whom I think I know. We line up successes and failures, just as we had lined the farms up before, we slap our cards down on the table and laugh at the losers who have just lost all their worldly goods. Grandmother knows exactly how much each property is worth, she knows how much sun each field and meadow gets, the fruit trees' yield, the quality of each farm's pork. As soon as she's had enough of "Business," she suggests a game of "Sixty-six" and we play for small coins and don't bankrupt anyone.

In her third lesson, she instructs me how to host guests.

One should always ask them to sit, even if they're in a hurry, because neighbors who don't sit down in your home cause nightmares, Grandmother claims. You should always have a good salami, farmer cheese, and bread in your pantry for guests and never, ever serve ham that's been infested with maggots like some farmers put on their tables when guests arrive like a rain shower. No one should ever claim we're miserly, that would be the worst thing anyone could say about our farm.

Elderly men from our area often come to visit Grandmother. Flori comes by almost every day because he's also leching after Mother. He has respect for Grandmother and doesn't grab her breasts every chance he gets the way he does with younger women. He has never reached his crooked fingers towards me, Grandmother says, and God help him if he ever tries! Flori lived on our farm before the War, she recounts, twice during the War she asked him to stay longer in the evening. The first time, she'd invited him and their closest neighbors to keep vigil with them because Grandfather had learned that our family was going to be deported the following morning. She cooked her best ham and the neighbors ate every last bite, but then no one came the next day to take them away after all. A year later, she'd asked Flori to testify to the police that the partisans had forced Grandfather to join them, that he hadn't gone willingly. But no one believed Flori.

Tschik, another regular visitor, doesn't have gnarled fingers like Flori, but he does have a hole in the side of his nose. He constantly rubs his hand over his dark, smooth hair. When I ask him how he got the third hole in his nose, from which he blows cigarette smoke, he reveals to me that he fell face-first on a nail. Later he tells me that the truth is, he jumped from a balcony and hit his head in such an unlucky way that the wound never healed.

Tschik lives in the sawmill near Rastočnik. He's got a stovepipe sticking out of his window. He calls Grandmother *teta*, even though she's not his aunt. He sighs when she brings up any incident that seems to connect them. Back then, when they came to deport her, yes, back on that October day when they arrested her, he was there too. He ended up in Moringen, in the children's camp, Grandmother says, where Johi Čemer was also taken and both Auprich boys, Erni and Franz.

A Gypsy man comes once a year and parks his van on the access road below the house. He sells duvets, tablecloths, and crockery. When he takes his plastic-wrapped wares and spreads them out on the farmhouse table and the wrapping on the embroidered and patterned fabrics gleams in the sun, the atmosphere in the sitting room is almost festive. He presents his wares and his young wife tells our fortunes. The cards say I will marry a rich man, live in a house, and be very happy, the woman claims. Grandmother is very satisfied. You see, you don't have to worry about a house, she tells me. She wants the Gypsy woman to tell her on which day she will die and the young woman answers that she can't read anyone's death in the cards. Doesn't matter, Grandmother says. In any case, Grandmother had a special loaf of bread made that she keeps in her wardrobe. When it starts to get moldy, she will die. Then she asks the Gypsy man to show her some towels and buys a few.

Our hospitality is lavish. Grandmother says I should be aware that the poor man has been through a lot and she asks him to show me the number on his forearm. He rolls up his sleeve and uncovers the number, which suddenly appears to lift off from his arm and hover above it. In my memory, the camp number rises from its bearer as in a dream that I might have dreamt once in which a number floats here and there until it has found the proper arm on which it can land like a black butterfly.

My number was 24834, Grandmother says, and at that moment she strikes me as at once sad and defiant.

She also invites Jehovah's Witnesses into the house when they stand in twos or threes at the door, wanting to explain to us the creation of the world. Grandmother sets the table while the Bible Students describe paradise, its inexhaustible rivers and streams, its wealth and the fruitfulness of God's pastures and fields, His strict watch over weak and guilty humans who, after the Fall, were expelled from paradise much too soon.

I suspect that Grandmother has secret powers because visitors show her so much gratitude. Their regard takes the form of gifts that she piles into the cupboards. Bottles of wine and spirits stand, unwrapped, next to unopened boxes of chocolates. When she finally opens a box of chocolates with great ceremony, removes the cellophane, and lifts the lid, most of the chocolates look like dried-up deer scat, Father says as soon as he takes a look. The chocolate is usually inedible and has to be thrown away. It doesn't seem to make any difference to Grandmother. She was delighted to receive the gift and shows her gratitude by keeping the chocolate and the wine in the cupboard for a long time without touching them, she says. Opening the presents right away would be vulgar and would show a lack of self-control.

I'm rarely surprised anymore when visitors appear in our house and claim they grew up in our family. They speak in muted tones as if it's unpleasant for them to admit they once relied on my grandmother's help. They ask after her health and Grandmother tells them she's convinced she will die soon. And so all of them try to talk her out of her illnesses, which spurs Grandmother to exaggerate her ills or her frailness even more.

T H A N K S to the construction of the municipal road that makes access to our farms much easier, Grandmother leaves the village more often. Once a month, she goes shopping in Eisenkappel. The evening before, she checks supplies in the storehouse, sets out her clothing, and counts her money. With the small victims' pension the postman delivers every month, Grandmother supports my parents. When she takes the money out of the envelope, she keeps in an old cardboard box with photographs and documents, she makes the sign of the cross over the bills before taking off the rubber band that holds them together. I've lost everything, my health, my happiness, she says, but now I have money to help.

In the morning, a neighbor or a relative comes to pick her up and drive her to the Eisenkappel. She begins her shopping day in the Perko family's foyer, where she sets down the bags of eggs and cheese she brought from home. After a cup of coffee with Maria, she sets off on her errands. First, she goes to the Majdič's store and greets the merchants with a handshake. They offer her a chair, from which she makes her requests. Mrs. Majdič serves her with affectionate courtesy and speaks Slovenian without lowering her voice when another customer enters the store. When she has finished her purchases, Grandmother again leaves her bags in the Perko family's foyer and walks to the Roscher general store. Her eyes gleam behind the lenses of her glasses when others recognize and greet her in the main square or when younger men raise their hats to her. In the Roschers' store, she's also served by the owner. Mrs. Roscher has a talent for placing the goods tenderly on the counter and Grandmother, in the meantime, also begins caressing a package of soup noodles here, a carton of breadcrumbs there. The goods pile up on the counter and an apprentice packs them in boxes, which are then stacked near the entrance for delivery to Lepena.

As she continues her errands, Grandmother explains that in Eisenkappel, you have to know precisely where you're welcome and to whom you can turn. She's already had some bitter experiences, but the Majdič, Perko, and Roscher families have always been cordial. She often thinks of how it was, after the War, when she returned from the camp to Eisenkappel for the first time to register as a survivor with the authorities. People were angry and afraid. Her own uncle, for example, threw her out of his house when she came to borrow a bit of flour or grain because the storehouse at home had been looted. She felt so ashamed, so humiliated, she wanted never to have to beg again in her life. Never again, Grandmother repeated. The Perkos, Majdičs, and Roschers, on the other hand, gave her clothing, stockings, underwear, shoes, and rye flour. That, she will never forget.

To conclude the shopping day, we visit Grandfather's grave and light a candle. Grandmother says that she will soon lie under this earth, next to Grandfather's bones and the ashes of her foster daughter Mici, sent home from Lublin. That's where I belong, she says and I realize that her longing for death has a hidden source.

Once a year she visits her eldest son, Tonči, and wants me to accompany her.

We take the postbus to Klagenfurt and then another to Oberglan. Uncle Tonči picks us up at the bus stop in his Puch 500 and drives along the curving road to the castle where he works as forester and custodian.

The attic of the castle outbuilding, where my uncle and his family live, smells of old wood, of dried herbs, of dust and melted schmaltz, of freshly laundered linens. As I climb the stairs with Grandmother up to our room, I secretly wait for this smell that calms and delights me. Surrounded by the thick castle walls, I feel safer than I do at home. The view from the window envelops me in a sense of security similar to what a fledgling might feel discovering an ancient and enormous stone egg into which it could retreat, confident that its shell has defied storms for centuries.

In the coming days, I will be given a new outfit and feel like I've been reinvented. I sit reverently at the beautifully set dinner table and am amazed that Grandmother doesn't find fault with the "waste of table-ware" as she always calls table settings at home. She praises her daughter-in-law's beautiful garden and marvels at her flowerbeds. She doesn't pluck indignantly at any perennials as she does in our garden. What a lovely place you've got here, she says sitting on a garden chair between two large pieces of cake, which she gobbles up one after the other without showing the slightest embarrassment or justifying herself.

She takes a walk with me before lunch, to stay out of her daughter-in-law's way in the kitchen, she claims. We go to the stables on the estate, and she asks the groom if we can see the horses. The beautiful animals impress her and remind her of two black horses on the farm where she grew up that were only hitched to the carriage or sled on Sundays and spared on the other days.

She explains castle etiquette to me and instructs me to greet the count and the employees on the estate in a clear voice and to give friendly answers to any questions. And I'm not allowed to tinkle in the yard or play in the castle's inner courtyard. I must cross the courtyard quickly. Even better, we should take the path that passes the stables to get to the garden. That way we won't run into his lordship.

At that very moment, the count comes towards us and greets Grandmother with a slight bow and shakes her hand. I, too, dutifully offer my hand. He says he hopes we're comfortable on the estate and asks after Grandmother's health. I'm astonished when she claims she's doing well and look at her in amazement. Grandmother is standing very straight and resting her right arm against her upper abdomen. It would seem she could easily begin chatting with the count then and there if I didn't know how hesitantly the German language crosses her lips because it's more or less just the language of the camps, as she maintains. I, at any rate, am waiting for the count to ask, as do all the strangers who stray into our valley, if I understand any German at all. I would say yes, of course, although I have my doubts, but the count doesn't ask any more questions and heads off towards the stables.

We walk on to the fishpond. The gravel path lays a veil of dust over Grandmother's black shoes, made for her by Perko the shoemaker. She's wearing her Sunday dress and has tied her kerchief at the nape of her neck. She has coquettishly turned up the sleeves of her blouse, revealing her sinewy forearms. At the large fishpond, we sit on the wooden pier. In the dark green, rather murky water we see trout and tench flit past against the shaded, swampy ground. On the way to the second fishpond, we miss the turn-off and search for the path in vain. Grandmother is irritated. We'll have to turn back, she says as if insulted. As we make our way back, one of the count's loggers comes towards us in a tractor. He stops and asks if he can offer us a lift, he has to drive past the castle in any case. We climb up on the hydraulic jack and are chauffeured, standing, to the castle. I've brought the runaways back, the logger says to my aunt who had come out of the house to see who'd arrived. Vera thanks him, and Grandmother is in a fine mood again. Everyone seems to know me here, she says. An ugly old woman stands out!

TAKING trips has come into fashion in Lepena. The neighbors all suddenly come down with travel fever. They mull over all the places they've wanted to travel, or where they might venture again after so many years. Excursions to the shrines of the Virgin Mary in Brezje and Monte Lussari as well as the Mauthausen and Ravensbrück concentration camps are discussed at great length, although Brezje in Slovenia seems to be the preferred destination.

Aunt Malka's husband, Sveršina, knows his way around Mauthausen. He, Malka, and my parents travel to the former camp with a group from Slovenia. On their return, they described how it was in Mauthausen, how many people were gathered on the grounds of the camp for the memorial service. The camp is now a museum, Father says. Sveršina showed them the barracks in which he was held and took them to the quarry where so many inmates died. Mother says she can't conceive of how anyone could survive the concentration camps. Grandmother gives her hostile and uncomprehending looks. Father tells us about a group of former Polish prisoners who had decorated a house near the camp with flowers. It moved him so deeply to see how the two men from Poland embraced the

- 44 -

owner of the house and thanked him for rescuing them that he couldn't help crying, and suddenly tears glisten on Father's cheeks. It's the first time I've seen him cry and I feel helpless and confused.

Grandmother decides she will travel to Ravensbrück this year. The trip will take a few days. When she returns and again lies next to me in bed, I'm relieved. She says the trip was very stressful. Women returned to the camp from all over Europe. She liked the speakers, she didn't understand everything they said, but their tone of voice pleased her. She tells me that former prisoners had gathered on the grounds of the camp. Many women stood at the edge of a lake and wept. They threw flowers in the lake and leaned against each other for support. She was hugged by two French women and by some Dutch women who were standing behind her listening to the speakers. She mentioned two names that she would always bring up from then on, Mici and Katrca, the names of her foster daughter and sister-in-law, both of whom died in the camp. She always thinks of Mici and Katrca, Grandmother says. She brought back two books. Books in which you can read about what happened in the camp. Grandmother says she'll show them to me, me and my unbelieving mother, when she's finished reading them, if that time comes.

Not long after this, we hear that Smrtnik from Ebriach has bought himself a van that seats eight people. A lot of people go on trips with Smrtnik, we're told. Grandmother doesn't wait long and organizes an expedition to Brezje. She decides I will have to go with them because it's time I went on a pilgrimage with her.

Early in the morning we cross the Seeberg Saddle Pass and are stopped at the border. I hand the Yugoslavian customs officer my first passport. He speaks Croatian or Serbo-Croatian and wants to impress upon us that we are at the border of a special nation that must examine all travelers who wish to enter it. Smrtnik takes over communications because he's had experience with customs officials. After we've crossed the border, the men on our pilgrimage begin recounting their border adventures in years past. The only story that makes an impression on me is how our neighbor Peter, whom I know well, smuggled the skeleton of a cave bear across the border in a basket over the course of several nights, but that was still before the war.

The church in Brezje is overflowing. With those who are praying, we push our way up to the altar on which a Madonna with a crown and scepter sits enthroned. A few women fall to their knees and shuffle on their knees up to the altar. To give my appeals weight, I imitate these women and decide that I'll just have to settle for dirty tights. Grandmother kneels, makes the sign of the cross, and stands up. Someone offers her his seat on the pew. During the mass I shift impatiently from one foot to the other and try to imagine what's going on in the minds of those who are singing and praying. Finally, I sit on Grandmother's lap. She tweaks my thigh to make me aware that I'm fidgeting. If you don't calm down, I won't bring you next time, she threatens.

When we step out of the church after the lengthy mass, the space outside looks to me like a high, shining nave and the inside of the church like a small cell in which we'd yearned to be outside, just as we'd earlier streamed into the semi-darkness to find purification. In the square in front of the church we pass merchants' stalls. Grandmother buys rosaries and wooden spoons. I get a pack of cookies and a devotional image with a picture of the church with the Madonna of Brezja floating on a small, round cloud above it.

We are shown to a table in the tavern on the other side of the square. We sit under the framed photograph of the president, who looks down from the wall under his garrison cap with a red star emblazoned on its front. Studying the photograph, Smrtnik claims that no matter which corner of the room you stand in, Marshal Tito looks directly at you, he follows you with his eyes, so to speak. You can test it when you walk into the room. Two men stand up from our table and go to the men's room so, they say, the Marshal will look straight at them when they return. Just as they come back in the room, our noodle soup is served. The two men don't linger on the threshold long, where they'd stopped to catch the Marshal's eye. From joy or relief at having prayed so exhaustively, they order wine to assuage their thirst. Grandmother announces that she can handle Cviček, too, and drinks a toast to her traveling companions. Besides, she has to fortify herself for the two remaining destinations, for Begunje and Bled.

The village of Begunje is not far from Brezje. We'll want to visit a former prison, Smrtnik says, many people were tortured and killed there during the War.

We get out of the car in front of a high, white wall and enter the former castle in which the Nazis had installed prison cells. Lists of those who were shot to death, signed by the Carinthian Gauleiter, hang on the walls of the prison wing. A woman guides us through the rooms and, before we enter a dark cell, turns on a recording of a child screaming desperately for its mother. Smrtnik describes for Grandmother how it was when the Gestapo deported his family from Trögern. He couldn't even cry, he says. I grab Grandmother's hand because the child's screams are upsetting. The screams cover everything there is to see like a blanket that cloaks what is visible and wrenches what is hidden to light. I don't know how to let Grandmother know that I can't bear the child's screams but she keeps listening to Smrtnik and thinks I'm misbehaving. Terror rages inside me like a hurricane. When we finally step outside, it feels as if half of my head were missing and I were looking at it from outside like a house with its roof torn off by a storm.

Bled enchants everyone. We absolutely have to visit the castle perched high above the lake and look down at the water from above, Smrtnik says. We park the car in a small wood and climb up to the castle grounds on foot. The smell of cooking wafts towards us from the doors and windows of the restaurant established in the castle. The pilgrims' moods revive. Soon after we've sat down on the terrace and ordered drinks and slices of the local cream pastry, a group of musicians start unpacking their instruments behind us.

For us? Smrtnik asks, that would be lovely!

For a double wedding, one of the musicians calls over, there's lots to celebrate!

The music starts up with the arrival of the first wedding party. A cluster surrounds the first couple. Waiters circle the happy couple with trays of wine. The second couple is led into the courtyard by a group of folk dancers who urge them to dance with laughter and cheers.

Grandmother stands up and toasts the wedding parties. Her kerchief has slipped back in the excitement and a strand of thin, white hair peaks out from under the cloth. Without a word, Grandmother sets her glass on the table and approaches the wedding guests. She tugs at a man's sleeve and whispers something into his ear. He bows his head, puts his arm around her shoulders, and starts to dance with her.

The elderly woman with round glasses dancing with a young man draws the photographers' attention for a few seconds. They turn away from the bride and groom and take pictures of the unusual couple.

In the breaks between the dances, Grandmother speaks animatedly with her partner and only after several dances does she allow him to lead her back to our table. Thank you for the dance and a lovely afternoon to all of you, the man says and winks at Grandmother. He's from Dolenjsko, Grandmother says. All I said was that I'm from Carinthia. That pleased him and he pleased me, it's as simple as that.

The pilgrims stock up on wine and cigarettes for the ride home. They discuss how best to smuggle the goods across the border, and one of the men suggests stuffing cigarette cartons in my clothes, because there's plenty of room under my dirndl. Grandmother considers the idea and gives me a questioning look. What happens when the customs officer finds the cigarettes, will I be arrested? I ask irritably. The pilgrims laugh.

The car bounces along the sparsely paved road towards Carinthia. We turn off into the Kokra Valley. One of the pilgrims becomes nauseous. Smrtnik pulls over on the side of the road and lets the man out. He throws up immediately. If he keeps vomiting at that rate, he'll sober up quickly, one of the men says, then there's no point drinking.

Smrtnik stops abruptly a few kilometers from the border. A second pilgrim has to vomit and dives into the bushes next to the road. In the dark, we can hear him heaving and breathing heavily.

Smrtnik asks the passengers to hide the wine and cigarettes, leaving only the authorized amounts visible on the seats so it doesn't look like we're bringing absolutely nothing back with us. A few bottles of wine and cases of cigarettes are stuck under the spare tire in the trunk, the rest are slipped into the sleeves of the men's jackets and draped inconspicuously. What about you, an older woman asks, should we stick a few cartons in your dress, the officer won't bother you because you're a child. I agree and open my collar so that Grandmother can slip the cigarette cartons behind the top section of my dirndl. You should wrap a woolen jacket around your shoulders so that your back isn't so noticeable, she says.

When we reach the border crossing, I lie stretched out on the back seat, stuffed full of cigarette cartons, with two cases beneath my seat, hidden there at the last minute, and I pretend to be asleep. The cigarette smoke tickles my nose. A customs official asks if the gentlemen have anything to declare and Florian answers that everyone each bought a bottle of wine and a few cartons of cigarettes, that's what's allowed.

And the girl, the officer asks.

I squeeze my eye shut more tightly and want to peek at least a little, to see what's going on.

She doesn't count, one of the men says, she's too young.

You're right there, the officer says and waves us on.

When we get out of the van on the access road below our house, Grandmother says that next time she'll make sure she knows which men will be traveling with them to Brezje. There are some people you simply can't go on a pilgrimage with.

Before bed, I lay my musty dirndl over the back of the chair. I'm exhausted and feel like my body has grown a few centimeters taller. Just wild growth, not at all useful, I might have thought had I not fallen asleep immediately.

T H E cigarettes we brought for Father don't cheer him up. He thanks us for the contraband and for a while no longer sends me to the tavern to get him two packs of strong, unfiltered Austria 3 cigarettes in a green package. He has other worries.

During the hay harvest his horse refuses from one day to the next to pull the cart. Father beats the animal with the straps. The stallion rears under the blows and pulls away the drawbar and traces, upsetting the cart. The panicked animal drags the splintering cart all the way back to the stables, where it comes to a stop, snorting and with foam around its nostrils. The shock ripples over its skin in constant shuddering waves. Father roars and yanks at the reins. I beg him to stop his cries of rage, but like the horse, he is beside himself.

Grandmother pulls me into the kitchen. She explains that from years of hard work the horse has become erratic and is at the end of its strength. For many winters, Father earned the money he needs to build the house with the dangerous work of hauling wood for the count.

He wants to build a house? I ask, astonished.

Yes, Grandmother says, but she'll know how to keep him from tearing down the old one.

Father decides to sell the stallion. One day the horse's stall in the stable is empty. The smell of horse sweat lingers for months. The stallion's perspiration fades only gradually and eventually cedes to the smell of the young bulls that toss their heads cantankerously, as if they wanted to shake off the chains that have been put around their necks.

One Sunday morning, Mother bursts into the kitchen in tears. She begs Grandmother to come with her, she doesn't know how she can help Father now. Grandmother seems to guess what the problem is and tells me to get a willow branch from the attic. Using the poker, she scrapes embers from the stove into a cast iron frying pan with a poker, breaks the willow branch I hand her in little pieces and puts it on the burning coals with a few herbs. It starts smoking right away. Mother has already run onto the outbuilding's balcony and is pointing at the apiary in which Father has holed himself up. Grandmother rushes past us with the smoking pan. I hear Father singing *Vigred se povrne*, a sad song about spring that returns every year and brings everything back to life, only for him there will be no more spring, for he will die. I ask Mother what's wrong with Father, but she just shakes her head and presses a handkerchief to her lips. Grandmother waves the smoking pan back and forth in front of the bee-house, covering the door with a cloud of smoke. Then she enters the apiary and comes right back out empty-handed. Without a word she returns to the kitchen. I stare at the apiary's open door and believe I can make out Father with a rifle in his hand. In any case, he comes out of the building without a weapon and sits on the threshold with his head in his hands. Mother whispers that we have to take care of him. I ask what we could do and Mother answers: pray. You should pray for him! And so I say an Our Father for Father. He lifts his head and looks at us reproachfully for a moment, then starts singing again and sets the smoking cast iron skillet down outside.

On weekends, Mother sends me to the tavern to get Father because, as she puts it, he forgot to come home. She doesn't want to fetch him anymore because he behaves impossibly on the way home and enough is enough, Mother says.

The kitchen at the Rastočniks' tavern is smoky and filled with cooking fumes. When I open the door someone inside yells that the command to retreat has sounded. Father sits grinning against the wall at the large guest table. I sit next to him on the wooden bench. You should come home, I say, as if he didn't already know. You think so, he asks and orders another beer for himself and a lemonade for me.

The waitress brings the drinks quickly and asks what's new at home and how things are at school. Are you happy about the new house, she wants to know. I nod and look at Father quizzically. It'll be something, he says, it will be my ruin.

Go on, says Pepi, one of my mother's cousins, you don't have to sign on to every stupidity. It's a good time to build, hasn't Father noticed there's a cement mixer in front of almost every house. Yes, goddamn it, Father responds and draws on his cigarette.

It's night when we leave the tavern. On the way home, Father argues with invisible adversaries. Sometimes he points at the sky and says, the Big Dipper, you see, or there, the Little Dipper. I walk beside him at a suitable distance and avoid touching him. Did Mother send you, he suddenly asks and he sounds more irritable than before. No, I lie, it was Grandmother. I see, he mumbles and walks on in silence.

At home Grandmother puts a glass of fortified wine and a cup of gentian tea on the table, the herb that cures a thousand ills, she says. Father should drink the tea before he goes to sleep. I ask Mother if Father is sick. He has stomach pains, she says, and lies awake almost every night. She can't sleep either when he groans with pain. But he refuses to see a doctor. Maybe it has to do with the coming changes, she supposes. We're getting a new house, and I'll have my own room. Am I not happy about that, she asks me. I nod, even though the thought of leaving Grandmother's room doesn't thrill me.

Father spends the next day resting on the bench near the stove. Mother has laid an herbal compress that smells of damp hay on his stomach. At night, the pain made him vomit, but only bile came out, Father tells me, a yellow slime. I give him a worried look and go outside with a guilty conscience because I can't do anything for him.

I T ’S time for you to walk to the Hrevelnik farm with me, Grandmother says, as long as I'm still on my feet. Soon it will be too late.

One morning she wakes me early and takes a willow rod taller than she is from the granary. Put decent footwear on, she commands, the path is steep.

We start at a leisurely pace, descending the sloping meadow below the house to the municipal road. On the road, Grandmother turns and looks back at our house and its whitewashed walls flashing between the trees. She can't get used to the idea that the old house is going to be torn down, she sighs. That house sheltered so many generations, how could anyone want to raze it!

We turn onto a road that winds its way through the pastures in broad curves up the shadowy side of the valley to the forest. The landscape dances and sways on the lenses of Grandmother's glasses. The pastures swing up to the crest of the hill, the tips of the spruce trees sink down into the shaded valley, a fragment of sky glints in the glittering stream running next to the road far below.

In the forest, the path narrows under our feet. After a clearing, it slips down to a streamlet then climbs steeply uphill, as if it wanted to prevent our advance. It is slippery and covered with beech leaves. Our steps set off small avalanches of leaves that slide gently into the depths. Walking is difficult. Grandmother stops and pants after almost every step. She would like to rest by the well up top, she says, there's nowhere to sit here.

At the beginning of the escarpment, I walk behind her and pass her on more even sections, wondering what I would do if Grandmother stopped and couldn't continue. In spite of my fears, she shows remarkable tenacity that you would never have suspected given her emaciated form. We climb slowly and doggedly until we reach the turn in the path at the top of the rise, behind which a well is visible. The water flows along a wooden channel into a wooden trough. Grandmother sits on the forest floor next to the well and looks at the house highest up on the valley wall opposite, now at the same elevation as we are. It strikes her that there are changes everywhere she looks, here something's been built, there something's been torn down, she says and points at a new access road. The road has torn a scar into the slope, Grandmother says and shakes her head.

After the well, the path runs almost level. Taking long strides, we approach the Hrevelnik property. It lies on the upper end of a gently sloping meadow. The shadow of a sundial vibrates on the whitewashed bulkhead of the main house. The buildings are abandoned. This farm was known far and wide for its sundial, now no one is left, Grandmother says and walks purposefully towards the stables. There was a path behind the stables that led to the Remschenig combe. This is the direction they came from back then, the women from Lepena who survived the camp, Grandmother begins her story. She was brought across the border near Koprivna illegally. When they climbed over the fence separating Yugoslavia and Austria, they laughed and wept. They flung their arms around each other's necks because it suddenly seemed so easy to make it home after their long odyssey. Once we crossed the border, walking wasn't hard at all, Grandmother tells me. They'd been walking all day. When they reached the Hrevelnik farm, night had fallen. She heard someone milking in the barn. She went in and said good evening. The milkmaid fell right off her stool, she was so happy, and the milk sprayed everywhere, Grandmother says. Milka jumped up and screamed, Mitzi, you're back! We thought you were dead! There are more with me, she answered and pointed at the women standing outside the barn, at Gregorička, Mimi, the Mitzis, at Frida and Malka. All these women who had lived on the farm, they all crowded together. At the Hrevelniks, they told Mimi there was no point in going home, because everything in Kach had been destroyed. Gregorička went to the Rigelniks, hoping they'd take her in, Grandmother says. The Gregorič's farm was destroyed, her husband died in Auschwitz, and the children were housed with strangers. The women were very upset. At the Hrevelniks they also learned that Grandfather and the boys were already home. Milka gave the women fresh milk to drink. She'll never forget the taste of that milk, Grandmother says and falls silent.

We sit on a wooden bench placed next to the front door of the house for solitary visitors to sit and rest. Grandmother gives a long, muted groan. After she recovers her strength, we set off. In the Hrevelniks' lower meadow, she stops and says that she was afraid at the time she'd no longer be welcome at home. My husband will reject me. I'm not the same person, she had thought to herself. I'll have to ask him, she decided, so that things are clear right from the start. It was very dark in the forest and in some spots she had to feel her way forward. It was early September.

When we enter the forest, the path is still easy to make out. Behind us, the light on the meadow collapses, as if someone had turned off the lights when we left the Hrevelnik farm.

That evening in bed, Grandmother tells me the rest of the story of her return, how she entered our farm when she finally made it home. She saw a light on in the sitting room, went up to the window and looked in. Her husband was sitting on the bench next to the oven, brooding. He was just taking off his shoes. He had one off already and had put his bare foot on the floor. The other was still on but the laces were untied. Your grandfather was staring into space, Grandmother says, he looked so strange that I had to gather all my courage to knock on the door. Grandfather looked up quickly, but didn't see her. Then she knocked again. He stood up slowly and went into the hallway. He opened the door and asked, who's there? She answered from the dark, will you take me back, do you recognize me? Mitzi, you're back, her husband shouted and hugged her so fiercely that her kerchief slipped off and fell to the ground. He hugged me so hard, the thing flew right off, Grandmother says and smiles. Then the boys, who were already in bed, got up. Mmm, I repeat after her, they got up, and I fall right asleep. Goodnight, *lahko noč*!

T H E time to tear down the old house approaches like an ineradicable evil. Father and Mother hectically discuss where to store the furniture and appliances from the old house during the construction. The outbuilding will be set up as temporary living quarters. The furniture that does not fit in the small rooms will be moved to the barn.

For days before the move, Grandmother paces through the old house. She touches the fixtures or sits on the oven bench and looks around the room.

She spent so many wonderful evenings here, she tells me, when the house was still full of life, when life had yet to become so sad. We danced and worked in this room, she says, we even put on plays and recited poetry when the girls still lived here. Katrca wrote poems and short plays. We learned them by heart and performed them.

I sit next to Grandmother and in my imagination I see blurry, faceless shadows flit past, their faces become distinct only later. I imagine a play that brings to life this passing parade of our family's and neighbors' ghosts. All those who once existed have brought along their clothing and furniture and they sing and act for us. They show us how people amused themselves in earlier days and what made them laugh. They strike poses and spin in circles, they pack up their things and disappear into a wall of emptiness and echoes. A bit of life seems to slip from Grandmother's frail body, like a puff of air rising to the ceiling. Her breath vibrates like a fleeting memory, a mere shadow of a breath, less than a sigh. The way she has begun to shrink makes me worry she might stiffen right there on the bench or dry up. Later, a hand could brush her slight body from the bench as easily as a dead bee.

Grandmother stands up and takes me by the hand. You know, I hate to give up this kitchen, your grandfather built it for me, she says. She'll miss the stove but will keep the sideboard no matter what. I follow her parting look as it sweeps over the entrance hall with the wooden stairs that lead to the attic and takes in the attic with its carved and painted chests, the cabinets, in which she's still hoarding provisions, the roof frame with rafters and beams, the laths and boards, the small skylight on the back wall of the house, the timbered balcony on the front of the house with bundles of herbs hung from nails to dry. I follow her into the smoke kitchen with its blackened walls, which remind me of shriveled or shining prunes depending on the light, and past the oven, which looks like it's set in the middle of an ashen landscape after a fire storm. Behind it, the larder with its unpainted wooden shelves filled with pots and jars. On the wall, the wooden pottery board holding fired pots full of cracks and held together with twisted wires. In the kitchen, the green sideboard and the food cupboard with tiny holes in its doors and drawer-fronts so the air can circulate, the prayer corner with the crucifix and pictures of saints, the benches along the walls, the square wooden table with inlaid decorations, the window casements and shutters with traces of mildew. Our bedroom in the back, its inner wall warmed by the tile oven in the kitchen so it's never cold, the wardrobe, the beds, the wall cupboard in which Grandmother keeps medicines and lotions. The house doors with their doorposts and cast iron locks, the cellar with its vaulted ceiling and shelves on which fruit is stored. The compartments for potatoes, the tub for sauerkraut, the barrels of hard cider.

On the day the excavator drives up to the farm, Grandmother stands on the outbuilding balcony and sobs, now it's all over, it's all over! God help me, Mary, Mother of God protect me! I'm so shocked, I start to cry with her. I grab onto her apron and howl so loudly that Grandmother begins hurling reproaches at Father who watches us helplessly, even this child understands what's happening right now, even the child! Toda, the excavator driver, lays his hand on her shoulder and pleads, calm down, Mitzi, the young ones want to have something of their own.

Grandmother stops weeping and only moans in protest as the last rafters are dropped and the excavator starts smashing the old walls. She pulls me to the front of the house and points at a number that has appeared under the yellowish plaster. 1743, this house has been inhabited since 1743 and now they say it's not good enough, she exclaims indignantly and begins looking for objects amidst the broken walls. In the past, she assumes, objects were always enclosed in the walls to protect the house from calamity. She scratches a few shards out of the rubble and, disappointed, tosses them away.

On his breaks, Toda sits with Grandmother. He tells her that lately he has been worried about his brother, who sometimes gets into a state in which he has no idea where he is. At night he escapes into the woods because he thinks the Germans are chasing him. He wanders about in a panic for hours, no one can calm him down. It's the camp, Grandmother says, it can only be the camp. His brother was still a child when the two of them were deported to the Altötting internment camp, Toda says, what can a child understand? A lot, Grandmother says, a whole lot.

I imagine the excavator driver's brother as someone who can also see the parade of ghosts and who follows those who have disappeared over hill and dale until he loses sight of them and their things in the dark forest.

When the shovel on Toda's digger reaches the basement, Father suggests he leave the cellar with its vaulted ceiling and only dig out the area for the second cellar. Maybe he did this to calm Grandmother down and give her the feeling that the new house would stand on the foundation of the old one. The old cellar survives the demolition like a stubborn molar that won't be extracted.

As the house's frame rises over the cellar and the first walls are being sheathed, Father is being persuaded to add a second floor to the planned one-story house. After all, his family will grow and the children will need room. Father agrees and asks everyone who comes to see the construction if it makes sense. He operates the monotonously grinding cement mixer, hauls the mortar to the building site in a wheelbarrow, the *cariola*, and lifts plastic buckets full of the heavy mash with a cable reel.

Since the whine of circular saws has replaced the mixer's chewing and, in the woodshed, bags of cement have been replaced by beams, posts, and planking, I can sense Grandmother giving in. Just as the builders are topping off the house with a spruce tree attached to the highest rafter, she decides not to move into the new house. She threatens to tell everyone who asks that she was thrown out.

A few weeks before we move in, the fabric merchant comes by.

Grandmother haggles over blankets, towels, pillows, and sheets – her contribution to the household, she says.

The Gypsy's van is filled to the brim with bed linens when he brings the ordered goods. He assures us he chose the best pieces for his best customer.

His wife can't read the cards fast enough because the construction workers are also hoping to be told of good fortunes. The piles of sheets and towels flaunt their white, blue, and golden-red flower patterns on the balcony of the outbuilding and are admired by the recipients for days.

The new house is furnished and occupied.

One evening I hear Father arguing with Michi, who had stopped in to ask how things were coming along. Michi thinks that Father shouldn't have cut costs and installed central heating. It's standard these days and is less time-consuming than heating with a small oven. Besides, Michi thinks a new house without warm water is old-fashioned. Father takes offense. He didn't want to go into debt, he protests. Furthermore, now there's running water in the house, so he can forego the luxury of central heating. As he is taken around the house, Michi does find a few things he likes, especially the bathroom and the new bread oven that has been covered with antique tiles.

Mother puts a set of dishes in mint condition into the sideboard, the set she received on her wedding day. She sews curtains and tablecloths for the kitchen and embroiders them with red carnations. She argues with Father over the wooden closet she ordered from the carpenter to keep her books and knitting supplies along with our schoolbooks. Grandmother moves into the outbuilding, and I move into a room of my own with no heating.

The new house is built on a vulnerable foundation. The slope, into which the old house seemed to have grown, has been removed. Where once a path led so close to the back of the house that you could support yourself with your hand on the wall, there is now an escarpment. Like an open mouth from which the jaws were extracted. The new house stands in this gaping mouth with no rear cover and cannot settle down. The badly insulated walls cannot store any heat. The first blotches and traces of mold appear in the stairwell. The old cellar revives memories of the past every time we set foot in it. When the seasons change, it emits strange odors that try to penetrate into the building above it. The new walls, however, send everything outside, eject all they cannot hold. Waves of odors waft around the courtyard, the musty smell of mold, the sour smell of apples, the sweetish smell of potatoes.

I'M delighted I can return to the castle in my summer holidays. In Gradisch, I hop up the wooden staircase to my uncle's apartment and plunge into the familiar mix of smells in the attic apartment. I want to play for hours with my cousins or lie in bed reading comic books.

The summer days have a glittering golden border and more of the color rubs off onto my skin every day. The days are painted with the colors of the flowers in my aunt's garden and blended in the water of the count's pond where we swim.

One hot day at noon, Iris, who works in the kitchen, takes Johanna and me to the pond. She is meant to keep an eye on us. In any case, she is older than we are.

We spread our towels on the dock and cautiously slip into the shallow water. Iris lets my little cousin climb onto her back and swims across the pond with her. Johanna squeals and laughs, but the pond's depths are quickly crossed.

After Iris set Johanna on the dock again, she offers to take me on her back. I hesitate because I can't swim, but finally picture myself flying across on Iris's back and I slip into the dark water. In the middle of the pond, Iris suddenly goes limp under me then digs her nails into my shoulders. We sink immediately, tenaciously gripping each other, trying again and again to surface. Iris holds me underwater but her grip grows weaker and when I pull myself up on her and scream for help, I don't hear a sound from her, not a scream or a groan, I just feel her yielding and I manage to tear myself away. I push off from her and swim, or at least move in a way that resembles swimming, the water around me a gelatinous mass. There's thudding in my blocked ears. The idea of surviving makes me feel light-headed, she could kill me, I have to swim, I tell myself until I feel the earth under my feet again and can stand. Johanna laughs. I gasp for air, turn, and see Iris floating, curled up, on the surface of the water. I scream for help and run to the castle, I call the workers, they rush down to the pond and pull Iris from the water. Her striped bikini top slips from her shoulders and bares one white breast, a thick light-colored substance gushes from her mouth. It's what she ate for lunch, says someone who is trying to revive her. The substance is orange now. She drowned, someone says. I killed her, I think. My aunt pulls Johanna and me away. I turn as we leave and see Iris, pale, so white and pale, lying on the sandy ground. I killed her, I think. A doctor arrives and says I shouldn't see more.

Later, the police arrive, too, and want to question me. But I can't speak German, I think, I can't tell them I killed her. So I tell a story, I say we were playing, that she sank underwater out of the blue, that I was able to get free from her, somehow or other. I run a fever, wake up screaming in the middle of the night, I'm galloping away on a flaming black horse.

The looks people give me over the following days are sad and wordless. They stick to the surface of my body that, like a snail's shell, is separated from my raw and tender interior, as if my skin were recoiling from the inflammation beneath it. I have landed in Death's quiver and have heard his breath, felt his maw. Death almost caught me. I'd barely escaped into life, into my scarcely eight-year-old life that had just taken its place inside me and refused to be chased away like a thief. Despite my bewilderment, I feel guilty for having survived.

When I'm brought home, my aunt says that they almost lost me, that I very nearly drowned, she can hardly forgive herself. Mother says, that's terrible. She says nothing else. I take a step to the side, invisible to everyone there, and watch myself standing on the front doorstep, crying. Am I really crying or am I only thinking of crying? The person that I'm watching or that I am would never be able to express how distraught she is. Grandmother puts her arm around me and says, sleep with me tonight, tonight you can sleep with me! At night, I press up against her so hard that, half-asleep, she scolds me. I hold her tight, as if her bony body were lying next to me like an island in the vast ocean.

W E are standing in the entrance to the old cellar when I try to recount how the disaster happened. I tell Grandmother a story that sounds strange and dull. The only thing I feel with any certainty is that Iris's death is overwhelming, that I can neither bear nor understand what happened, and that I'm afraid of the police. I thought they were going to lock me up, I manage to squeeze out.

Grandmother takes my hand. I'll show you how to act when the police come, she says. With your tongue, you have to make the sign of the cross on the roof of your mouth. You have to make three crosses and repeat that a few times. You see, she says and opens her mouth to show her tongue making a crossing motion on the top of her mouth. In this way, silently, invisibly, she prayed on the day the police took her away and she had to say goodbye to her oldest son and her nephew who were in the house at the time. I crossed myself with my tongue and with my foot, I drew crosses on the ground, Grandmother tells me. You have to pray for a safe return and convince all the powers that be that you want to go home. On the 12th of October in 1943, many of the neighbors who had been arrested with her died, Marija Mozgan, the Mozgan's maid, Bricl, Luka Čemer, Miha Kožel, Poldi Topičnik, the men in the Kach family, Jurij, Hanzi, and Franz, the Kach women, Marija and Ana, they all died in the camp. The only ones who came back were the Mozgdan's daughter Amalija, the Čemer children, Johi and Katrca, Tschik and the Auprich boys, Erni and Franz, Paula Maloveršnik, and Grandmother herself. They were all that was left of the procession led away towards Eisenkappel that day. I also prayed silently during each roll call in the camp, Grandmother says. Once, in the first winter, they had to stand late into the night on Christmas, it was snowing, the women had to endure the cold in their light work coats. One woman was missing, no one knew if she'd escaped or died. They had to stand until the prisoner count tallied. The snow stuck to the women. We were so frozen the snow didn't even melt, but piled up on our thin coats, Grandmother says. Late into the night, she constantly repeated her prayers and made the sign of the cross with her tongue so she wouldn't collapse. She was saved, yes, but whether or not she's glad she's alive, that she can't say.

I slowly begin to emerge from my torpor and realize there are disasters much greater than mine. I should stick to Grandmother, I think, since she knows Death, because once you've smelled Death, you can chase him away, scare him off, as soon as you feel him approaching. I'm not reassured, just admonished and distracted, spilled like a glass of water that can't be put back in the receptacle, that has changed and evaporated where it was spilled.

T H E colors of summer slowly return. They flicker in the sunlit trees and float up from the sun-warmed meadows as we cross them. The hay harvest sets the rhythm to our days and I bury my horror in a remote corner of my consciousness. Despite the heat, an icy shadow flits through me from time to time and envelops me in its darkness.

Uncle Jozi brings two baby goats to our farm for the summer. It is my job to tend them because, left on their own, the two kids would get lost or run away from the farm. One day, when I'm crying, the playful animals discover my tears taste good and lick my face with their small, rough tongues. I can't help but laugh and from that day on, I bring lettuce leaves to the pasture to lure the kids to me. I give them the run of my face and let them clean my nose and ears with their tongues. It tickles and drives away all dark thoughts. Their soft, light-colored bodies calm my fingertips as they relentlessly rub the kids' fine coats, trying to absorb some of their whiteness.

Before the start of the school year, Mother sends me to the seaside with a group of farmers' children. I need to learn to swim, she tells me, and to get some rest. She lays out all the necessary clothing, stitches my initials into each item, and takes me to the office of the Farmers' Insurance Association in Klagenfurt where the other children are already waiting with their parents for the bus that will take us to Bibione. On the bus we are each given an orange cardboard nametag to hang from our necks and a large snack to ease the pain of saying goodbye to our parents.

In Bibione, I struggle against an overwhelming anxiety that paralyzes me as soon as I go into the water for swimming lessons. Every little wave that touches my face, every mouthful of salt water that runs down my throat makes me frantic. When the salt water stings my eyes, I fear I won't ever be able to see again and shoot up from under the water like an injured fish fighting to stay alive. My fear of drowning darkens the sun-drenched days. The colors of the long, sandy beach and the grayish blue of the sea cannot push aside the baleful shadows of the count's fish pond.

Then, one day, I pluck up my courage and swim in shallow water. My arms and legs move as if revived from rigor mortis, still panicky at first, but gradually more confidently and smoothly. Life looks more promising, I think, as long as I'm certain I can feel solid ground beneath my feet.

I make friends with one of the girls, and as we walk along the beach on the last day I tell her that I have to say goodbye to the sea because this is probably the last time I'll ever see it. I can't confide to her that I've already started getting used to seeing things for the last time, the glittering ocean of stars in the night sky, for example, or the beach chairs and umbrellas on the seaside, or Father at home kneeling down to repair a chainsaw, or Mother holding up a bunch of carrots as she comes in from the garden, or the angry, green-tinged lizards I pester with wooden sticks when I'm tending the cows. My friend gives me a surprised look and I can't explain even to myself why, from time to time, I'm convinced life holds no future for me.

Two decades later, my aunt will tell me as we swim in the count's pond that Iris suffered from epilepsy and had an attack in the water. Why are you only telling me this now, I will ask her. Because it needed to be said, Vera will answer, whenever she swam in this pond, she always thought of that tragedy. If I'd known, then as a child I'd have been able to deal with the fact that I survived much better and wouldn't have been terrified every time I went into a swimming pool, I will exclaim. I wouldn't have lain in dark water for entire nights, alone and invisible, a tiny corpse that could talk and lived among people constantly bumping into her.

T H E small wood behind our house, which I have to cross on the way to see Michi and his family when I want to watch television, is growing rampant. I thought I knew it inside out. I've walked in this wood countless times and could find my way through it with my eyes closed. Now I have to summon all my courage just to set foot in it. I used to think I could smell every section of the path, every little clearing, the places where the trees had grown tall or were still short, and, with my eyes closed, could sense the sequence of hazel, raspberry, and willow bushes, or tell when the canopy of fir trees opened up or closed in above me. Now the wood is no longer familiar. It has joined with the forest and turned into a sea of green, full of prickly needles and sharp-edged scales, with a heaving, surging underbrush of rough bark. As soon as I look out my bedroom window, the wood creeps into sight or lurks with its rippling, jagged surface behind the meadow. I'm afraid it will overflow its banks one day and leave the forest's edge, flooding our thoughts the way I now feel the forest occupies the thoughts of the men who work with my father or visit us to go hunting with him.

Going into the forest, in our language, not only means felling trees, hunting, or gathering mushrooms. It also means – as they're always telling us – hiding, escaping, and ambushing. Men and women slept in the forest, they cooked and ate there, too, not just in peacetime, but also during the war. Not into our wood, no, it was much too sparse for that, too small and too easily controlled. They set off into the larger forests. Many people took refuge in the forests, a hell in which they hunted and were hunted like game.

The stories revolve around the forest, just as the forest encircles our farm.

In the forest were hidden the best places to hunt, to gather berries and mushrooms, and the best feeding grounds, secrets you never disclose. Even more secret are the places that no paths or tracks lead to, places you have to track down over hunting trails and streambeds, the hideouts and refuges, the bunkers in which our people went to ground, as they say.

This year a windstorm causes a lot of damage to the count's forested slopes. The gales leave behind a broad swath of destruction in which trees lie split, broken, and uprooted on the ground. Loggers from all the count's crews are called up to clear the fallen trees. For weeks, the whine of saws, the dull thuds of axes, and the cracking of trunks hang over the valley.

On weekends, the loggers gather at our farm to sharpen and repair their tools. Their trousers are spattered with pitch stains that gleam like small swamps. Circular buds of dirt spread from the middle of these swamps and seep into the cloth like shadows of pitch clouds. The loggers' shirts are soaked with sweat, the sweaters and jackets they lay over their shoulders are fraying at the sleeves and hems.

Father sits on a bench, repairing a saw he calls "the American lady." He hammers gently on the saw. It bobs up and down to the beat, making a humming noise.

You're making the saw dance, Michi says. As soon as I put her in your hands, she's in a good mood. Uncle Jozi tells his crewmates that he'd like to do a radio show. In fact, he's already put in a request for a recording device from the Slovenian department of the Austrian Broadcasting Corporation. He wants to talk to people and record their conversations. If they don't mind, he'd like to do a story about them, too: Count Thurn's loggers.

You're not loggers anymore, Father says, you left the forest a long time ago.

You have think of the future, Michi answers, you can't just go into the forest every day as if there weren't anything else, as if there were no other way of earning a living. He's signed up with the Socialists, he announces. They'd promised they would find him something else.

You want to go into politics, Father counters, but you'll never be mayor, there's no way they would ever let you, a Slovene, be mayor.

You have no idea, Michi says.

I know what I know, Father says.

Father tells them that earlier in the week he crossed the green border into Slovenia from the Mozgans' ridge, where he's been cutting wood for the farmers, and had a beer at the Kumers'. The women were amazed that he ventured across the border. They asked after people in Lepena and told him to say hello to everyone they knew. Thanks, thanks, the loggers say as they set off on foot for home. Only Jozi climbs onto a motorcycle and drives off with a wave of his hand.

WHERE is the border, actually, I ask Father.

Up that way, he says and points at the ridge that encloses the valley in a semi-circle.

I'd like to go to work with you one day, I say.

Father is so surprised by my request that he promises to take me to the logging stand the next day. He has to take some tools up anyway.

Early in the morning, his motorcycle is outside the stable, a Puch with a dark, gleaming gas tank that looks like the body of a black dolphin. Father ties the knapsack bulging with tools and a canister of fuel onto the luggage rack. I sit on the back seat and wrap my arms carefully around his waist. He tells me to hold on tight so I won't fall off on the way. In the first curve he yells, you're wobbling, hold on tight or we'll start skidding. After the initial fear that floods over me when Father brakes into a curve, I let myself get carried away as he accelerates on the straight stretches.

He parks his motorcycle behind the Mozgans' farm, slides a few iron clamps under his belt, and shoulders his backpack. We start off walking slowly. The gasoline sloshes in the canister. You have to stroll on steep terrain or you'll get out of breath, Father says. Then he picks up his pace.

I lag behind and take advantage of flat stretches to catch up with him. Were you here during the war? I ask.

Yes, we had a bunker higher up, he says. Your grandfather ran the couriers. I did the cooking. It was very dangerous.

Were you afraid? I ask.

I should think so, I was only a child, a few years older than you.

Behind us we hear frightened game take flight.

It got a whiff of us, Father says.

Under the crest of the forest, between mighty spruce trees with thick branches that almost reach the ground, a hut appears. It is completely covered with bark, layer nailed upon layer over a wooden frame. We used to sleep here when we were felling timber, Father says. He opens the lock and stores the tools and the fuel canister next to the unused cots.

First I have to go to the logging stand, he says, then we can cross the border.

His work area looks neat and is marked off by piles of branches. Stripped and unstripped logs are arranged on the ground, with branch stumps or pared, as Father says, and between them, fragrant piles of sawdust. The logs have sloping edges, the cut surfaces of the trunks shine like freshly carved wooden plates.

Father stands in the middle of the clearing and looks over the stand, then he gathers the scattered splitting wedges and covers them with branches. I'm looking forward to a beer now, he says and points toward the border.

To my surprise, the border runs close to the logging stand. From the crest of the forest I can see the Yugoslavian side of the slope and to my amazement it looks exactly like the Austrian side, just a continuation of the familiar landscape. Father leans his weight on a fence post as he leaps over the border. He tells me to crawl across under the barbed wire, lifting the bottom strand so I don't get caught on the twirling spikes.

Suddenly he is in a hurry again. With long strides, he rushes downhill through a sparse wood. Fern leaves slap at my face. He waits for me below the wood. He sits on the grass, looking down at a low-lying valley that seems to disappear in the depths.

Over there, behind the Raduha, Father points at the ridge of a mountain, that's where I went to school during the war, he says. Not long. Fourteen days it must have been. I went to school there, in Luče. He and his brother were the band's couriers, on a farm. After they ran away from home, they were only allowed to stay in the bunker with their father for two weeks. Then they were taken to the Savinja Valley because it was liberated territory. They had to abandon their command center in January because the Germans attacked the valley. The Germans fired so many shots over the field, that dirt sprayed everywhere, Father says. He and the other couriers buried the typewriters in the ground. They dug a hole, threw in some straw and piled the typewriters on it. Then they spread more straw on top, and then dirt, and grass, and snow, until nothing was visible. They set off in the afternoon and walked all night. The next day, Germans chased us again, Father says. The snow came up to my hips. One of the commanders told me I wasn't going to make it.

He spits hard as if he needed relief after telling the story.

At the Kumers', we are greeted by two women who know his name. Zdravko, they call, Zdravko, how nice that you've come back! They serve Father a beer and me a slice of bread with liverwurst.

On the way home, Father looks at me with an absent smile. I think how good it would be if Father took me into his confidence and repeated the story he told me earlier then asked me what I've been through and I could tell him how I'm bullied on the way to school and that I dream of him confronting my classmates and demanding they stop threatening me at once. In the hope of being able to count on Father, I make him a silent promise that I myself don't understand, a commitment to accompany him on his way home and on his way to school, through this very landscape, maybe, or in his memories. As we make our way uphill through the forest I wonder if I should stay in my child's body or should grow out of it, and for this day I decide to stay in my short skirt, cotton tights, and rubber boots.

When we arrive at the customs path below the border, I look for footprints in the soft ground, in which puddles have formed. Father says the customs officers must have the day off because it's Sunday, and laughs at his own joke.

We reach the Austrian side without being seen, and Father asks if I'd like to go with him as a beater on a hunt now that he's seen what a good walker I am. I say yes and resolve to overcome my fear of the forest. On the way to the Mozgans', there's a clearing with a view of the farms scattered throughout the valley. We pause and look out from the green undergrowth. Like two fish, it occurs to me, peering out from the seaweed. I saw the perky fish on television and imagine Father and me peeking out from the thicket with our big eyes and disappearing into it again, raising a small cloud of sand that slowly sinks back down in the murky water. A sea of stalks, I think. Soon we'll reach the shore.

When I climb up behind Father on his motorcycle, I'm happy. I wrap my arms tight around his waist and press up against his back. It is late afternoon as we drive down the winding Koprina Road. The sun hovers level with us. Father stops in a hairpin turn and smokes a cigarette. There used to be a fence here, he says and exhales a puff of smoke.

Before we reach the bottom of the valley, we cross a wooden bridge toward a rundown house hidden amidst plum and apple trees. As we climb off the motorcycle, Jaki, one of Father's fellow loggers, stands leaning on his scythe in front of the door. The mown grass lies in waves around the house.

I was going after the thistles, Jaki says. Were you at the felling strip? Father nods.

If you don't mow regularly, it all gets overgrown, Jaki says. He was up at the Blajs' place earlier today. The grass has grown high there, too.

Father looks up at the lonely property still in the sun.

Too bad no one is farming the place, he says. Who'd have imagined it would turn out this way.

How many brothers was it who died in the camp? Jaki asks.

The three older ones, Jakob, Johi, and Lipi, Father says. Lipi's ashes were sent from Natzweiler, the others died in Dachau.

I hear the resounding name of Dachau, which I'd heard before, but Natzweiler is a new one, and I forget it again immediately.

His uncle died up there, too, Jaki recalls. He had just deserted, Jaki says to me, feeling my gaze on him, and he was wounded in the first battle with the Germans. He dragged himself over the field to the Jekls' and lay bleeding below the road behind a bush. The German patrol passed him without seeing him. But then the last soldier looked down and shot him. The Jekls had to bury him next to the road.

That's right, my father says, I know the spot.

The dead leave their chill in this spot from which the sun has now withdrawn. I wonder if the cold that is making me shiver also has something to do with the evening and with the forest creeping up to the houses. The light rushes up into the sky. Father sinks into immobility. I ask him if we can finally go home.

Yes, yes, he says and tells me not to *tschentsch* him like my mother. He only decides to get back on his motorcycle when Jaki wheels his own around the side of the house. The three of us drive down the gravel road, but at the fork where we should have turned left, Father turns right and stops at the side of the road.

You can walk home from here, if you want, he tells me, I'm going to have a beer.

I take the shortcut across the field that belongs to the inn, where lethargic, sated cows switch their tails. I balance on the two tree trunks laid across the Lepena stream and hurry up a bank behind which I can hear our pigs squealing in their sty.

T H E forest has not been able protect its solitude since men sought refuge it in, since it lost control of their straying, since loggers and hunters have ranged through it searching for prey, since it was declared bandit territory.

The way someone went into the forest or came out of it revealed everything about him, it was said. Was he carrying a gun, did he have a red star on his cap, was he wearing two pairs of trousers at once and two coats so he wouldn't freeze, was his shirt unbuttoned, his trousers torn and stained with pitch, was he carrying a dead deer in his backpack or bringing bacon to the Green cadres up near the highest fir trees? Was he carrying a basket of mushrooms, a bucket filled with berries, or courier letters in his pockets? Was his shirt clean, did he smell of pitch and bark, or did he stink, rank and unwashed, of dirt and cold sweat, of blood and scabs?

My father's hunting friends wear ironed trousers and jackets the color of trees, they carry the smell of moss in their hair and put fir twigs in their hat bands when they've bagged their prey. The heads of horned game dangle from their backpacks. A gun was trained on each animal, then they were felled. Blood and sweat still drip from their muzzles, the dew of the last breaths they took. The dark gleam of their eyes will continue to shine a while from their delicate heads. Their skulls stripped of pelt and fur will simmer in peroxide baths until they are bleached and lifted from the cauldron like trophies.

Hunting is part of the family myth, every hunting day is a celebration, that's how it has always been, Father says. He still goes deerstalking at dawn and at dusk, oils his rifles and shotguns, cleans the scope, counts the cartridges. The game is still boiled and braised in the kitchen, the smell of chamois stew whets our appetite. His hunting friends still come in and out of our house telling their stories. He still looks forward to the annual hunt and to the drive he will take me on since I am such a good walker.

When the day comes, the hunt is discussed early in the morning, the hunters are served doughnuts and hot tea. The area is divided up, sections of the forest assigned, positions designated. I'm to go with old Pop, whom I know well. Pop's face looks like a coarse-grained desert landscape. He is the oldest in the group and, it is said, the one with the worst eyes. Once they wanted to test him and his eyesight, the story goes, and they stuck a house cat in a rabbit's pelt. They wrapped the fur around the cat and tied it on with string. Hissing and scratching, the cat fled up the nearest tree and Pop couldn't believe his eyes because he could have sworn he saw the first rabbit that ever climbed a tree.

Grandmother pulls me aside. She has heard that the hunt will end at the Gregoričs' farm. She wants me to say hello to old Gregorička for her. She carried me out of the camp when the camp was being evacuated and I was too weak to walk, Grandmother says. For three whole days, Gregorička carried me, helped me walk, and pushed me in a wheelbarrow until the SS had disappeared. Gregorička lost her mind in Auschwitz, even before she was transferred to Ravensbrück, and from that point on, she swore that the devil who put her in the camp would lead her out again. When she was younger, she was a strong woman who could take on any man, Grandmother recalls. I nod and say that I'll give Gregorička her best.

Pop holds my hand as we walk towards our section of the forest, beating our sticks against the trees and bushes. Shotguns over their shoulders, the hunters have hurried on ahead of us. The dogs drive hares and foxes in their direction, we hear only a few isolated shots and see only a few animals take flight.

The line of game laid out in front of the Gregoričs' farm that afternoon is as short as a wake, and the schnapps is soon drunk. We're invited into the farmhouse. They say they've cooked up some goulash for the *Schüsseltrieb*, the closing feast. Old Gregorička is sitting on the bench at the table. I go up to her to pass on Grandmother's greeting and give her my hand. Hers is cold and moist. She smells of urine. Gregorička does not understand who is sending their good wishes and looks at me blankly. Sveršina tries to explain. The strong old woman nods and sways her powerful body back and forth while we eat. I watch her from the corner of my eye and can't help thinking of Grandmother and how this Gregorička was capable of throwing men into the air and carrying my weakened grandmother out of the camp.

One hunter tells us that a neighbor of his, who had fought with the partisans during the war and had just died, once told him that he saw a white stag when he was out on watch, not in a raised hide, and he had an intuition that his partisan bunker had been betrayed. He warned his comrades, but they wouldn't listen. The police did, in fact, raid the bunker the next day. It was a sign and you have to heed signs, the hunter says. Sveršina says it's nonsense. Intuition, what do you mean, intuition, he blusters. The fear of falling into the Gestapo's hands had nothing supernatural about it. After he brought Kori to the partisans, it wasn't long before the police showed up at the Brečks' farm. Someone must have gotten wind of it and the next thing you know, he was off to Mauthausen!

Father asks the hunters if they still remember who was the best shot in Lepena. Well, he says, well, you don't remember. It was old Farmer Mozgan's wife, he says after a short pause, as if playing the queen of spades. She was a legendary poacher and bagged some powerful roe. What do you say to that, Father wants to know, what have you got to say with the puny little hares you've bagged, you can only dream of being as good a shot as Mozgan's wife. She sat up in the hide with her knitting and when a deer came grazing, she didn't bat an eye, just raised her rifle and bang and done! But she didn't make it through Ravensbrück, Sveršina throws down the joker, that was the end of her, yes, the end of her.

Night is falling when the hunters head home, and I realize that Father has had too much to drink. He stands unsteadily and complains about the long way he has to go to get home. They press a flashlight into my hand and send me off with the words, you know how to look after your father.

I lead the way and try to light up the path for Father and me. He tells me how often he has gone this way alone and how well he knows it.

The forest begins to draw in the darkness. A keen-eared silence surrounds us and seems to be lying in wait for our footsteps. I wonder how I can keep Father talking so the stillness won't get the upper hand. As we step out of the forest and stop in the field behind the Auprichs' farm, I ask the name of the farmhouse we can see higher up, outlined below the top of the wooded hill. That's the Hojniks' farm, Father says, the Nazi police went on a rampage there as well. The family was supposed to be hauled off, but old Hojnik refused to leave. He was beaten to death on the spot. They shot his son and daughter-in-law and threw all their bodies into the cottage and set it on fire. Father's voice cracks suddenly. He speaks in a strained tone. I find it irritating.

A light wind sets in. The trees begin to groan as soon as we step back into the forest. Amid the rustling of the leaves, I can just make out the sound of voices and screams. I ask Father to give me his hand. He laughs and takes a big step forward to reach my hand. At that moment, he loses his balance and slides sideways down a steep scarp and ends up lying flat on the ground behind a bush. The flashlight, which fell when he grabbed for my hand, goes out. I can barely see him in the dark and hear him swearing far below. How the devil am I supposed to get back up there, he moans. I think he is hurt and get ready to slide down to him. Stay up there, he shouts, stay right there, I can make it up on my own. He starts to crawl up the slope on all fours. The flashlight's gone, how am I supposed to see anything in the dark, Father complains and kicks his boots into the ground to get his footing. When he is near me, he says, you can pull me up now, and I pull with all my strength. I just need to rest a bit, he says, and then we'll keep going. He sits down on the forest floor and seems to fall asleep a second later. I crouch next to him and feel my eyes fill with tears. The forest and the darkness let all their ghosts loose and they grab at me wildly. I raise my head and try to make out the moon that tonight is hiding behind the clouds. A dark sphere in the sky seems to be sinking towards me. I'm afraid I've drawn it down with my crying, and I close my eyes. The darkness takes hold of me and fills my chest intoxicatingly.

Father lies next to me, as if drugged. After an eternity, he opens his eyes and says, you know, the best thing to do when you're afraid in the forest is to sing partisan songs. He often did, and it always helped. Do I know any, he asks. I don't. Fine, then I'll sing, he says. And Father sings as best he can some partisan fighting songs, though he can only remember a few verses and repeats them over and over until we finally reach home.

Mother is waiting up for us in the kitchen, angry and worried. I don't want to upset her so I don't say anything about the calamities on our way home. I'm afraid that death has taken root inside me, like a small black button, like a lattice-work of dark moss creeping invisibly over my skin.

T H E   WA R is a devious fisher of men. It has cast out its net for the adults and traps them with its fragments of death, its debris of memory. Just one careless act, one brief moment of inattention, and it pulls in its net. Father is immediately snagged on memory's hooks, he's already running for his life, trying to escape the war's omnipotence. The war suddenly looms in hastily spoken sentences, strikes out from the shelter of darkness. It leaves its captives trembling in its net and withdraws for months at a time to prepare a fresh attack as soon as it's forgotten. If ever it grows feeble, they welcome it into their homes and smile at its armor, certain they can win it over, they set a place at the table, make up a bed for it.

Father was the youngest partisan, his cousin Peter tells us when we're gathered in the sitting room to celebrate Grandmother's birthday. The youngest partisan, do you still remember, you were barely twelve years old. Yes, Father says but he'd much rather forget all about it. At night he sometimes wakes with a start and has no idea where he is. In my dreams,

I'm still running for my life like I did back then on the Velika Planina, Father says.

Mother of God, the others say, now that was a dog's life!

The day our provisions ran out and the commando came, it was up and out, down the mountain, through the German soldiers, over, out, Father recalled. That was some kind of noise. At two in the morning, they slid down the mountainside in deep snow, down a chute that was used to send tree trunks into the valley below. The Germans trained searchlights up from Kamnik. It was so bright, every movement was visible. There was shooting in the valley, and all you could see were red and blue streaks. Leaves and branches rained down from the trees and one partisan was lying on the ground yelling help me, help me, Father tells us, but he just ran as if the devil were on his heels. They'd gotten separated while escaping, he and two other partisans ran across the road and right in front of a German soldier with a machine gun. I'm a dead man, Father told himself, now I'm going to get shot, but the German made it clear that he should disappear. He waved Father on. Quick, quick, the soldier said. He was a good one, Father says, one of the good ones, I'll never forget him. Father's group reached the river and the commander yelled: Cross through the water, we'll never make it over the bridge! The first one who stepped in the river vanished, washed away like nothing. They'd clung to each other and made it across. The water rushed over him and his brother – and this in January. Because in war it's like being hares in a hunt, only much worse, Father says.

Yes, Peter confirmed, we were the hares and hunger was our commander.

He often remembers how hungry he was then, how his stomach was at the core of his delirium and put him in harm's way. When he thinks of it now, how careless he and Lojz were at the Kebers' farm because they believed the farmer's wife would give them bread, he still gets goose bumps. I can hear the Germans, Peter says. Shoot, shoot, bandits! they'd shouted. Lojz had fired and Peter had shot his revolver. There was no possible retreat, they couldn't run up the mountain so they ran across the field, Lojz in front and Peter behind. Then the police dog caught him and tore his pant leg. He fell head over heels and lost his gun. The officer chasing him yelled: Stop, boy, stay where you are! But he kept running like mad. Then the Germans started shooting, all at once, terrifying, but the mountain swallowed them up, him and Lojz.

ON days like these, Father sometimes loses his grip. At the beginning of a celebration, he seems almost shy, wants to be put in the mood, drinks a lot of hard cider or wine. The family's high spirits get him cracking jokes. The relatives convince him to get his accordion and finally make some music. Father plays with abandon, calls everyone onto the dance floor and stamps his foot to the beat. After a while, his look changes. A second being inside him pushes its back up against his eyes. They turn blank, like false windows you can't see into or out of. He becomes irritable. Our relatives decide they can no longer take him seriously and start to think about leaving. The nervous ones whisper that it's about time to go and clear their throats. It was so much fun, they say, we should do this more often because it does everyone such good to sit together, to dance and sing.

As soon as the last guest is gone, Father's eye-demon takes full possession of him and leads him in a wild polka, flinging him in all directions. The polka to the left throws Father into utter dejection, the one to the right sends him into a mad rage that erupts in ear-splitting cries and is sparked by small misunderstandings.

My brother and I are sent out of the room and in our distress we don't know what to do. We stand around the kitchen or run outside. We're convinced the war has moved into our house for a few days and is not prepared to give ground.

We play partisans when once again Father, hunting rifle in hand, threatens at the top of his voice to shoot us all. We run up the slope into the forest, huddle behind a hazel bush, crawl on our stomachs along the edge of the forest, our invisible weapons at the ready, and, lying in the grass, we look down at our parents' house and debate when it would be safe to leave our cover and go back to our rooms.

One time Mother flees with us, which makes us anxious because we're afraid she'll draw Father's attention to our hiding place. Our numbed lungs can barely expand. I look at my brother and hope he doesn't understand everything that's going on, but I'm not quite sure. I watch Father, how he wages war with us in a new form, and I see myself floating free from the husk of my body, and I look down at myself as if at a doll lying in the grass, head drawn in between its shoulders. Even if I'm hit, I won't die, I think, because I've left my body.

A dormant cannon, an undetonated missile has wandered out of the past and onto our farm by mistake and is seeking shelter under the plum trees in our wood. We're the unintended targets, which we never should have been but in the heat of the battle, we're forced to stand in for the real thing.

As soon as Father, overcome with exhaustion, nods off and the gun slips from his hand, we exhale. Mother takes his gun and locks it in the hunting closet. We clean up our hiding place and gingerly hurry past Father as he sleeps, his head propped on his elbows. He seems to sigh in his sleep and lies like a gnarled plum tree branch in the field behind the house, on the floor near the doorstep, or on the corner bench in the kitchen.

The dance in the opposite direction opens with Father's self-incriminations. He rhythmically repeats that he's worth nothing, never has been worth anything, a dog is what he is, a dog hiding under the table. Come, little doggy, he says, come out from under the table. Come on now, tu tu tu tu, he coaxes, tu tu tu tu!

But the little dog won't move. It has crawled into a corner, as have I, already guessing what will happen when Father leaves the house. That's not true at all, I try to reassure him. How could he possibly say he's a little dog, how could he even think it, I ask and see my sentences hanging in the air like a line that has broken off before reaching its goal.

Father takes a deep breath to drag his voice up from deep in his belly. He squeezes it into his throat, where it's honed to a cutting edge. Then he fires sentences from his mouth like blistering projectiles. At some point he breaks off mid-sentence and walks, or rather runs, out of the house. Nothing we can say, no amount of pleading helps. Even Grandmother shrinks back and gets out her rosary. Rivers of darkness flow from the small black opening inside me.

Mother says she can't stand it any longer, whether she wants to or not she has to go see where Father's run off to, somebody has to stop him from hurting himself. I grab her hand and try to tell her with the pressure of my fingers that I want to go with her, that she shouldn't even try to shake me off. She does try to pull her hand away. Stay here, she says, you have to let go of my hand! There's no way I'm letting go, and I start to cry. I cry because the dead woman from the pond is stirring inside me. She moans and I scream that we have to do something right away so nothing terrible will happen. Mother is surprised by my determination and lets me go with her.

We run across the courtyard to the barn. Our hearts beat in our throats. We listen intently to hear if anything is moving on the barn floor or in the hay. Our ears are so keen, we would hear even the tiniest mouse scrabbling, but in the barn all is still. Then a shot rings out from the bee-house. The stray shot has hit the mark. It has shredded the breath in my windpipe and the air sacs in my lungs exude a gas that makes me dizzy. I sway and hurry after Mother racing blindly towards the bee-house. Go away, she screams, get away from me. But I'm determined. If it has to be, then I, too, want to look Father's death in the eye.

We stop at the south side of the small outbuilding and cautiously peer around the corner. Father is lying on his back in the grass below the bee-house, his rifle at a slant beside him as if it had slipped from his hand when he fell. Mother clutches at her heart. She tears herself away from the wall and approaches Father warily. She stops a few steps away and stands looking down at him for a long time, then turns around and walks back to me. He's breathing, she whispers, he didn't shoot himself, he's only playing dead, there's no sign of blood, no wound. Tell Grandmother she should come down and take Father's gun away. If I tried to touch it, he might go after me, you never know, Mother says. Grandmother is already rushing over with a bowl of holy water, which she sprinkles on Father. Holy Mary, Mother of God, what has our family come to, she moans and gropes for the gun.

Father rolls onto his side. He mumbles something I can't understand.

I turn away from him as I'll never turn away from him again. I feel he wants to rob me of my childhood. I feel he's carved a notch in my back, which now hunches slightly, and I'm afraid people will see my back, see how it leaves him behind, even if it's not far or forever.

I was planted in my childhood like a wooden stake in a yard that is shaken everyday to see if it can withstand the shaking.

My thoughts are fuzzy. There's a rushing in my head that spreads through my limbs and floods my ribcage, which I look down at, perplexed.

Old men from the neighborhood pass by with their strange, moist eyes. Their gazes cling to my shoulders, my face. From time to time, Flori grabs my chest to see if anything is happening. He says he wants to marry me when I'm old enough.

Stefan, who has been renting the garret in our outbuilding for the past year, hides something unrestrained behind his reddened face. He drinks and smells of acrid old sweat. He has a habit of talking past people, as if he can't bring himself to look anyone in the eye, and his words are meant to cheat their way, as if in passing, into the ear canals of those he addresses. He works as a logger for the count and is making himself comfortable in our family. He sits in our kitchen and drips schnapps into my youngest brother's tea. I'm embarrassed for him and don't know if I should tell Mother because she probably wouldn't believe me. Grandmother can't stand Stefan, but Father is grateful when Stefan helps him work in the forest or bring in the hay harvest.

I can't figure out what I'm really living. My feelings aren't on speaking terms with the words I say. Before, if I aimed my words at objects, emotions, and grasses, I'd hit them, now my words bounce off the objects and emotions. Before, it seemed to me that the feelings took on the words, but now I'm left behind with everything for which there is no language, or if there is, it's one I can't use.

Walking defines me. I walk to school. I walk home. I walk across the field and back again. I look up at the treetops and reach for the fruit. I walk to the mountain stream; its splashing fills the valley from the bottom up with invisible bubbles like a tub filled with a foam of noise. My thoughts are spiraling chimaeras, conjectures about Death who's peeling off his old skin and still isn't sure when he'll show himself, when he'll show everything in its true light. Presumption.

It's always different with the children in my schoolbooks. There's never anyone like me. I consider withdrawing from childhood because its roof has grown leaky, because I run the risk of foundering with it. I also think that much more has happened to me than could possibly be good for any child and that I already should have changed into something else, although I have no notion what that might be.

And there are still those words standing around in pretty crinolines, balancing like ballerinas on the tips of their toes, and rumors of being

sent to another school. These thoughts seep into me like a clear caril-
lon, and I imagine how changing schools could cut me off from these
surroundings.

Secret thoughts become vain. Timid, burnished thoughts begin circling in my head. They smell of lilies of the valley and look like they've
just emerged from a beauty bath. They wear princess dresses and fur-
lined high-heeled shoes.

After school, I like to go see Aunt Malka who lives with Sveršina in the
Auprich cottage. She was one of the girls on our farm, Grandfather's
youngest and prettiest sister, who'd married the widowed Farmer
Auprich and, because he died in the war, now lives in the small cottage
with Sveršina.

Aunt Malka is the only one who finds everything I say enchanting.
She doesn't just smile at me when I visit her. She beams, she claps her
hands, and strokes my cheeks. She gives me a hug. Good Lord, she says,
good Lord, my girl, my darling girl, what do you want, what would you
like me to give you? She makes me *palatschinken*, pancakes spread with
a thick layer of jam. She slips me pieces of candy that glow in my book
bag like small spheres of bliss that I keep for myself and don't share with
anyone. She sits with me while I eat and wants to know what's new at
home. Oh, nothing, I say, Grandmother's doing well. And your father,
she asks. He's doing well, too, I answer. The two of them suffered through
so much, she observes, enough for several lives. Does your grandmother
tell you how things were then, she wants to know. Yes, sometimes, I say,
I know a few stories. You should ask her, Malka urges me. She, too, had

told her children many stories once they started to be curious, how she and the others were arrested as partisans and taken to Ravensbrück, how the war turned their lives upside down. Of course children shouldn't be frightened too much, it could make them as strange as their parents and grandparents, as crazy as she is. Her fear of planes, for example. Every time she sees a plane in the sky she has to run into the house and hide. She has become so childish with time, she says, terribly childish, as if she's turned into a girl instead of an old woman. There's no explanation for it and none for the horrifying dreams she has. Sometimes Malka dreams she's back in Ravensbrück, and she constantly has to calm Sveršina down. When he can't sleep, he also talks about Mauthausen, but he doesn't say much, he's never very talkative. But your grandmother has kept her pride, she hasn't become as fearful as I have, she's not as skittish, Malka tells me.

Sveršina, on the other hand, doesn't want to hear anything about me when he joins us at the white enamel table. He never asks after my parents or Grandmother. He sits there without saying a word. He seems to know more about them than I do.

FATHER avoids us for days after the most recent incident with the gun. He works in the forest and rarely comes home. The mood on our farm is like after a deafening explosion. An inner numbness has us in a stranglehold and makes talking difficult. I wonder if Father's condition might have something to do with me or with Mother's attitude. I can't come up with anything about me that would drive Father to such episodes, so I watch Mother very closely. I'm suddenly suspicious of her loud laughter. I silently reproach her for never joking as boisterously with Father as she does with the acquaintances who come to visit or whom she meets after mass.

But Father is also friendlier outside the house than at home. As long as he's not drunk, he smiles engagingly. He drapes his arms casually over various seat and chair backs. His tongue loosens and he becomes talkative and says "I" and "I have" and "I".

I begin to suspect that he's automatically drawn to those who were hunted by the Nazis and that he thinks there's something fishy about people who, as he says, pretend to be better than they are. This doesn't surprise me. I can't remember ever finding it surprising. Grandmother also never stops complaining that Mother wants to be something better, that Mother knows nothing about people or the world because she never suffered a day in her life, because she has no idea what suffering is. I debate whether I should take sides in the argument smoldering between Mother and Grandmother and in the end decide to side with Grandmother because she has been through so much in her life and Mother is always finding fault with me.

Father begins to withdraw from social life. When Michi asks him to sing in the Slovenian Cultural Association's mixed choir, Father declines. They should just leave him in peace with their cultural activities, he says. He never wants to step onstage again, his days of acting and music-making are over. Michi is sorry to hear it and asks if Father would at least consider joining the association's yearly excursion, it's always great fun. Yes, Father agrees, for that he'll go along. He also refuses to go to parent-teacher conferences at school. That's only for people who think they're important, he says. He's never been full of himself, he's never been one of those people.

Now and then I go collect him from the neighbors' place, where he's gotten stuck, as he says, after work in the forest. He likes to sit in the kitchen of the Peršman farm with Anči, who survived back when the SS shot the entire family. She was seven years old, Father says, and she was hit six times. You can still see the bullet wounds on her chin and hand.

She was able to play dead, but the younger children cried and were shot and killed.

When I arrive, Father is usually sitting at the end of the kitchen table with a bottle of beer in his hand. Anči presides near the stove on which she keeps her children's dinner warm. As soon as I enter the kitchen, I start to examine her face and hands for scars. She was able to hide behind the stove, Anči says, but her little brother, who was in her arms, was shot.

On the front of the house is a marble plaque with the names of the children, the parents, and grandparents, engraved and gold-plated. Father says he could never live in a house where he'd be reminded of the dead every day, several times a day, every time he went in or out.

W H E N I come home from school one day, Grandmother tells me that old Pečnica is dead and that she wants me to go with her to the wake.

As darkness falls, we cross the field behind our house and walk through the woods up to the Pečniks'. People stand by the front door, talking in hushed voices. Grandmother and I enter the room where old Pečnica is laid out. Neighbors sit and pray on the wooden benches that line the walls. The coffin is set before an open window and is surrounded with wreathes and flower arrangements of glowing red and white blossoms.

Grandmother cuts a small chunk of bread from the loaf handed to her. She gives me a bite and says that with this bread, she's cut off a bit of eternity, that by this bread we'll recognize each other in the hereafter, by the bread we eat at wakes. I'm not sure I want to eat this bread because the thought of meeting the dead in the hereafter scares me. I quickly slip the bread out of my mouth and hide it in my coat pocket. On a small table at the foot of the bier are two white candles, a statue of the Virgin

Mary, a framed photograph, and two teacups with holy water to sprinkle on the dead woman. Only now do I notice that the coffin is encircled with intertwined red carnations that look like they're growing out of the corpse. Grandmother tells me to take the small twig of boxwood from the teacup and sprinkle the dead woman with holy water. The only part of her I recognize are her strong hands, folded on her stomach. At the head of the bier, Grandmother lifts me slightly so that I can see the woman's face. I see an unfamiliar, round, waxy face, bordered by a dark kerchief and I quickly make a few motions in the shape of a cross with the boxwood twig. Done, I say to Grandmother, who is groaning under my weight. She lowers me to the flowers, lays her hand on the dead woman's forearm, and makes the sign of the cross with her fingertips. After we've sat down on a bench set close to the bier, I notice that Michi is also sitting on the bench, crying. I ask Grandmother if Michi is related to the dead woman and she says no, but Pečnica was very good to the neighbor's children.

On the way home, Grandmother tells me that on Christmas in '44, Pečnica took in Michi and his sisters, Zofka and Bredica, after the police had surrounded the Kuchars' house and had shot at Michi's mother and the partisans who were staying there. Luckily, Michi held his mother back so she couldn't run out of the house. She would have been immediately mowed down by the patrol like Primož who ran out ahead of her. The seven-year-old Michi, his entire body trembling, stepped out in front of the house with the two Knolič sisters, Anni and Malka, who were also partisans. The Knolič sisters were arrested at once and taken to

Ravensbrück. Michi had to step over Primož's body and saw the police beat two more partisans who had surrendered with their butts of their guns. One of the wounded partisans was her own brother Cyril, whom I must know, Grandmother tells me. The children went to the Pečniks with just a few possessions. Pečnica warmed them up and took care of them until they'd calmed down enough to go stay with relatives over in Lobnik two weeks later.

After Pečnica's burial, for which Father and Mother drove to Eisenkappel, I overhear a heated conversation between Father and Grandmother in the sitting room.

He knows exactly, Father claims, Beti told him, or maybe it was old Pečnik, back then in January '44, the two of them had gone to Hojnik's to see what happened after the police had killed old Hojnik, who was in bed with pneumonia, and had shot the farmer's family. They'd heard the shots from the Pečniks' place and could see something was burning. The dead bodies had been thrown, half-burnt, onto the manure pile. After old Pečnik went to Eisenkappel to report the incident, the police came back at night, poured gasoline on the rest of the Hojniks, and set them on fire. Nonsense, Grandmother counters, old Hojnik wasn't ill, his son Johan was in bed with pneumonia when the police looted their house. Old Hojnik was beside himself because the police not only wanted to arrest his sick son, but also to take away his daughter-in-law Angela and his grandchildren, Mitzi and Johan. The police had filled two ox-drawn carts with stolen goods and blankets and ordered old Hojnik to come with them, but with his crutches he could barely walk in the snow. He sat down on the side of the road and said he wouldn't let them take him away from his farm. So then, the police officers beat him to death with his crutches. Bits of his brain stuck to the surrounding trees, that's what eighteen-year-old Mitzi told her in Ravensbruck, where she'd been sent after the arrest, Grandmother says. Mitzi and her brother Johan, who had to pull a fully loaded cart, were forced to watch as their parents and grandparents were murdered. Mitzi Hojnik, by the way, was killed on the very day Ravensbrück was evacuated. An SS man was shooting wildly about because he was drunk and Mitzi happened to step out of the line at that very moment. On evacuation day, you understand, just like that, by chance, Grandmother says, her voice rising. She was denied a homecoming. In any case, Grandmother continues after a pause, little Klari, whom the police left behind with her younger siblings, all of them alone on the farm, she refused to leave the house for three days. Pečnica took in the terrorized children who had barricaded themselves in the house, paralyzed with fear. She went and got Klari, ten-year-old Roki, three-year-old Rozika, and thirteen-month-old Mihec and brought them home to the Pečniks.

Hojnik above Pečnik, Kuchar below Pečnik, the farms one on top of the other and our farm nearby. I stand near the door left ajar and listen.

As I listen, something collapses in my chest, as if a stack of logs were rolling away behind me, into the time before my time, and that time reaches out to grab me and I start to give in out of fascination and fear. It's got hold of me, I think, now it's here with me.

The child understands that it's the past she must reckon with. She can't just focus on her own wishes and on the present. The sprawling present that allows the grownups to survey the past as from a distant shore, the same past that blocked their view of everything then. Childhood is naturally oriented towards the future, but against the backdrop of the past, the future proves lightweight. What could it possibly bring, where will it lead? Isn't it enough, when it simply makes life possible, thinks Father, and the child occasionally thinks so, too.

In the books I read, bodies remain intact and rise up to heaven with a blissful expression or are caught as they fall. In our graves, however, it suddenly occurs to me, bodies are always ravaged, destroyed as a warning to those who remain. Here the rashest dissipation holds sway, here life is squandered, here bodies are brought low, it's a crying shame. One day when I enter our neighbors' kitchen, Loni pushes me emphatically back out. Help, she screams, help, we need a doctor right away! I see her brother Andi lying on the kitchen bench, groaning. He is as white as a sheet. A kitchen knife is sticking out of his stomach. Andi's mother screams, don't pull it out, don't pull it out, get a doctor, now! When I have just taken my younger twin sisters to Rastočnik for ice cream, Rosi and Filica speed past on a moped and crash in the curve behind the barn. Rosi runs towards me, blood streaming down her face, screaming for help, while her sister lies dying on the side of the road, her neck broken. The echoes of the family's weeping have barely faded in my mind when Stefan hangs himself, our boarder Stefan, who for weeks has been leaving smudges and drops of blood on all the chairs and benches he sat on. He hangs himself near the door to the stable, under the ramp that leads up to the threshing floor, as if he wanted to dangle right in front of my mother's eyes, since she is usually the first one in the stalls in the morning. She had a nervous breakdown, Grandmother says as we stand around the kitchen in shock from the news. First, she needs to calm down, and we children must stay in the house until they've taken the corpse away. But without waiting for the hearse, we drag the hanged man into the house with our watchful eyes, we pull him out from under the wooden bridge that hides him, we picture to ourselves what he must have looked like, we imagine we're kneeling on the bridge, peering down between the planks and catching sight of his swaying legs, his dangling, lifeless legs in blue work pants. By the time the doctor arrives, we have already looked down from the bridge several times in our imagination. The way you look from shore into raging water, from life we look at eager Death. Death disguised himself in work clothes. He wanted to remain unrecognized under the barn if possible, pushing the corpse before him without being seen. But we recognized him and felt a hint of his presence.

Mother cries for days, never again will she be able to go into the stables without fear, she complains, Stefan hanged himself under the barn to punish her, he could have hanged himself somewhere else, somewhere she wouldn't have been the one to find him. Grandmother says it serves her right.

Before long our farm is too small and too loud for Death. He finds refuge at the Auprichs' farm, where he takes cover and is not noticed for a time until the farmer, a friend of my father's, startles him and shoots himself a few months later. The morning we were told that Franz shot himself in the head with a rifle, but his aim was bad and all he did was shoot out his own eyes, I feel things getting tight, I feel that Death hasn't given up his attack on Father, but has only taken a detour so he can get closer and ambush him. Father says, now he's done it, he's really gone and done it. I think his thought through to the end, which immediately gets me worked up. I think I understand how serious things have gotten and that I have to fulfill my duty. It's now up to me to save Father.

After Franz's burial, I watch Father with suspense. I know that work protects him during the week, but his unease is palpable on weekends. It's as if he were constantly observing his life and had no idea what he should feel about it. On Sundays, bare-chested, he shaves in the kitchen and washes his underarms with the water brimming with stubble and bits of foam. He combs his hair with an old comb dipped in aftershave. He smells of soap and sometimes, when he catches me looking at him, a smile lights up his eyes like a gentle taunt, like a nod to better times which he has also had, though there is no point in thinking of them now.

Would I like to know what he'd been thinking at Franz's burial? I nod. He was thinking that it's only at a funeral that people realize whom they've just lost. Only then do they understand what the person they're carrying to the grave meant to them, what his true worth as a human being was. When it's time to say goodbye, people are overcome with emotion, they weep and grieve, but at that point it's too late, because it makes no difference to the dead whether or not they're being buried with honor, do I understand? I nod again. A person is honored for the first time, everyone throws flowers on his coffin, they make speeches in which the community thanks him for his work, for the sacrifices the dead man made in his life, but it's all pointless. At his own funeral, Father tells me, he's going to make sure he spoils some people's joy in weeping and wailing, they'll be stunned, they will realize for the first time that they did him wrong and for the rest of their lives, they won't forgive themselves for treating him like a mangy dog. He will reject their tears, he won't relent, no matter how much they whine and plead for his forgiveness, that much he has promised himself, Father says.

I picture a procession of people following Father's coffin, the mourners beating their hands against their chests with remorse and gathering around the open grave, their heads hanging low. I agree with Father and have to work hard to keep from giving way to tears because I think I can also make out a tone of mockery and rancor in his words.

My uneasiness grows when Father goes to the tavern on Sunday afternoons. As soon as evening has fallen and I can hear him swearing behind the stable on his return, I sit by the living room window, from which I can see the stable and, more importantly, the ramp to the threshing barn. Mother asks me to watch how long Father stays in the barn. If he isn't back in half an hour, someone will have to go check on him. With its beams and rafters, the threshing barn is a place that gives people ideas, Mother says.

I'm sure I once heard Father threaten Mother that he would hang himself in the barn after she took away the cartridges for his rifle. As a hunter, he has a right to his cartridges, and it's downright indecent for her to have taken them. There isn't a single woman in Lepena who would dare take away her husband's bullets.

As soon as Father has staggered up the wooden ramp to the threshing barn, racing thoughts set my body on fire, the fever spikes, and I start to melt like beeswax put too near the flame. Father usually comes down again, but a few times we wait for him in vain. We hurry into the barn with bated breath and find him asleep in the hay.

One Monday morning, as I am checking my schoolbag before going to school, Father comes into the sitting room and sits on the bench near the oven. In his hand, he is holding a calving rope and he sighs. This time I don't hold back my tears and I sit down next to him. He looks at me, astonished as if he only just grasped what I thought I'd understood. But my girl, he says, you don't need to cry! I only thought about doing it, and when I wanted to do it, when I put the noose around my neck, I could feel something holding me back, a kind of angel, you see. I thought I saw someone. I can't do it, that's one thing you need to know! I can't bring myself to do it, Father says.

Mother is suddenly standing before us and she starts screaming at Father, does he realize what he's doing to the child, does he have any idea that I immediately get a fever when he gets up to his stupid tricks, he should just stop terrorizing the children, she screams, he should finally get a grip on himself! Well, the girl, at least, loves me, which no one can say about you, Father taunts Mother. Besides, he's planning on moving in with his brother.

At that moment, the despair bottled up inside me comes flooding out. I wail and beg him not to go, he has to stay with us. I cling to him tightly, I will hold on until he finally understands that he can't sneak out of our lives.

She's about to faint, Mother says, I've never seen her like this, the child is out of her senses, she tells him I have to be put to bed, I can't go to school in such a state. Now Father can see what he's done, he's scared the child out of her wits.

They carry me to bed, and I toss and turn under the sheets. Mother holds my hand, she sits at my bedside as she has never done before. She brings me warm milk and apple compote, she'll even bring me red currants from the cellar storeroom if I'd like. I have to calm down, she says. She tells me I should pray, if I prayed properly, God would put everything right, she believes. I don't.

For the next week, Father can hardly sleep. Through the long nights he sways his upper body and aching head back and forth. He moans and groans, his headache is like a purgatorial fire, he has no idea how he could have earned such pain, he can't imagine why God would punish him with a headache like this.

One evening, Grandmother has him stand in the doorway to the house and toss cooled embers over his head behind him, one piece of coal for each stab of pain.

Throw your pain behind you, without looking back, hold your breath, say a prayer! You have to believe, Grandmother says. You have to call the saints because to hear is to obey. Michael, Raphael, Gabriel, Souriel, Zaziel, Badakiel! Flee illness, a god is chasing you out! Flee illness, a god is chasing you out!

O U T of exhaustion, I begin to withdraw from my sentient body. I wonder why no one has thought of casting a protective spell for me, too, a spell that would shield me from excessive danger. I wonder why they all forget to cover me with defensive words that will preserve me from this reality that makes me shudder at every new occurrence. I could grab any hand, could press myself against any tree or animal I pass. I speak with the calves and let loose on the imperturbable cows when I drive them off the field and into the barn.

Grandmother keeps making signs to come near her, she wants to tell me something. She asks me if I'd like to sleep in the outbuilding with her, I could share her bed. I do want to! But only if your mother doesn't object, Grandmother says with a slight, triumphant trembling in her voice, you have to ask her first, of course.

Sometimes I ask Mother before even speaking to Grandmother. I just invite myself to Grandmother's room. I don't want to be alone.

Grandmother's bedroom is a site of memory, a queen bee's cell, in which everything seems bathed in a milky liquid, a breeding cell, in which I'm fed with Grandmother's nutrient juices. It is in this nucleus, I realize only years later, that I will be formed. Grandmother guides my sense of orientation. From then on there will be no passing by her markers. My senses will project Grandmother's vibrations onto this world and will perceive the possibility of destruction everywhere. They will wait for fateful coincidences, for moments in which change is possible, because one must hope and prepare for salvation, yet without good fortune, everything falls apart.

From the moment Grandmother decides to bring me into the two years of her life that marked her most profoundly, the pamphlets she brought back from the commemoration ceremony in Ravensbrück, *The Women of Ravensbrück* and *What does it have to do with me?*, lie on her night table next to the arnica tincture and the bitter mugwort liqueur. Occasionally Grandmother hands me a pamphlet and asks me to read out loud to her from it. I sit down at the old kitchen table and read: In Ravensbrück there were the *Lagerkommandanten* (camp commanders), the *Schutzhaftlagerführer* (preventive detention camp leader), the *Verwaltungsführer* (head of administration), the *Arbeitsdienstführer* (head of work details), the Gestapo officers in the political department, the camp doctors, the SS nurses, the *Oberaufseherin* (senior camp guard), the *Aufseherinnen* (camp guards), the SS *Wachmannschaften* (security guard details).

Give it to me, Grandmother says and pulls the book impatiently from my hands, I'll show you the guards. She leafs through the book and shows me a group of women sitting in dock in a courtroom. She points at a young, blonde woman. She was the worst, Grandmother says. She had a dog that she set on prisoners when they collapsed during roll call. Grandmother can still see the bloodhound, how it pulls at the leash before crouching to leap onto an exhausted woman. A Polish woman from her block was bitten by that dog. She had real holes in her legs. A Polish doctor ordered the wounds washed in urine, it helped, they didn't have anything else, no bandages, nothing at all.

It was this guard, Grandmother says, laying her index finger on the woman's face, which disappeared beneath it. She was very young and very evil, very depraved. Good Lord, what people won't do, Grandmother exclaims and spits on the photograph. Then she wipes the pages with her sleeve so they won't stick together.

Sometimes she spits at the photograph of the SS camp doctor as a substitute for the SS doctors she came across when she was brought into the infirmary. The things these doctors did to the women, *čudno, čudno*, Grandmother says and, again, means *terrible* when she says *strange*.

She believes that, because of these books, no one will be able to accuse her of making up stories anymore. No one can call me a liar anymore, she says.

Every now and then she takes a stained red notebook out of the table drawer. My camp diary, she says and opens the notebook, look, on the inside cover I wrote *knjiga od zapora Maria H.*, the prison book of Maria

H. A fellow prisoner gave her the notebook on the way home. That prisoner had been given the notebook by a French woman. She tore out a few pages. But look, Grandmother says, in Prenzlau, I started to make notes. On April 28th, they drove us out of the camp, the trip was amazing, she reads out loud, *čudovita*, because once again she can't think of the Slovenian word for terrible. The SS forced them north along the front or in circles, she recounts. No one knew where they were heading. She can barely remember the first days because she was so weak, Gregorička had to carry her. One time, she can still remember they were marching through a forest that just would not end, the bodies of the dead and the exhausted were lying everywhere, along with gutted cars and munitions. Gregorička got hold of a wheelbarrow, put her in, and pushed it. Then the 1st of May came and the SS disappeared, they vanished on the spot. Thunder and gunfire all around them. The women wandered along the battle lines in groups. Her group spent the night in a pigsty. The Russians were going to shoot at the sty. Only when a woman in a striped camp uniform came out did the Russians realize concentration camp prisoners were in there. Then they slaughtered a pig for everyone to eat.

They moved on the next day, devastation everywhere, villages bombed out, the planes flew very low over them. They searched for food and clothing in the abandoned houses. A woman from Ljubljana led her group, they stayed with her because the Slovenians were supposed to be taken home as a group. The Slovenians waited until the middle of August to go home. The Austrians wanted to struggle home as soon as the fighting had stopped, Grandmother says.

As soon as Grandmother starts undressing, I do the same.

She sits on the bed in her undershirt and undoes her thin braid, which she wears wound into a bun on the back of her head. I kneel on the bed behind Grandmother and start combing her hair. Her thin, gray hair falls between her shoulder blades. She alternately lays her left or her right hand on the side of her head I am combing. Careful, she says, careful, and sometimes after a sigh she continues, it was the 13th of November, the day she arrived at the camp. The women who were marched there with her through Fürstenberg had to get undressed after they were admitted. There was an air-raid alarm in the very first hours. They had to wait, naked, for two hours until they were examined. Then their heads were shaved. As soon as she says shaved, she pushes my hand away as if I were touching her hair without permission. With a few quick flicks of her hands, she weaves a braid and winds it back into a bun. She sighs. She had to lie on a table, she says, and they injected something into her vagina and it burned beyond belief and that was probably due to women's trouble. One woman had just gotten her period and it all ran down her legs. The uniformed men looked at her like she was a cow, she was one of the older ones. The younger ones had problems because of their looks, they were taken from block twelve, where they were locked up for four weeks and brought back completely destroyed. Every day, morning and evening, they had to stand through two-hour roll calls, complete confusion, tears, it took a long time until they were all counted, and the disparaging looks measuring what you were still worth and what kind of work you could do.

I catch myself scanning Grandmother for the looks that appraised her. I see strangers' eyes covering her like a net and wonder if traces of horror were left on her skin. But there is no sign of the terror. It leaves no visible scars. Grandmother's body is as angular as a skeleton, her horizontal collarbone, her shoulders, the protrusion of her lower cervical spine, her rib cage, her upper arm bones, over which her skin stretches like light gauze. She has no muscles anymore and no chest, look, she says, lifting her undershirt, my chest is a big wrinkle. I look reluctantly, but Grandmother purses her lips and says I shouldn't shudder at the sight of old women. She's seen a lot of naked women in her life and once you have, you stop being prim. She's seen women in every possible condition, good Lord, she says, young and old, frail and beaten down, women with their skin hanging off them in tatters, dead women with skin like paper, like yellowish paper you could peel off their bones, she says. In the beginning she had to clean the latrines, you can't imagine how it stank. The smell stuck to her, she couldn't wash it off. Angela Piskernik, the professor from Eisenkappel, complained about the stink, but what was she supposed to do. Dirt is dirt and shit is shit, Grandmother says.

She rubs her hands along her thighs, which are covered with cotton underwear to her knees, and tries to straighten her back by pressing against her legs. She asks me to pull her woolen tights off. The garters leave marks on her lower legs. Grandmother says her legs swell badly since the camp. It all started in the camp, the heaviness and swelling in her legs, with such pain in her joints and bones that she could barely stand at times. She asks if I want to see her throbbing big toe. I bend over her feet.

Her big toenails look like barley sugar, I say and Grandmother laughs at the comparison. Like candy, she says, pleased, I didn't know I have barley sugar on my feet! The skin below her knees has a bluish tinge, the capillaries hover over her calves and shins like webbing and cover her feet in a thicket that looks like a river delta.

Should we eat a few cookies before we lie down, Grandmother asks after a pause.

I nod and she gets a tin of wafers out of the kitchen sideboard. She prefers the crumbly ones that fall apart in your mouth right away, she says and unwraps her false teeth from the handkerchief she always keeps on her night table. Grandmother only uses her dentures to eat. She decided not to wear her dentures anymore once Grandfather died, why bother, she asks, she's not going to get another man anyway. She keeps them in reach and often has them in her apron pocket. Most of the time, her false teeth feel superfluous, she claims.

When I'm stretched out on the bed and she sits near me, telling me about the camp, she likes to talk about her foster daughter, Mici. Oh, she sighs, oh, if you only knew how my Mici looked when I saw her in the roll-call square! Mici threw her arms around me, Grandmother says, she cried Mother, Mother what are you doing here! I couldn't hold back my tears, Grandmother says, it made me so sad! Mici told her that on the day she left the house to register with the police in Eisenkappel because she'd been summoned, she stopped in at Šertev's to ask if it wouldn't be better to hide with the partisans. The partisans had a bunker near Šertev's, Grandmother says. The partisans said there was nothing to worry about,

Mici told her, the police couldn't prove anything, she was still very young and going to the partisans just as winter was setting in was very hard for women. As long as she wasn't in immediate danger, she should wait and keep calm.

Mici went and registered with the police. They told her that others had sworn she worked for the partisans. She denied everything but the judgment stood. She was deported to the camp. Mici was filthy and disturbed, Grandmother recalled. She sensed Mici wouldn't survive the camp and she'd given up. On that day, she sensed it would be the end of her foster daughter. Three months later Leni wrote that Mici's ashes had been sent from Lublin. That was too much for me, Grandmother said. I wept the whole night through. The women in the barrack told me not to give in, because in camp strong feelings are heralds of death. Mici was gassed in Lublin, she was gassed in Lublin, Grandmother repeats as if trying, again, to grasp that fact. From that day on she was no good for outside work, she could barely stand on her own two feet, she continues. But before that, look, on May 10th, Grandmother says and leafs through her camp notebook, on May 10th, I saw a sign in the sky. I saw my brother Miklavž, Katrca's husband, and I told Katrca, who was your grandfather's sister. Katrca was already in the infirmary. I described the sign and told her it boded no good. Not long after that, Katrca heard that Miklavž had died in Dachau, Grandmother recounts. She lost her will to survive. She said she wanted to join her husband. She wrote more poems on her sickbed, she always wrote poems. It was a very dangerous thing to do.

A Russian woman was beaten to death for writing poems in the bunker, but Katrca wanted her poems to be smuggled to freedom. Grandmother tells me she doesn't know if it worked. She visited Katrca, she always visited Katrca, even when she herself was in the infirmary and had to spend fourteen days in the ward with the dying. Those who died in the infirmary during the night were piled up in front of the baths, the emaciated bodies lay on the ground like sticks of wood and we tripped over them. Katrca had an abscessed back, Grandmother says and, lying on the bed, in my imagination Katrca's back looks like a painted cloth, saturated with circle upon circle of red, mixed with wilted rose petals, covered with a pustulent crust. Lying behind my grandmother's back, staring at the image of Katrca's back, I float in the past as in a drop of time that circulates within my mind.

Grandmother breathes heavily and gasps for air. She stayed in the infirmary for fourteen days, she reports, then she recovered a bit. There were also Czech women doctors in the infirmary. They could speak German and they tried to help. The Czechs stuck together, she could sense it. The *Blockova* assigned her to inside work after she'd recovered. She had to wash the big cauldrons in the camp kitchen. That kept her alive, Grandmother says, because she could often steal what was thrown away and eat it. She stashed away what was left lying around and brought it to the other inmates. She could even save turnip or potato peelings for Katrca, now and again, and that was lucky because the food for the inmates was garbage that at home would have been given to the pigs or thrown away.

Katrca died on the 1st of July, on a Saturday afternoon. I went up to the window of the infirmary with a scrap of turnip in my hand, looked inside and saw that Katrca's bed was empty, Grandmother says. A Czech woman told her Katrca had been taken away. Grandmother often remembered this and hoped that Katrca didn't have to live through what happened to Jerči Vivoda from the Lobnik Valley. Jerči was still alive when they threw her on the pile of dead bodies. She managed to climb out of the stack of corpses and crawl back three times to block six. I prayed for Katrca's death, Grandmother says, and hoped she didn't go through what the young Jerči from Upper Lobnik did.

When Grandmother mentions food rations in the camp, she is overcome with a nervous hunger. She opens the tin of cookies again or takes a jar of apple compote from the cabinet in which she keeps several jars of preserves as reassurance rations.

If she places a glass of grape compote on the table, I know she is happy with the way the evening went. She takes a large spoon from the table drawer, the camp spoon for the top brass she stole from the camp kitchen, she says. Look, she says and points to the engraving on the back of the handle, RAD, *Reicharbeitdienst*. Then she dips the spoon into the grape compote, lifts a few grapes from the jar, and lets them slide into her mouth. The next spoonful is for me. I close my eyes and open my mouth. Grandmother carefully rolls a few grapes onto my tongue. Sometimes I choke because the spoon fills my mouth. Not so greedy, Grandmother laughs, not so greedy! She took her own camp spoon, too, a simple aluminum spoon, she stores it with the documents, as a piece of evidence, she says, so it won't get lost.

Now and again she pulls a gray box of photographs from the dresser. Where has Mici got to, she murmurs as she rummages through the black and white photographs, which are mostly of wedding parties. I look at the photographs she lays out on the bed for me as if from a great distance. Only Mici grabs me as a child, perhaps also Katrca's melancholy gaze. What interest me most are the photographs of Grandmother as a girl my age. I remark that we look alike. After thinking about it for a long time, Grandmother says, maybe, maybe we do look alike, she's not sure. The white dress she's wearing in the confirmation picture is pretty, I say appreciatively and with her finger Grandmother caresses her girlish head adorned with a crown of white flowers. Then she starts to tell me about the worst times in the camp.

Early in 1945, more and more transports arrived in Ravensbrück. There was no more room in the barracks, the women had to sleep three or four to a bunk. Many women from Poland and Slovenia arrived, many city women from France, Belgium, Holland, good Lord, how those women fought for their dresses and furs, Grandmother says. They sat in the admission block and couldn't believe their eyes. We were already deadened, Grandmother says, we'd already gotten used to a lot. She was completely emaciated that winter, there was less and less to eat, sometimes nothing for days. She saw women carted away in trucks and brought back as corpses for the crematorium. In the spring, she was selected for the gas chamber at one roll call. For death, my God, I was lying on straw in the typhus ward, waiting to be transported to the gas, and praying, Grandmother says. Suddenly a woman from Vienna said to her, we Austrians have to stick together! We Austrians have to stick together! The woman from Vienna switched her camp number with one of the dead. She told Grandmother to hide and so Grandmother locked herself in the toilet before the transport. It was horrible, Grandmother recalls, there was banging on the door the whole time. It was unbearable. She would never do it again. From then on, she never went to any selection roll calls and hid in the barracks under the bunk bed, barricaded behind the packages that were sent to the women from home. She spent the final days in the camp as a dead person, illegally.

On your way through life, Grandmother says in conclusion, I offer you this: Never lock yourself in the toilet after a selection, share whatever packages you get from home with others, take good care of the few possessions you have. Things get stolen right and left in the camp. Make sure you get along with the other inmates so you won't die alone, without anyone to help you.

As soon as I am in secondary school, Grandmother will ask me to help her write a letter to the woman from Vienna who saved her life. She simply has to find out her address and her exact name, then we can compose the letter, Grandmother tells me. After she came home from the camp, she wrote a few letters, but eventually the correspondence dried up and they lost touch.

Grandmother pulls a postcard out of the carton. Here, read this, she says and pushes the postcard into my hand. I read: *3/9/1946, Dear Mitzi! Many thanks for your precious words. I'm very happy to hear you made it home safely. How are you? Are you and your children well? Have you had any news of your husband? I am always in the best of health and my boy is lively and alert. He will be four already in June. Dear Mitzi, I was released on February 13th and was happily at home by the 16th. I was very happy indeed to have gotten away from that gang of SS. Dear Mitzi! Do you know what happened to Sabine Bauer, was she still with you? Please write and let me know. I have one more question, do you know Sabine Schwaiger's address? I'd like to write her. I hope to hear from you soon! Your friend Anna Weilaner.*

I give the postcard back to Grandmother. She smiles. Then she hands me a letter. I have trouble deciphering the handwriting: *April 30, 1946; I was only able to answer your card today and would like to send you my sincere thanks. Do you remember the many hours we lived through together, hours that brought so much suffering? But still, we made it – today we are free and can even feel that we're free! Well then, how did things go for you in Wesenberg? And why did it take so long for you to get home? I arrived in Graz on July 10th. What are you doing now? Are you running your farm again? I hope everything was returned to you! Things are looking meager indeed for me. To date I have not gotten a single thing back from the inventory of my apartment. Do you still have your "best coat"? – Another little momento of Ravensbrück. If the train connections were better we would have lots to 'grouse' about. This is all I can manage today and look forward to receiving a sign of life from you again soon. And now I'm going to go have a coffee à la 'care package'? And we don't even need to 'filch' things anymore! With sincerest wishes, your fellow sufferer, Elisse Siegl, Graz. "Clara Zetkin."* Grandmother smiles again. She has no idea who this Zetkin is, she says, and by the time I could answer her question, Grandmother was no longer alive.

She sets the camp notebook and the letters on the table, turns off the light, and starts to pray softly. I turn onto my side and press my back against her ribs. After making the sign of the cross, she turns towards me and puts an arm around me. This is her favorite position, she says. She cuddled up with Grandfather like this with bent knees. I press my back against her chest and long for her to hold me even tighter. Occasionally, she pinches me lightly with her hard nails when she wants to show me how they used to squeeze lice. It always went snap when a louse burst, but lice rarely come alone so there was no chance of sleep, Grandmother says. I, on the other hand, fall asleep right away next to her, and in the morning I open my eyes, bewildered. The bed next to me is empty. Grandmother has already gotten up and hurried into the house. When I come into the kitchen, she will be standing by the stove and will say that she feels cold. Then we will drink her barley coffee and sit without speaking, as if we had come too close the night before.

IN THE evening, the child stands in the field behind the house in the open doorway to night, which rises like a princely palace over the landscape with tinkling, twinkling stars, with the forest's breath, and the plashing of the stream at the bottom of the valley. She enters the house of night and leaves it again. The child, hovering between past, present, and future, thinks that, actually, she would like to die, that she has had enough of life, and she thinks that she shouldn't have such thoughts, but she would like to die anyway because death has come so near her. She thinks she should let go of the dead or bury them, the dead she drags behind her like a rickety wooden horse on wheels, even though she has yet to see an open grave, even though she has only ever seen people on their way to the grave. She wants to bury her dead, the drowned kitchen maid, those who were beaten to death, shot, or hanged, the unknown dead in Grandmother's stories.

The child would like to recover the immediacy of things, a state in which no words intrude between her and the world, where nothing she touches pulls away from her. She wants to pluck the words from things, the names *buttercup* from the buttercups and *white nettle* from the white nettles.

She crouches in the grass and doesn't stand back up. She shrinks to a dark, shimmering stone with glittering sparks of light trapped inside it and shining like water and fire and fluorescing like the air. Her breath draws rivers through the stone, her laughter welling up from the core of the stone like columns of cloud that freeze as they expand.

The child has turned inward, into the hollow that hides her and keeps her warm.

T H E C H I L D who rose from the grass with her awkward, supple body may well have been me, the strange me who discovered crying as a well to wash out of the body everything piled up deep inside it, who discovered crying as a pit cage to descend deep down into the body's core and bring up to the light the metal that poisons and feeds her. That night, I learn to push through, sobbing, to something warm and velvety, to something dark and light that crushes and reconciles me and lets me see the child who is far away as if she were inside me.

From that point on, I am the awkwardly assembled girl, it seems to me, the girl with dislocated limbs and overblown thoughts. My arms stick out sideways, my legs, as if badly fitted, hang in the air with a new heaviness. My head is hollow, emptied out for everything and nothing.

I go back into my parents' house, crawl into bed, and stare into the darkness. In the morning, I rinse my swollen lids with cold water and walk numbly into the kitchen.

Through the closed door, I hear Mother say to Father that it's time to make preparations in case the girl goes to secondary school. She says she spoke with the teachers and the chaplain and everyone agrees that a change of school is a good idea. She already missed the registration deadline once, but the girl could enter the second year class in the fall if she studies hard.

Father asks what that's supposed to mean, "go to secondary school," yet again she's making decisions behind his back. He is not at all of a mind to send the girl away to school, he won't allow it. She wants to take the child away from him, that's all she really wants. Mother tells him to be reasonable, you have to take advantage of opportunities that come with state funding, Michi is sending his daughter to secondary school, too, and his brother's daughters have been going to the Slovenian middle school for some time now.

She should leave his brother out of it, Father shouts, he doesn't care what Tonči and the others do, he's not going to let the girl go, period, the end! He's put all his money into the house, where would they find money to pay for school, she'd better not dare spend his money. Then I hear a blow and glass splintering on the floor. I burst through the kitchen door and I stop in the doorway, shocked. Father has broken the pane of glass on the front of the credenza and is holding a coffee mug he had just taken out of it. Mother is standing next to the door and says, her voice trembling, once again you've shown what you're capable of, the girl has to know where things stand, we can't wait another year. Father throws the mug on the floor and rushes out of the kitchen, she should stop taking him for a fool, he shouts.

I tell Mother that if Father doesn't have any money, then I just won't go to school.

Nonsense, Mother says and picks up the mug, it will work out. She registers me in the secondary school, and after an entrance exam, I'm enrolled as a student.

At the beginning of the school year, we take the postal bus to Klagenfurt. On the way to the student dormitory where I'll be living, I stop and refuse to go any further for reasons that are not clear to me. I yell at Mother, who is becoming embarrassed, that I don't want to go to school, I don't want to live in the dormitory and I don't want to go to Klagenfurt! Mother says, just pay attention to the way, so you'll know how to get back to the train station. I don't care, I bawl at her, I definitely won't remember any of the streets, because I'm going home right now. Mother calls me *lojza*, which means ninny in our language and is what we say when we don't want to call someone an idiot. *Lojza*, Mother says, you're a complete *lojza*, stop your tantrum, people are starting to stare.

I sense Mother's intransigence and am filled with a bewildered sense of despair. I believe I cannot leave Father alone, I could never forgive myself if he hurt himself, I doubt I can live with the thought that he has spent what little money he has on me. I don't want that to happen, I think to myself, and can't hold back my tears. In a sharp tone of voice Mother says, come on, now come along and let's go!

In the dormitory, sitting on the bed assigned to me, holding the key to my cubicle, I wipe away the traces of my tears. I look at the other girls kissing their mothers and fathers goodbye and realize that I have never yet kissed Mother goodbye. Mother looks into the room a last time, she tells me she's discussed everything with the directors of the dormitory and shakes my hand. Make sure you behave, she says in parting and leaves.

That night I cannot sleep. I feel like a traitor. I wipe away the tears stinging my cheeks on the bed sheets. I am almost intoxicated by the sadness washing over me, which I can only bear lying down. I decide not to give in to this intoxication anymore and resolve not to speak about my feelings and to do whatever is required of me. No one is going to learn anything about me I don't want them to know. They aren't going to see through me, would be the right way of putting it.

First I have to get used to afternoon classes because the Slovenian Secondary School does not have its own building. For more than ten years, they have been hosted in another school building in the afternoon. The German-speaking students hurry home at midday while we Slovenian speakers wait at the side door so that we can enter the school through the basement coatroom. Living in the student dormitory and waiting with the others outside the side entrance makes me a part of the group. I feel like I belong and sense that it will be difficult to hide.

On one of the weekends I spend at home, Father protests one last time against my being away. At night, after we have already gone to bed, he jolts us awake. Mother got what she was after, he roars from the staircase, this is what she wanted and she has put the girl in harm's way. Why is it necessary to send the girl away to school, why send her to Klagenfurt now when the bilingual road signs are being torn down all over Carinthia. But no, Mother has to get her way, no matter what it takes. I'm a human being, too, and my voice should also be heard. I am a human being, Father shouts in German.

It makes me sad to think that I'm the cause of Father's distress, at least I'm convinced I am and that everything about me is embarrassing and oppressive. My body, tall and lanky after a growth spurt, feels that the speed with which it is growing is inappropriate. I'm also convinced I can no longer wear my traditional provincial dress because, in it, I look even worse than usual, unbearably so.

I suspect Mother is waging war against my stubborn nature because she sends me to mass every weekend I spend at home. She makes me feel that she only let me out of her care unwillingly and that from now on I am responsible for my own progress, for my own laundry, for my success in school. At eleven-years-old, I bear a special responsibility because I was allowed to leave our inhospitable home, according to her unspoken charge, which, out of defiance or despair, I assume as a burden.

Mother clings to this last parental duty and urgently works to fulfill it. She believes she has to make sure I meet my obligations as a Christian. That immediately provokes my protests, which in turn reconciles Father with the course events have taken. He abandons his resistance to school and resigns himself to the thought that his daughter's path through life will always be foreign to him and that he'll never be able to follow her.

GRANDMOTHER and I begin to draw apart. She harbors her strength in order to cope with her growing fragility, and I am heading towards something vague in the future. Grandmother doesn't try to hold me back. She lets me go in a peculiar, occasionally affronted way. She grows ever more thin-skinned and intolerant. One day, after I've decided to kiss my parents goodbye every Monday morning before I leave for the dorms, she stops letting me show her affection. As soon as I bend towards her, she shakes her head energetically and pushes me away.

That summer I wear a bikini at home for the first time. When Grandmother sees me, she grabs her cast iron pan and envelopes me in a bitter cloud of willow twig smoke. She is furious. I get dressed quickly and go to her room to placate her. Never flaunt your ass or your money, Grandmother says. A young woman should know what becomes her, she says and pulls a dark blue satin dress from the bottom drawer of the dresser. Her Mici wore this dress to her uncle's wedding. She looked very elegant in it, Grandmother says with a look of reproach. A woman should always adorn herself with a small bouquet of flowers or a brooch. When she went to church, she always carried a few carnations, greenery, and southernwood made into a fragrant bouquet. It smells nice and looks festive. If you dry it and keep it in the closet, it will also keep the moths away, she claims.

In the open drawer I can see old yellow candles and ornate silver-colored candleholders, a black-lacquered wooden crucifix with a pedestal, as well as white cloths and sheets embroidered with liturgical motifs. In my time, Grandmother says, a bride had to bring winding sheets along with bed sheets as a dowry, so that the household was equipped with all that was necessary. She had recently gotten everything ready for when her body would be laid out and has another piece of advice for me. When you have your period, don't ever stick paper or anything like that in your vagina. In the camp, a Polish doctor had warned the women in her block against it because a few women died from having put dirty newspaper up inside themselves. She has been wanting to tell me this for the longest time, Grandmother says, but now that I come home so rarely, there was no opportunity. This conversation puts an end to our intimacy. We can no longer be close because she withdraws into her diminishing self.

On the weekends I spend at home, I hear Grandmother explaining the branches in our family tree to Father and correcting him when he mixes up his first and second cousins. She lists all the neighboring properties and the names of those who lived there and who survived the camps or died in them. She sketches the holdings without writing, weaves a fine net from farm to farm, drawing the names together over the hills, a curious network, a secret community of the overpowered.

Grandmother lists the holdings in the Lepena Valley, the Dimnik holding, along with the Knolič, Šertev, Gobanc, Hirtl, Gregorič, Auprich, Hojnik, and Skutl holdings, and the crofts that belong to the Hrevelniks, the Winkels, the Kožels, the Peternels, the Čemers, the Blajs, the Kokežs, the Potočniks, and the upper Mozgan croft, in the Remschenig Valley, the Kach, Makež, Papež, Črnokruh, and Struz crofts, and the Šopar, Ponovčar, and Tonov holdings, in the Lobnik Valley the Vivoda, Brečk, Topičinik, Mikej, the Stopar, the Wölfl, the Tavčman crofts, in Ebriach the Peruč croft, the Jereb and the Pegrin croft, the Pegrin farm, and those of the Smrtniks, the Šajdniks, the Urhs, in Vellach the Šein, the Kristan, the Podpesnik and the Vejnik farms. The names of the camps hang upon the murdered and on the survivors like small labels with inscriptions and they fade on those who have passed away. They disappear with the farms and holdings, are overrun with grass and underbrush, they are no longer visible, hardly a trace or pile of debris is left, not even a moldering wooden shed or an overgrown footpath.

As always, Death makes his yearly rounds. He watches a young neighbor hang herself and her suicide will devastate everyone as never before. Another one gone much too young, they say, another one who slipped, crashed, fell backwards while the living grasped at life and refused to look into the abyss that makes them dizzy. Grandmother says it's time for her to go. She uses the deferment Death has granted her, as she puts it, to spend time with acquaintances and to talk. She laughs with

Malka Knolič, whose cheeks turn even redder than usual when she and Grandmother recall their return home from Ravensbrück, and Grandmother lets Tonči drive her to see her sisters-in-law. A shawl draped over her shoulders, she sits with her sisters-in-law in their new kitchen, which they show her proudly. She breathes with difficulty and rests her bony hands, covered in thin, liver-spotted skin, in her lap. Her head has shrunk, her nose and chin protrude from her skull like two sharp bumps. Grandmother looks like a distillation of herself. She is held up by a bony frame that houses her shallow breath. She has arrived at the goal, she says, now she finally looks like a woman from a concentration camp.

IN THE dorm, I find my retreat in the Slovenian school library on the building's ground floor. I go there almost every day. My worries about Father and Grandmother's stories coalesce into a thought world, which I guard well and which hides a secret, the secret of the menace that always hangs over humanity. I believe I should not talk about this secret because I have a sense it is a precarious mystery and because I assume that in speaking, I could expose the awkwardness and the fears that form my inner nature, that lie at the very core of my being.

The census for minority groups in Carinthia is a school in itself, and I get the point of the slogans emblazoned on posters: Vote German if you don't want to become a Slovene! So the Slovenian language is not welcome in this land, I think and side with the publicly disparaged because in my eyes, and in the eyes of those I live with, it is important and because for the first time I understand how many shades of meaning the word "belonging" can have.

I have grown into a group and have a recurring dream in which I march at the head of a procession of Slovenians. I know them all, but they don't seem to see me, even though I am naked. When I notice my nakedness I think, nothing can happen to me now because I'm dead, no one can harm me because I've become invisible.

Despite my nocturnal invisibility, my body plays tricks on me. It seems to be working against me internally and relentlessly. Under my skin, it multiplies and extends itself, it strives and ferments. It won't stop growing, it won't stop calling attention to itself even though I want to disappear. My body sneaks up on me from behind and knocks unexpectedly at my door. It wants to be let in, wants me to open myself up to it although I am still not considering doing so. Sometimes it appears as a little toe or gapes at my birthmarks, it protrudes from my chest as nipples or stirs like a hairy slug on my crotch. My body sits grumbling on my shoulder or crouches on my back just as I myself am always on my own back, butting my head against the inside of my skull, presumptuously straining towards speech.

I am overflowing with language, brimming with Slovenian word-shapes I release into the void because I don't know what to do with them. Sentences surround me like a haze that rises towards me from the books I read. Sentences like undigested word particles that move about freely, that I can exhale, that I can breathe out of my lungs again. Sentences like a membrane with which I can hold off anything that might be touched or should be said, but not by me. I am, as they say, a funny girl, who wears a mask to distract others from the melancholy that has spread inside me. For months, I feel like an animal caught in the process of molting, its head caught in the skin it's shedding, unable to free itself. I could lash out if anyone came near me, but I don't realize that.

FROM the day Grandmother can no longer get out of bed, our farm is in a state of emergency. It's the middle of winter. Mother has just given birth to her fifth child, a girl Father refuses to recognize as his own. I am outraged, but my protests don't make the slightest impression on him.

My second Grandmother, whom I call Bica, and Leni, one of my grandfather's sisters, take turns visiting and helping out on the farm. Grandmother complains of shortness of breath. Her heart simply doesn't want to go on, she says. In February, she sends for the priest to administer the extreme unction. Her cheeks are sunken, her skin finally molds itself exactly to the bones underneath. We know that the relatives and neighbors who drop in when they happen to be nearby are here to say goodbye to her. During the day, Father is busy clearing snow because the snow refuses to let up this February. Then the weather turns abruptly warm. The snow melts unusually quickly. By the end of March, the ground is dry. Traces of snow linger only in secluded corners and shadowy nooks, as if to spice the air with a hint of wintery cold.

Classes, in the meantime, are taught in the mornings because politics finally decided to build an appropriate school.

One morning in mid-March, I am called out of the classroom. I am told that my Grandmother has died. Even though I've been expecting this, I'm in a state of shock. I picture myself repeatedly rising up, inwardly, in horror. On the bus trip home, I can only think of how horrified I am.

Grandmother is already laid out when I arrive home in the late afternoon. She lies somewhat elevated below a south-facing window in the living room. Her winding sheets are draped over the improvised trestle table that supports the casket. Mother's sheets have been used in the arrangement, with her embroidery adorning the front of the bier. As usual, a small table has been placed in front of the casket with the silver-colored candleholders, the black crucifix, and two bowls of holy water to bless the dead. Two more candleholders have been placed near Grandmother's head and their candles will not be lit until evening. Grandmother's body is dressed in her Sunday best. She is wearing a black skirt and jacket and a silver-gray kerchief. Her pale hands, folded together with a rosary wound around them, stick up over her ribcage.

I go up to the coffin and lay my hand on her cool, stiffened fingers. Through my tears, I study her face, which is particularly clear in its emptiness. I look at her body as if at a shuttered house and would like to make my presence felt, I would like to call out to her, but I remain behind, a poor hapless thing, among the living. While I weep, Grandmother enters into me as one of the departed. In my thoughts, she grabs the rake leaning against the side of the house and begins to rake the freshly mown grass into piles under the linden tree near our front door. She tries to convince me to slip a few stones into the backpack of a guest who wants to buy some of her smoked ham so that he'll have something to carry. She taps me on the crown of my head with her long fingers and says, we get along just fine, don't we?

Father sits, blinded by tears, on the bench near the oven. Leni bustles back and forth between the kitchen and the pantry. She gives the impression of having taken charge of the household as she did once before, when Grandmother was arrested.

The first mourners arrive. The living room gradually fills, those leading the prayer kneel before the bier and lean their elbows on the wooden bench. The prayer for the dead begins like a choral murmur, like a singsong in monotone.

I have time to get used to having Grandmother's dead body in the house. Mother is still at work in the stall and my baby sister is asleep in a carriage on the second floor over the bier. In the pauses between prayers, hot tea and cider is served with coffee cake. Steam and smoke rise from the large pots in the kitchen under Aunt Leni's and Bica's supervision. Father and Tonči want to keep vigil tonight, the rest of us should get some rest because there will be a crowd of mourners the next day. News of Grandmother's death won't reach most of our relatives until tomorrow, observes Tonči, who has taken on the task of letting everyone know.

Early the next morning, the first wreaths are delivered and they are propped against the wall behind the casket. I go to Grandmother's body before breakfast. For a moment, I have the feeling that she had slept through the night like the rest of us and has only just passed. Mimi, a neighbor, is sitting on the wooden bench, staring fixedly at the dead woman. Tears as round as peas roll down her cheeks in a slow sequence and drip from her chin onto her hands. Since I first met her, I have been struck by Mimi's powerful hands that form a whole with her sturdy body. I found your grandmother in the barrack right after she'd crawled out from behind the boxes where she had hidden. She looked so pitiful, I barely recognized her. For a few moments, Mimi's tears seem to fall faster. Mimi had been transferred to Ravensbrück from the girls' concentration camp in Uckermark and was told to go to block six, where they were all politicals. There she ran into my Grandmother and other neighbors with whom she later made her way home. They arrived home together, Mimi tells me. I know, I say, Grandmother told me. Mimi wipes her eyes and cheeks with a handkerchief and resumes her earlier posture.

I go into the kitchen, following the others' voices. Leni is serving coffee and trying to convince Father that he should be happy to have another girl in the house because houses where girls are growing up are always full of people and are never dull, boys come to visit and you're never home alone for long. Girls bring good luck, she says. Father gives a pained smile and dunks his coffee cake in his coffee. I also want you to send your children to school, Leni continues, when I've reached the point where your mother is now, I want educated people standing at my grave, you understand? You have to educate the young people, let them learn! It's alright, Aunt, Father says. For a moment he looks like a little boy being scolded by his mother and actually seems to duck his head.

The conversation bores me, and I secretly wish Leni would start in with her preaching again. And, in fact, after a pause she says, you can't go on like this Zdravko, you can't spend your life thinking only about dying. You have to stop! I know how it feels not to want to live any longer, but you're going to destroy everyone around you. Father turns pale. He stands up and puts his coffee cup on the warm stove.

You can't even be left in peace at breakfast, he says and leaves. Leni turns to Bica, who was listening, and asks, am I right, I am right, aren't I? Bica nods. After a pause she says, but my daughter is part of the problem, too. Why does she have to be so cold and turn her own husband against her.

The women are busy in the kitchen all morning. Coffee cake is baked for the mourning guests, and the bread oven in the room where Grandmother is laid out gives off so much heat they've opened the window to keep the decomposition of the corpse from accelerating. During the day we are drawn to her and believe we have to make ourselves useful around the bier. The burning candles must be watched, the melted wax cleared away, the wick trimmed, the wreaths propped against the wall made secure, the winding cloth with the white lace smoothed, the water in the vases changed, the bowls of holy water refilled. The dead woman is our sweet babe that must be cared for and dressed up for the guests.

Mother asks me to offer my room to relatives. Someone might want to stay overnight and we need to keep a few extra places to sleep ready for them, she says. I tell her I could sleep in Grandmother's bed without giving it another thought.

In the evening, the expected mourners begin to stream into the living room. Those who can't find anywhere to sit in the room stand in the hall or in the open doorway and, craning their heads, try to keep the body in sight as they pray. The house seethes with the murmuring of the mourners crowding around the corpse. The mood is gloomy. It seems as if something were brewing deep inside of each of those present that looks like grief for the departed but is, in fact, a long suppressed sentiment, a knot of emotion that demands release. I wonder if the mourners are actually weeping for themselves. The dead woman allows them to lament without drawing attention to themselves, allows them to grieve without looking ridiculous.

In the intervals between prayers, I serve tea and pastries.

Later, after most of the mourners have left, a few of the more persistent take a seat in the kitchen. They drink coffee and prepare to keep vigil through the night.

I go to the outbuilding, lie down in Grandmother's bed and, feeling comforted, fall asleep immediately. Past midnight, I wake with a start. It suddenly occurs to me that I'm sleeping in a deathbed. The initial sense of familiarity evaporates at once. I consider jumping out of bed because

I sense I won't be able to cope with the waves of anxiety breaking over me. Premonitions of death wash over me, stiffness, numbness, carrion, the verb "to pass," the raging sea with the ship of death, the black sail over the dead water, the quicklime, too much to bear. Through the window, I can see the brightly lit kitchen in the main house and the living room illuminated with the glow of the candles. I put on my clothes and step outside. The night is clear, the clouds swept from the sky with its bright, twinkling stars. Three men stand below the house with their backs to me, peeing. They're talking and do not hear me coming. As I get closer, I recognize Father with a cigarette hanging from the corner of his mouth. Stanko is telling them that whenever he sees a cigarette glimmer in the dark, a firefly flutter past, or even someone strike a match, it's always a shock for him, because it reminds him of the partisans who smoked in the dark. Suddenly, in the night, the partisans would be standing behind his parents' house or behind his back. To him, those faint gleams were signs that things could get serious again, that they would have to see to the wounded or offer provisions.

Yes, well, Father says and spits, are you coming back inside with us?

No, Stanko answers. He wants to go home and marvel at the peaceful night. He says goodnight, not before adding that I am probably also one of those who startles people.

Father brings cider up from the cellar and goes into the kitchen with Sveršina and me. I can't sleep in Grandmother's bed, I say to explain why I'm awake. The mood in the kitchen has lifted. Cyril sits at the table with Leni, rubbing his hands, because he won at cards. A loud snoring comes from my room over the kitchen. That's my wife, Cyril says, she's asleep in your bed. At home she snores so loud you can hear her out on the street. Sveršina slides in behind the table and says, since Zdravko isn't allowed to play cards he'd like to take the opportunity to ask Leni how it was when she took over the farm. I can tell you about that, too, Father says. What is it you want to tell, Leni interrupts Father, you were such a mess when we told you your mother had been arrested that you threw yourself on the ground in front of my house and started eating the grass. Do you remember? Leni asks. Father answers no. There you go! A week after they tortured you, your mother was arrested. It was too much for you. I can still see you as a ten-year-old boy, Leni says, I know how you were doubled up with cramps.

I am suddenly wide-awake. What happened? I ask. Well, they hanged him, Leni says. Who, I want to know. Your father, she says. How come? I ask because nothing else occurs to me. Tell her about it, Leni says to Father, for whom the conversation is now uncomfortable. He scratches his head and says, they just wanted to know if Grandfather had joined the partisans and if he came home now and then, that's all. What do you mean, that's all? I ask. The police came from Eisenkappel to our farm, very early, I took care of the cows before going to school, they gathered around me in a circle, down there, by the mill. They asked about Grandfather and if I knew when he was coming home, Father recounts looking around at us to see if we even want to hear his story. He sees my astonished expression and continues. After I protested several times that I didn't know anything, the police officers took ropes out of their knapsacks and tied one around my neck. Then they hanged me from a branch, a branch on the walnut tree that stood next to the mill. They pulled me up with the rope until I started to faint and then let me down again. Then they pulled me back up, three times in a row. Then Grandmother ran out of the house and begged them to let me go, she begged them to let me go for God's sake because I still had to go to school. Ain't gonna make it to school, the police said and went up to the house and turned everything upside down. After that, they took him to the Čemers' farm, Father recalls, they'd just arrested Johi Čemer and beat him so badly that Father couldn't bear to look at him. One police officer spoke to him in Slovenian and told him that he would beat the two of them even worse if they didn't tell the truth, they should just finally tell the truth. All day long, they dragged him and Johi to one bunker after another that had been betrayed to them, but they didn't find any partisans. At two in the morning, they brought him to the police station in Eisenkappel and let him sleep on the bare ground. They threw me a blanket, but that was it, Father says. In the morning they took me to another room and hung me up on a hook in the wall, a kind of clothes hook. Then a police officer beat me with a whip, Mother of God, Father says, beating a child with a whip. It was a thick whip with lots of cords. As the officer was beating him, he kept asking if Grandfather was at home. But I didn't say a thing, Father announced. So they let him go. The police officer told him Mici had to report to the station. Then I ran like the devil. Mother met me on the way home. I was beaten black and blue, all over my face and my legs. I was terrified, Father says looking a little surprised that he spoke so long.

After you got home you were so scared you couldn't open your mouth, Leni says. Your neck was full of bruises and your legs covered with blue welts but you absolutely refused to say a thing. Yes, that's how it was, Father says and falls silent.

I am completely upset and want to leap up and ask questions I can't put into words. They rebound through me like a loose flock of arrows, speeding about in all directions and ricocheting off each other. I try to look over at Father who is sitting next to me, but I cannot move my head. I'm afraid to look him in the eye now, it would be an offense against something. His story has become mine, I observe, although in the moment I'm not perceiving anything, I merely have the feeling that he told me a part of my own story. I recoil from this thought just as I shrink away from Father's story, which I find horrifying and incomprehensible. I turn that incomprehensibility onto my own story and am incensed at having to think such thoughts. I don't want to have to think about it.

Leni recounts that, when she saw Grandmother being arrested, she scooped up little Bredica and ran to our farm. It looked as if everything in the house was topsy-turvy and, you wouldn't believe it, a neighbor was already in the cellar trying to fill a sack with apples, Leni says. That's why she decided then and there to stay at the farm; they'd have carried off the entire house and cleaned out the stable. In early November, three weeks after Grandmother's arrest, Grandfather came, accompanied by another partisan, close to the farm and called her up into the forest. That's the first time I saw my brother as a partisan, Leni says. Grandfather was so frantic about his wife's arrest that Leni had to reassure him. She promised she would stay on the farm until the end of the war and would take care of his children. Then she collected some sugar, salt, and dried fruit and carried it into the forest. A few days later all hell broke loose. I still wonder who it was who reported that I took a basket of provisions into the forest, Leni says. From then on, the children had to stand guard when a partisan came to the house. In late December, there was a lot of snow on the ground, my brother came back and suddenly appeared in the hut where we prepared the slop for the pigs and where I brewed schnapps with the children. He had come alone via Globasnitz, there had been a gunfight, during which his group had been torn apart and they'd had to flee. One of his friends had been killed. My brother said that it was all pointless, that he was going to turn himself in to the police, that he was bringing trouble on his whole family, that he couldn't stand this kind of life any more. He cried like a baby, my brother cried like a baby, Leni says. She made him some scrambled eggs and a cup of tea. She gave him clean underwear and dried his clothes. She and Tonči, his eldest son, convinced him not to rush into anything, the Gestapo would send him straight to the camp or would have him tortured, it made no sense to turn himself in, and it wouldn't bring his wife and foster daughter home. At that, your Grandfather calmed down a bit. Before it got light, he darted back into the forest, Leni says. What times those were!

It was a dog's life, Cyril says. As a soldier, he'd gotten used to quite a bit, but the uncertainty, the lack of supplies, the cold, and how they always had to be on their guard... Being with the partisans, he lost his sense of humor even though he sometimes had an itch to pull some shenanigans, but that always risked putting someone in danger. Šorli the courier, for example, just could not give up playing his accordion and running after women. He was snagged by a patrol and fatally wounded at the Wögel's farm when he tried to jump out of the sitting room window and his accordion got caught on the window frame. He gave up his life for a few happy hours, I suppose. That's how crazy people were sometimes, Cyril says. He himself couldn't give up hunting, he just had the itch. He got his hunting rifle from home and then it happened. When he jumped over the damn fence, a shot went off and right through his hand. Jesus Christ, Cyril says. So I had to be treated illegally by the doctor, whereas until then I was the one taking care of the sick and wounded in the bunkers. They had to build a bunker near his farm so his wife could take care of him in secret. His sister had to get bandages and medicine from the community physician who sympathized with the Germans. Naturally, the doctor could guess who the medicine was for, but he just gave it to her and grumbled, as he had on other occasions as well, and didn't blow anyone's cover. After my hand had healed, I was assigned to be an escort to the commanders. I knew all the paths and tracks, the neighbors trusted me, Cyril says. The wound was good for something, he had thought to himself, maybe it was meant to happen. After he decided to desert from the Wehrmacht in Finland where he had been deployed with an anti-aircraft battery, he had an old Carinthian doctor in Klagenfurt bandage his arm when he was on leave so he could return home. The doctor looked up at me and asked if he could bandage up my good arm, Cyril says, he didn't say any more than that. Surely he knew I was planning on deserting.

To a certain extent, people were completely naïve, Sveršina joins into the conversation. That lasted until they realized that in our valleys, it was a life and death struggle. For a while, the farmers and the farmhands believed the partisans were adventurers they could badmouth. No one had a clue about conspirators. Sveršina says he'd often racked his brains about why so many people from our valleys ended up in concentration camps and why the police were always so well-informed.

Dear Cyril, Leni says, in all the time since that disastrous winter when you and I were arrested as partisans, I don't think we once sat down together as long as this. She stands up. You were a brave fighter, aside from that accident with the hunting rifle. You even grabbed the grenade the police had thrown into my house and threw it right back outside. You saved the lives of my children and everyone living in my house at the time we were betrayed. Even if you just stick to your woodcarving now and don't have any time for us politicals, you contributed a great deal to the liberation of our land.

It was horrible, Cyril interrupts her, the way they mowed down Primož and tortured you in prison.

I'm not finished, Leni says and takes a deep breath. She believes that today's wake is a special one, which Mitzi, her sister-in-law, now laid out, could well have been listening to. She was proud that the Slovenian people did not back down during the Nazi years, that they started to fight for their survival. On certain days she can feel the scars on her neck, back, and bottom left from the Gestapo interrogation. It's the past knocking on my door, Leni says, it calls out to me and starts tormenting me. That's when she's sure that they, the older generations, have the obligation to pass on what they know to the younger ones, so that they don't end up one day with no memories of their families. She'd like to close, she tells us, by saying that she's very happy that Zdravko went the whole evening without raising his voice once and remained calm. As everyone smiles with embarrassment, Father's face freezes. He asks me if I'd like to keep vigil now since he has to lie down. I agree because I hope it will help quiet my mind.

Leni goes with me to the casket in the living room and with a cloth dries the holy water from Grandmother's face, which has gotten wet from the many blessings. She changes the candles and backs out of the room, as if she wanted to pay homage to Grandmother one more time.

I remain alone with the casket and watch the candles' flickering tongues. A few drops of holy water that landed on Grandmother's jacket look like little soap bubbles. I can hear the sound of creaking chairs in the kitchen. I open the window and sit back down on the bench near the oven. My thoughts begin to sink into my belly, where they look for a dark place to settle.

Silence emanates from the bier. Outside I can hear the first birdcalls, they float into the room as a warbling, chirping wave of sound. The birdsong flows around the silent core of the bier and envelops Grandmother in something in which she can return, something that will take her back.

Cyril comes from the kitchen and says that Sveršina has fallen asleep on the bench. Cyril wants to say more prayers for his sister. He sits at the head of the bier and takes a rosary from his pocket. In silent prayer, his fingers unroll the rosary, bead by bead, sentence by sentence. I stretch out on the bench and fall asleep.

Mother, who has gotten up to go to the stables, wakes me. She says I can lie down in her bed. I see Cyril still sitting at the head of the bier and stumble, drunk with sleep, into my parents' bedroom. When I get up, it's midday. Those who kept vigil all night have left.

In the evening, the mourners bring more bouquets and wreaths to the house. The sweetish smell of flowers spreads through the living room and turns, by the next morning, into the sharper smell of wilting flowers. After midnight, as the last mourners leave, Father decides to put the coffin lid on because, as he says, she has started to work. The window is opened, and the room is fumigated. Before the coffin lid is brought into the room, Mother approaches the bier and grabs jerkily at Grandmother's hand. She starts to whimper softly and then says in a voice loud enough for me to hear: When you were alive, you were not good to me, but I always respected you. May God grant you peace. I've made my peace with you. Mother's outburst, which rises to loud sobbing and subsides, disconcerts me. When the men lay the lid on the coffin, Mother tears herself away from the bier. She blows her nose in her handkerchief and begins to pray in a hoarse voice. We are forced to answer her and stand perplexed in the room, which suddenly resembles a bird's nest on a high cliff, from the opening of which the dead are thrown down into the depths.

Tschik will take over the final vigil, so that he can take his leave from his KZ companion, as he puts it. The wreath from the Ravensbrück Concentration Camp Association with the red triangle in its center rests against the front of the bier and gleams.

The pallbearers come to the farm early the next morning. The dead woman in her coffin is lifted out through the window and set down on the doorstep one last time so that she can say goodbye to her home and those she leaves behind. Then the coffin is set on a trailer, covered with wreaths, and driven to the graveyard.

Grandmother's burial is a solemn one. I move through the throng of people as if I were using my body for the first time. As the coffin is carried through the market square, a pair of warbling thrushes frolic above the funeral procession and the massive wreaths.

After Grandmother is laid to rest, I am also offered condolences, which surprises me since I had not considered myself an adult. At the funeral dinner, I look at Father, and he strikes me as a man who has just lost his entire family.

At home I sit in the empty living room that still has faint traces of the sweetish smell of decay. Along with the smell fading from the room, I can feel Grandmother retreating from me. She shifts inside me, as if it were time to part. She stands up, lays her knitting on the table, draws the curtains, closes the door, and walks out from inside me. A tenacious pain settles into the space in me she once filled, a pain that will not yield for a long time. My eyes linger on the primroses outside along the near edge of the field that stretches up the slope behind our house. Everything is about to change, I think.

On the following day, after helping Mother clean the house and scrub the living room floor, I crouch in a warm hollow behind our house near the forest's edge. I look down into the valley and wonder if I shouldn't start writing after all. I could divert words from their constant rotation around me, I could pull them out of their dark course and have them tell my own story, but a story of my own is nothing more than a Fata Morgana.

AFTER Grandmother's death, the order of things in our house is reconfigured. Her legacy is distributed. I get her straw hats and kerchiefs, her white linen petticoats, a couple of teacups and glasses, as well as a few photographs. These objects are my body's fitments, I find, they give me shape for the first time.

Mother arranges the household according to her own ideas. She buys herself a moped and, when necessary, drives it to the remote regional capital to take care of official matters or to make purchases. She loads her purchases into a large knapsack she carries on her back or into the bags she fastens onto the luggage rack. Little by little, she takes over the organization of the family. Father complains that she is rising above him, but leaves the official and domestic decisions entirely to his wife.

He begins leading a double life, one life for the neighbors and another for his family. He tries to maintain the illusion for his neighbors that he leads a light-hearted existence. In public, he wants to display his cheerfulness, his confidence, and his diligence. He wants to be considered the hardest worker, the most accomplished and circumspect hunter in the area. He wants to be a daring motorcyclist and the jolliest clarinet and accordion player around. He wants the neighbors to remember him for his extraordinary practical jokes and feats. In winter, even though he does not know how to ski, he lets himself be talked into strapping on skis and barreling down the steep escarpment for others' amusement. He enters sled races with a heavy old farm sleigh so he can play the clown, swallows raw eggs until he feels nauseous, climbs onto every overloaded cart and up every tree if asked. He drinks to excess because he doesn't believe in moderation, because as long as he can remember, his life has been filled with extremity, enormity, and transgression. At home, the slightest thing can unsettle, irritate, or exasperate him. He loses patience easily. When he doesn't understand something or someone contradicts him, he refuses to speak for days at a time.

After Grandmother's death, Father stops talking about suicide. The destructive rage he used to direct inward, he now turns outward. When he's drunk, his body becomes an instrument that emits shrill, ear-splitting shrieks. His voice is catapulted out of his wiry ribcage in every possible pitch and at every imaginable level of intensity. His rages are like the howling of a man condemned to death. In this state, he runs from room to room or entrenches himself behind the kitchen table, which he hammers with his fists. He threatens to show us just how much he's worth, he will show us children and Mother, we who want only to destroy him. He vents his fears and anxieties, launches his rage against us in a barrage of words that buries us and from which we will arduously have to dig ourselves out hours later.

Father's thoughts revolve around death. He is susceptible to destructive tendencies. When he comes home spent or from the Rastočniks', he begins to fantasize about murders that were committed in the region before, during, and after the War. He shouts that he knows who killed that nymphomaniac Katharina, who was discovered stabbed to death in the Lepena stream before the war, he knows who killed Peternel when he came home after the war, he knows who did away with the partisans in Benetek Valley, he shouts that he feels he's under threat, he, too, will be murdered one day, murdered by his wife who already has it all planned out and set up, she's got the pickaxe and spade ready so she can hide his body after she has killed him. He is utterly convinced that Mother is responsible for all his bad feelings. He accuses her of humiliating him as a man, of betraying him, and always saying the wrong thing. She doesn't understand him and is ruining his reputation with her ways, she has no pity for him. He claims she, the daughter of a simple day laborer, is not grateful enough for the social status she now enjoys from having married into a farming family.

Mother is far from feeling any compassion for Father. She gives him sullen and reproachful looks because she feels misunderstood and insulted. She makes it clear that he has disappointed her, that she dreams of leading another life, and that she believes marrying him was a mistake.

Father's fits of nerves over the years infuse us children like an invisible poison, drop by drop. We watch how he undermines his role as father, how he tries to turn us into sidekicks who have to put up with his raging fury, how he draws us into his old horror and tries to impress his pain on us, pain we can intuit but not grasp, how he wants us to undo his devastation with ours, and wants us to understand that horror is the essence of life. He feels betrayed by everyone around him and betrays us to all those who are ready to credit his suspicions. After the storm dies out and life continues soberly, Father remains silent for days from horror and regret, from the shame or satisfaction of having once again expressed himself fully.

I can only recover with difficulty from the havoc wreaked on me by staying up all night with Father, nights in which none of us can sleep because he will not calm down. I'm worn out from his fits and cannot find the words to describe the impact of his outbursts. My attempts to speak are no more than meek stammering and silence because I'm embarrassed by my incomprehension and am ashamed for Father.

In spite of it all, I come to his defense, as all his relatives instinctively do. They seem to have come to an agreement that his outbursts must be respected, that there is no point in asking anyone for advice since, in any case, you can never be sure of being understood or receiving assistance. The reigning attitude is that you cannot escape fate. You have to accept your destiny like the old family names because those who do try to flee vanish in the distance, disappear like smoke.

I write my first poems, mere groping for words, and live through the period before my final examination in the student dormitory as in a no-man's land, where I have been granted an interval I can fill with day-dreams and nocturnal fantasies. I hope I will be able to find or invent the right language, and I conceive phantom sentences that I launch into the future. All that is thought and felt, experienced and feared, will only come to words later, they will meet or be joined in a phrase, I hope, some day, when the time comes.

IN CONTRAST to the combative Leni, who was politicized by the war, Father is suspicious of politics and refuses to take part in the demonstrations that follow the anti-Slovenian *Ortstafelsturm* or "place-name sign storm" when bilingual road signs were destroyed throughout the province by German-national Carinthians, because he believes you should let sleeping dogs lie. He and his companions from the war years did not want anyone swearing or spitting at them on the street. Even Michi is convinced, after a rally of Slovenian Carinthians in Klagenfurt, that for decades to come, the German Carinthians in Klagenfurt would resent the Slovenians, the children of the farmers, laborers, and clerical workers from the southern part of the province for publicly protesting and demanding compliance with the Austrian State Treaty, especially for demanding that Article 7 of the treaty be followed, in other words, demonstrating for something that means absolutely nothing to the majority of the population. The majority, on the other hand, feel that the national treaty is more a castigation than a state contract, a punishment meted out to them after the war on terms dictated by the occupying powers.

Father has lost the conviction that getting involved politically is worthwhile, or maybe he never had it. The idea you can change anything is foreign to him. Father believes that engaging in politics is to put your life at risk. He believes absolutely everything is at stake, not just individual interests. He cannot separate his own interests from his survival. He is skeptical of anyone who acts under the protection of a political organization or looks for support in an ideological creed. He can't recall a single political slogan he could believe. The only thing he has to say about his time with the partisans is that, as a child, he was never assigned to a combat unit, that the partisans saved his life, and that almost the entire time he had the feeling he was on the run.

I remember that I rarely saw Father emerge from his political reservation as fully as he did following a rare excursion to Slovenia with the Partisan Association.

On his return home, he raves about how well received the Carinthian partisans were in Yugoslavia. He describes how much pomp and circumstance surround the partisans in Slovenia, how supportive they appear of their state and how conscious of their power, how there is still something militant about them, which you can only say about the functionaries when it comes to the Carinthian partisans. He mentions the impressive partisan chorus from Trieste and hums a few fighting songs, as if for emphasis to show that he can still sing or hum along. Here, partisans are always bad-mouthed as bandits and murderers, he says, like after that ceremony in Klagenfurt when we were given awards sent by the Yugoslavian president Tito in recognition of our service in the resistance against National Socialism. It turned into a riot in which his cousin Peter grabbed one of the hecklers and threw him in the bushes. He felt then that they had kept some of their fighting spirit, Father says. In any case, he and few companions quickly drove to Eisenkappel and ordered goulash and beer at the Koller inn. We left the certificates in the car or there would have been another brawl at the Koller, Father says.

A few years later, Father receives a medal from the Austrian president for his service in the liberation of Austria. Father says that he's proud of his medal and that he's going to have the certificate framed. All the same, he is convinced that politics are a swindle and simply lead people like him around by the nose.

Political occasions of the Carinthian variety, funerals, or family reunions trap Father in the past and he has difficulty finding his way out again. He's tormented for weeks after an encounter in an inn during which someone he had been drinking with told him he was responsible for his own misfortune and it was his father and mother's fault that he ended up in this situation. If his father hadn't joined the partisans and fought against Hitler and for the Slovenians, then nothing would have happened to him. Why does he get so worked up, whoever says A, also has to say B, the boor said and none of the others wanted to speak against him because alcohol had gotten the better of them all. Father is hit hard and I am distressed because I sense that he loses any capacity to defend himself when he drinks, that it renders him vulnerable to every provocation, every insinuation, every rumor, and that he is immediately ready to doubt himself and defer to those who are taunting him.

Only visits from his closest relatives, his brother and his brother's family, or the cousins with whom he lived through the war years, make him strangely happy. We children are glad when our sitting room is full of guests chattering happily around a full table. They laugh, tell stories, and sing songs. Occasionally, one of the guests will stand and give a speech. Father weeps without embarrassment and sometimes others cry too, especially his cousin Zofka, of whom Father is particularly fond. When they reminisce about the dramatic day on which Grandmother was arrested and Peter and Tonči recall how humiliating and painful the slaps were that a police officer searching the house had given them, they always mention an older, more restrained, red-haired officer who had tears in his eyes when he looked at the desperate boys. The tears of the policeman who had assisted with Grandmother's arrest bring tears to the storytellers' eyes, too, as if the stranger's emotions were making their own sorrow possible, as if their despair were reflected more convincingly and more vividly in the unknown policeman's eyes than in their own souls. Michi tells of the Šporns' daughter who was her age at the time, in other words still a child. Policemen beat her unconscious with the butts of their guns on the bridge to the Kupitz inn in the Remschenig valley because her parents joined the partisans, he says. Her classmate, who later became her husband and who accompanied her home was also almost beaten to death by the police. He still has scars on his ribs from the beating. Father knows about it. He also claimed that Count Thurn saved the children's lives. Since the policemen did not stop beating the children even after they were lying on the ground unconscious, the Count stood in front of the children and then had them taken to the Kupitzs' to be cared for. The police would have taken away thirteen entire families in the Remschenig Valley in a single day if some of them hadn't been able to escape to the partisans during the arrests, Michi says and asks, can you imagine, in a valley with not even twenty holdings.

IN MY final years of secondary school, Father develops a bashful interest in my academic progress and shows it casually and shyly. He looks at my report cards and reads the names of the subjects out loud because the bilingual designations appeal to him. When the snow is high one winter morning when I have to leave early for Klagenfurt and Michi, who always drives me to the bus in Eisenkappel at the beginning of the week, can't get his car out of the garage, Father gets up at four in the morning and starts to plow the driveways with his tractor. He drives to Michi's house and, in reverse, pushes the mounds of snow from the access road. Sometimes he stops on the main road and waits until Michi drives up next to the tractor and gets out. The two men share their first morning smoke in the dark and discuss the weather. They are burned in my memory as two shivering men, standing in the drifting snow and blocking my way to school.

When my parents are invited to the graduation ceremony, my father doesn't want to come. He can't imagine himself going to a school event, never, Father says. He is angry with Mother when she goes to the ceremony because, in his view, she is adorning herself with borrowed plumes.

To me, my future after graduation looks only like a white cloud bank, and I convince myself to move toward it, out into uncertainty.

My parents restrain themselves, not a single suggestion passes their lips, they leave my choice of study entirely to me, they don't try to meddle in something they do not know or have ever taken into consideration. Their daughter should do whatever she wants as long as she doesn't bring shame on them, because a concept like shame means more to my parents than the word "studies." They use that word warily, like all foreign words. After months, Mother hesitantly pronounces "theater studies," the title of my chosen program, and Father doesn't even try to remember it. When asked what his daughter is studying, he says that it has something to do with plays and that's enough for him since he doesn't know anything about intellectual work and would rather not think about such things.

I decide to pursue theater studies because I'm convinced, after seeing many plays, that the stage could become a space for me in which I could face all my complications and despair without danger. The catastrophes on stage are all contained, the protagonists all survive no matter how many times they die. They present their disappointments, dreams, and malice, their love and their hatred, they can yield to their emotions and their nagging fears. A performance has to start with a beginning and does not have to have a happy ending. Yet it always has an ending. The theater can't attack you from behind the way life can, even when it flails about. It's all a game, all up in the air.

In Vienna, I start trying to write again and write in Slovenian as if I could recollect myself, as if Slovenian could lead me back to the feelings from which I have become estranged. A mourning that doesn't yet know what it is called or even what it is lies waiting to be named, waiting for me to solve its mystery. It wants to be bound to me with words like all the other emotions that swirl nebulously inside me. My sentences are clumsy, as if they were composed of fragments of random letter sequences. They resemble letters that cannot be attributed to anyone or traced back to their senders and don't want to betray who had written them.

Mother writes that she is considering leaving home. She can't bear it any longer and is going to find a job.

When I come home for Christmas, she tells me that she talked it all over with Father. He has promised to change, she says uncertainly, as if she were aware this means giving up some of her hopes. She is determined to take small liberties, to go to a spa, join excursions, or go on Sunday hikes. She needs to get away from home now and then and be exposed to new ideas so that she's better able to bear the weekdays. I encourage her in her new resolutions and ask if she ever imagined living in the city or ever considered a divorce. But for Mother divorce is out of the question.

In the winter of my second year of university, I arrive in Eisenkappel late one evening, wondering how to cover the seven kilometers to Lepena with my suitcases since I had not been able to find anyone who could pick me up and drive me into the valley. I stand in the snow-covered main square and decide to look in the inn where I am bound to find men from Lepena.

As I pass the church, I see Father's tractor with a trailer parked in front of the Slovenian savings bank. Three sacks of flour lie uncovered and exposed to the cold on the loader wagon. I check the Koller inn, but one of the waitress says he has not been there. So I go the Bošti, a run-down inn with dark, low-ceilinged rooms. I do, in fact, find Father there. He greets me with a loud well, hello there! This one's mine, he beams, she came all the way from Vienna to get me!

As the men at his table squeeze together to make room for me, the guests at the next table barely glance up. I put my suitcase down, hang up my coat, and give Father a kiss on the cheek. The men pick up their conversation, which I had interrupted. Tine, whom they jokingly call the

General, was just recounting an incident from their time as partisans and they wanted to hear the end of the story. The next table is noisily occupied. The men burst into frequent ear-splitting guffaws.

Tine tells them how, as company commander, he had to leave three wounded men with their relatives in Koprivna. The farmers gave them medical attention in secret. It was especially bad during the last winter of the war. His company had had to evacuate their infirmary in Solčava and they received orders to transport seventeen wounded fighters through deep snow to a distant valley. Three severely wounded men died during the transport that night. I could hardly bear it when partisans died, Tine says, and the political commissars' mania for control and for issuing orders. They were constantly inspecting everything, they searched his backpack and forbade him from writing letters to his girlfriend, whom they'd classified as unreliable. They meddled in our private lives and issued pointless orders, Tine says. One of the men at our table asks what happened with Peršman, after all, Tine's company was near the farm. Tine takes a deep breath, yes, Peršman, he says, every day they expected news that the war was over. He and his company had waited near the farm for almost three weeks with two other units. Even then, Tine had thought it was irresponsible, but the commander wanted to wait. The partisans had even been practicing dancing for when peace was declared, that's how foolish we were, Tine recalls. A man from Globasnitz fell asleep on his watch and didn't see that SS units were approaching the Peršman farm. Then the catastrophe occurred, just ten days before the end of the war. No one expected it. The partisans had withdrawn after a skirmish because they wanted to avoid a battle, then an SS unit attacked the entire family. After the massacre of the Peršman family, he had been beside himself, Tine says, the dead civilians from his time in the Wehrmacht in Poland and Russia came back to haunt him, before his eyes, the entire war became a tower of civilian corpses, horrible, he says, horrible! That night everything was mixed up for him, the Russians hanged in the Ukrainian villages, the burned down farms, the smell of burning flesh that spread over the Peršman farm.

At that moment, one of the men at the next table said, that's a lie, it was the partisans who murdered the Peršman family. How's that, Tine asks and raises his head.

I suddenly have the feeling that the men at Father's table have fallen into an ambush.

You did nothing more than terrorize the local population. You all fought for Yugoslavia. You are traitors to your country plain and simple, the man at the next table shouts. You mean we terrorized those in the population who were loyal to the Reich, Tine says gradually getting ahold of himself, that's something I know inside and out! You still believe that under Hitler's Germany you were fighting for Austria. For the expansion of German territory, sure, but not for Austria! A free Austria was written off like never before. So is that still your country, the German Reich, even now when you call us traitors, Tine asked threateningly but the man remained obstinate. You should all be called up before a military court, he persists, the English should have locked you up instead of the respectable citizens who did their duty.

The English were with us during the war, Tine counters, we belonged to the Allies, if that name rings a bell! But there's no room in your head for that, is there? After so many years, you people can't think of anything to say about the Nazi period other than repeating your propaganda, Tine says in disgust. He should have relied on his intuition and gone home.

So now he wants to go, someone roared from the next table, during the war he would have shot us on the spot, but now he wants to go home!

He wouldn't have shot you, but I would have, if I'd caught you, a man at our table says with a threatening stare.

Echoes of the war surround us for a moment. The inn is transformed into a battle ground on which the opposing sides are taking stands.

I'll remember that, the cowed attacker says.

Father is nervous. Tine tells the man at our table who had leapt up angrily, sit down, come on now, sit down!

The next table renews the attack.

And you, Zdravko, the loudmouth says to my father, you were nothing but a snitch. Your stateless president can give you all the decorations he wants. For me you're just a bandit like all the others.

My heart is racing and I have an overwhelming need to hurl something at the attacker and protect my father, but nothing else occurs to me than to call him a Nazi. You Nazi, I say and I'm shocked by my faltering voice. Father laughs a short, pained laugh and says to the belligerent man, I'm a bandit and you're a cretin!

I'm going to get my gun right now, the militant defender at our table announces leaping to his feet again.

If you go to get it, you can stay home, the waitress says firmly. I will call the police this instant!

The front is breached. The opposing armies fall back.

I ask Father to pay, wanting to leave right away. Father raises his hand defensively. I'll decide when I leave, he says. Check, Father calls after a frightening moment and throws some money on the table. The waitress's hands tremble as she pulls out her pad and adds up the bill. Father gives her a generous tip and tries to stand. He sways. There should be a bag of groceries around here somewhere, he says, we can't forget it. I hold his winter jacket out for him and point to the grocery bag on the floor.

Well then, Father says after picking up the bag, let's be on our way! He seems to consider launching another round at the hostile table, but when apparently nothing occurs to him, he opens the door.

We step out onto the street. The main square is empty. I hope no one stole the sacks of flour, Father says as we turn towards the church. The tractor stands in the cold like a forbidding ghost. I put my suitcase in the trailer and Father lets the grocery bag drop with a crash. We climb into the driver's cab. After several attempts to start it, the engine springs to life. Father's legs rise and fall like the limbs of a marionette as he steps on the clutch and the gas pedal. His driving sends chills down my spine. I ask him if he has anything against my driving home. For a while, Father drives along the winding curves of the slippery, snow-covered road without answering, then he stops. You want to drive, he shouts, you don't have a driver's license or the slightest idea! Be my guest, he says and leaves me the driver's seat.

I immediately have problems putting the tractor in gear and Father jeers, what did I say, the show-off, doesn't know a thing, doesn't have a license, but she wants to drive!

The road is slippery and I'm frightened. Father is getting more and more worked up. He calls me a snitch, Father says, outraged, calling me a snitch and a bandit, I won't put up with that, I'm going to teach him that no one calls me a snitch or a bandit. Stop, he orders, I have to go back, I have to tell him, Father shouts and grabs the steering wheel.

I stop the tractor and beg Father, who is getting ready to climb out, to stay in the cab. It's the middle of the night, the other men went home long ago, there's no point in getting upset about comments by some imbecile. Easy for you to say, Father says. No one can treat me like that, period! He looks at me, his eye wide and gasping for air as if he were suffocating. I stare doggedly at the road, decide not to pay him any attention, and put the tractor in gear.

The steady throb of the motor calms him. As I drive the vehicle across a level part of the valley, where it opens outs and the wooded slopes recede from the edge of the road, Father seems to have fallen asleep next to me. Suddenly he wakes with a start and says, I've lost my gloves, my gloves slipped out of my hand. We have to turn around and drive back! I can't turn the tractor around, I say, we can look for them tomorrow. He'll go back the few meters on foot, Father grumbles. They can't be far, he just had them in his hands, he says and tries to stand up. I stop. Father gets out onto the road and says, I'll be right back. Swearing, I climb down from the driver's seat and watch Father's dark silhouette draw away.

The cold grips me like a painful shudder. In the night silence that sparkles around me, the creak of the running engine sounds like a ticking music. The winter night is turning into a fixed image of moonlight frozen on the gleaming snow. Then the layer of snow lifts abruptly as if it were wearing a feathered mantel that rises breathlessly. The stars in the sky are like falling snow crystals or flakes of ice rising further and further into the endless expanse. The valley widens beneath the burning air. A stream's icy water crackles next to the road.

Father has not returned. I run back along the road and call hesitantly, *ati*, Papa, but the stream swallows my call. Near the end of the level stretch, I notice a dark spot on the embankment. When I get closer, I recognize Father lying on his back on a pile of snow.

Are you not feeling well, I ask, should I get help?

Let me lie here, Father says, just let me lie here. I don't want to go on, I'm going to stay here. Sveršina showed me how it's done. Sveršina can sleep in the snow like a partisan and I can too.

What about the gloves, I ask.

They're under my head, Father says.

I have run out of patience. I grab Father's hand and pull him up, stand up, stand up, I scold him, but Father just lies back down in the snow and crosses his arms. If everyone else is acting crazy, why shouldn't I, my thoughts race desperately and I scream in a Hitler imitation, On your feet, Comrade! What is the meaning of this? Stand up, fall in, move, march, march! And I raise my hand in a Hitler salute. Father laughs a laugh that sounds like a scream. He stands up immediately and salutes.

Heil Hitler, he says swaying but this time from laughter. I spin around in a goose-step and start belting out a partisan song. Father stumbles after me, yelling, Heil Hitler, Heil Hitler, *ta je pa dobra*, this is good, this is really good! I manage to start the tractor before he climbs in and sits down. I sing the partisan song without stopping, even as I drive, because I am worried that Father will want to get out as soon as I stop. But he is happy to follow my lead. He laughs, conducts, sings, slaps me on the back and keeps repeating, the two of us, we're the real half-wits, we're fighting for freedom and bread!

At home, in bed, I lie awake for a long time. The room is cold, I'm chilled to the bone and a cold rash covers my arms and legs. The frost has crept under my skin. It wants to spend the winter inside me, it seems, and I'm too tired to fend it off.

That night I dream I'm running away from home. I'm waiting for a train coming down from the mountain that is very delayed. I just manage to climb onto the last car. I lie face down on the roof of the last compartment so that we can climb the steep mountain slope faster because the man who doesn't want to let me go is on the lookout just under the summit and he wants to pull me from the moving train. He created a bloodbath in our house. He killed all the children by cutting their throats. Even my father shouldn't see me, he is not to know I am there. I can see him in the compartment below me, lying on a hospital bed, and I am afraid he might fall out of it. He is very small and frail.

T H E trips between Vienna and my hometown turn into expeditions through time, into trips through different periods and versions of history that exist in parallel. The closer I get to my hometown, the stronger the feeling grows that I'm traveling into the past, and the further away I am, the faster hours and days speed by. Traveling back and forth, I feel like someone who has been flung through eras, who has dropped from the future, or who has arrived too late.

Since I started at the university, Father's cries for help have taken on a societal, even political dimension. I start thinking in larger, public contexts. I am convinced that this country's general stance toward the past is what makes our family stories appear so strange and relegates them to such isolation. They have almost no connection to the present. Between the official version of Austria's history and its actual history stretches a no-man's land in which it's easy to get lost. I picture myself shuttling back and forth between a dark, forgotten part of the cellar in the house of Austria and its bright, richly furnished spaces. No one in the bright rooms seems to guess or wants to imagine that there are people in this building confined by politics to history's cellar, where they are besieged and poisoned by their own memories.

In a Slovenian anthology, I come upon two poems by Katrca Miklav, my grandfather's sister, which were saved from the camp, and I am strangely moved, as if a long forgotten embryonic memory had stirred in my thoughts. I am startled that it exists. In the explanatory notes I read that three days before she died Katrca wrote a few poems on small scraps of paper and gave them to Angela Piskernik, a fellow inmate from Eisenkappel. Katrca believed Angela would appreciate the poems since she respected the written word. Angela had the poems published in a Slovenian cultural magazine after the war. And so they were preserved, the notes say.

After several of my poems appeared in magazines, a publisher takes on my first volume of poetry. I can hardly believe it: a book that will bundle my Slovenian poems into something daring that could give my life as a student a new direction. It will compel me to express myself with more clarity, more precision, I hope. It will delay the disappearance of the Slovenian language in Carinthia, I think enthusiastically, it could create the illusion that this language still has a role.

Writing about cultural politics is easier for me than writing "I" in my texts. My self does not say I. It plays on its own stage. It speaks in coded language, it is hidden underneath old and new costumes, it randomly tries on languages like attractive or functional clothing as it searches for its real face. It rummages through stockpiles of explanations and meanings.

I doggedly train myself to discern at least the tone of my thoughts, to recognize it among the multitude of other tones. I have barely heard it and it's gone because it's too faint, because it gets lost in the tangle of voices, in my efforts to pull together a sense of my self.

Convinced nonetheless that I've heard that tone, I cannot get away from it, I constantly seek it out, I long for another encounter with it in which we can throw off sparks and devise a melody that will unite us in a wonderful fashion.

IN MY third year of university, Father writes me one of his rare letters. Greetings, *Mic*, he writes. He is home alone, Mother is off taking a cure. That's why he has to write me a letter and ask how I am. He is not doing well. He is forwarding the mail that came to my old address along with money. I should spend it however I like. He closes with the phrase 'with regards from the worthless one,' *od ničvrednega*, he writes, as if he crossed himself off with that signature.

At the beginning of summer, a friend drives me home. Father is beside himself.

After the young man has left and Mother has shown me her new flowerbeds, Father locks the front door, leaving us outside. He yells out the kitchen window that he refuses to let me in, tramp of a whore that I am. I am so hurt I threaten to call the police immediately if he won't let us in the house. I can do without a father like that, I shout.

Report me to the police if you want, Father roars back. If nothing occurs to you other than reporting me, you can stay outside and your mother can too.

He's jealous, Mother says, we'll wait a while and then climb in through the kitchen window. I wonder if I should feel sorry for myself or if the situation is simply too grotesque to take seriously. I'm relieved that the kitchen window is not latched. Mother takes me through the garden one more time and when we come back the door is still locked. In the woodshed I find an old milking stool, which I set under the window so we can climb over the window boxes, onto the windowsill, and into the kitchen.

Father is in the living room, sitting on the bench next to the oven and looking out the south window at the other side of the valley. I go to him.

Hand me the key, I say. He gives me a wild and reproachful look.

Get out, he growls, go on and call the police!

Where is the key, I demand.

Here, he says and throws the front door key on the floor.

I pick up the key and give him a sidelong glance.

Go on, get the police, disappear, he says.

Just then I am seized by a fierce, defiant rage. Not with me, I think, not with me! On a sudden impulse, I go up to Father and caress his head twice. As if I had been doing an experiment, I gently stroke his hair. Father caves under the palm of my hand. His head dips towards his chest as if his neck muscles suddenly abandoned their duty. He swallows a sigh, yes, Mic, he says, yes, and then, a shit life, *kurc, pa to življenje*!

For a moment, I am reconciled. I could smile, but the smile on my face turns into a mask of rage, indignation, and sympathy. That's all it takes to intimidate Father, I think, that's all it takes. But I made the calculation without taking him into account, because Father will not let me change him.

That night, I stand in a bathroom in front of the sink and my job is to hand a pill to each man who enters the room. Men I think I recognize come in. I give each of them a pill and they all swallow them willingly. Then they immediately double up with cramps and die. After a while I begin to doubt my executioner's duty. I don't want to watch them croak any longer. A stranger comes in. He's the one I've been waiting for. We fall into each other's arms and sink to the floor with complete abandon. A window above the sink opens. Half of my family is peering in and pointing at us. I stop our lovemaking and go around the corner into a palatial room in which an enormous table is set for celebration. Father and Mother are sitting at the head of the table and they invite me to join the feast.

T H E hills of my home region have turned into a trap that reaches for me and snaps shut every summer. It is more and more difficult for me to find a connection between my current life and the place I was born, and I contemplate creating escape routes to smuggle my self-confidence out of the valley. I try to find solace in the landscape, to sniff out a place I can live without feeling threatened. I hope to creep under the landscape's skin over the course of the summer, to discover its secrets so that I won't leave with empty hands, with nothing more than my own skin.

How can I master the scene of my childhood? How can I visualize its forms? Should I start from the fact that the valley is designed as the landscape's cul-de-sac, in which all roads and paths come to a dead end? Should I claim that it looks like an open sock wedged between the hills to keep them apart? Confirm that all the hillsides sink into a valley floor marked by a river and a road? That the valley tries to defy its narrowness and even succeeds, here and there, in padding sections with level meadows and fields? But the meadows must soon adapt to the constriction and nestle up against the next escarpment. Anything expansive has retreated from this landscape.

A cold breath of air rises from the stream. This chill is spread throughout the landscape by the adenostyles' flat leaves. It rises to the edges of the meadows and hovers over the mixed forests. Above the tree line, rock shimmers under a thin layer of humus, like the bones of the mountains' skeletons pushed down into the valley by avalanches of snow. Buzzards, hawks, and eagles circle above the trees. They emerge out of the forest silence, isolate and unexpected, soar over the deep valleys, circle, and disappear into invisible cracks in the mountainsides. They rarely swoop down to the ground to snatch up prey. They're in no hurry. The prey is theirs for the taking after they've driven it into the narrow valley.

Men have established their properties on flat stretches above the slopes. Here and there you can find a meadow like a hammock, a level surface with room for several buildings and gardens to sprawl. On spring days, the mountainsides seem to rebel against the people moving over them. Yet in midsummer, carpets of light and heat stretch out in front of the farmhouses and exert an irresistible allure and draw the inhabitants straight to them. You see them sitting alone or in groups on the grass or in front of their houses, lying on the edges of the fields, abandoning themselves to the sun, exhausted by the heat. They swivel their heads in all directions, their eyes directed at the neighboring properties and forests and seeking out the hues of shade in the hollows and on the hummocks of the valley. The landscape solidifies with the approach of autumn. The familiar chill rises again from the hollows. Only the abandoned tunnels in the forests seem out of place with their small mouths gaping above rock piles overgrown with scrub. Some are still accessible, protected by bluffs, cages of stone.

I think of Grandmother, how she scanned the landscape every morning, of Father's gaze, how he first examined the sky, then the position of the sun or moon, before looking at the ground. Every day the state of nature was palpated by eye. Today it's time to harvest or to plow, they'd decide. Today the ground is ready and the air is warm enough, Father would say. The cloud formations, the evening light, and the shriek of an owl are ill omens, Grandmother would prophesy. Her secret landscape was marked with her own particular names, the old wheat field, the abandoned potato field, Chestnut Hollow, Fish Spawn Spot, Sun Boulder, Dripping Cliff, Devil's Gap, Ghost Knoll, Lily Field, Carnation Slope, Yarrow Meadow. The meadows and slopes facing the sun have names associated with light, the shadowed knolls and sites have shaded names that don't appear on any map. The forest paths lead past places of death: Fritz was killed here by a falling branch, Grandmother knew, here three men were charred by lightning, in Lightning Glade next to the Death Beech near the stream, the screeching girls in the stream on the Poset farm, where the dead walk and wail, the Wild Valley where they found the skull.

For all my efforts to get closer to it, the landscape of my childhood leads me astray. It lies awkwardly at my feet and leaves my questions unanswered. It remains unmoved. The paths through the landscape are nothing more than obstacles. They contradict themselves and lead me in the opposite direction when they were supposed to reach the center. The area won't admit a single straight line, just crooked slopes and hills entangled around a higher peak. The forested sides of the valley are recognizable in their telescoping contradictions and defiance of all cardinal points. As soon as I think I'm on the right path, I get lost. I have to climb up to higher elevations to get a view of my meanderings. Up high, under the wide-open sky, I can untangle the snarl below. It becomes clear to me that the landscape conceals itself and does not want its puzzles unraveled, that it swallows those who are impatient and spits them out undigested the moment they expect it to be accommodating and mild.

Once in a while, after a long hike through a steep, overgrown wood, the countryside rewards me with unimagined views that reveal a gentle and friendly side of this land. Rough cliff faces look softer, the regions' sharp edges are smoothed and rounded. An unexpected expanse opens before my eyes and lets them range over the valley and cross the narrow canyons without effort or vertigo. From such viewpoints, I can see the Košuta's craggy white cliffs to the west where the flatlands meet the mountains. The white mountain face will assert itself longest against the darker blue-green color of the beginning plains. To the south, the sea is mirrored in the light blue sky as if the firmament were looking with one eye at the Adriatic and winking at the valleys with the other.

As soon as I leave this spot, my eyes are pervaded by sharp grasses and plants, overgrown with scrub, and are finally exhausted from constantly turning to the sky, the only orientation point. And as soon as I leave, I feel like a visitor whom nature has cast adrift on the street after a lavish feast and who grudgingly hurries away because the rich landscape lies heavy in her stomach.

The underside of this stretch of land, its dark reflection, will be my refuge, the nocturnal area that will swallow and absorb every place I have ever been, the avenues, the cities, the busses, the trains, the airplanes. It will gather everything in and toss it all into oblivion. High-rises will spring up in the middle of the fields and theater stages will be built into the mountain and surrounded by forests. The sea will creep up close to my house and linger in the depths of the valleys. The sky will be a retractable roof and on many nights will rise up from the darkness to its firmament.

The landscape in which I'll find refuge that summer will blaze in the strongest colors. Light will flood over the hills, the air will shimmer. Hawk-eyed, I will direct my gaze into the valley. I will feel my way through the land with the waves of heat streaming from my scalp. I will scan my surroundings with hidden sensors. A group of men will stride over the high valley. They will go up the mountain where a railroad runs that will take them to their places of work or into the city that hums at the base of the mountain. My brother and I will get on a tram that stops in front of our house and we'll ride it to France. In the valley basin behind my house, I'll get on the tram again and introduce myself to all the passengers. It will be evening by the time we arrive in Provence and we will enter a tower. Outside, golden fields of wheat will swell around hills covered with light green grass. The sky will be deep red, velvety black. Why does the wheat field glow?

GRANDFATHER'S sister Leni has recorded her memories of her time with the partisans on audiotape. The transcription is translated into German and published as a book. It is to be presented in Vienna at the State Secretariat for Women's Affairs. For my relatives, it's a rare occasion to travel to the capital. Father decides to accompany his cousins. It's the first time he will see Vienna. I'm to collect him from the *Landesgericht*, Vienna's Civil Court, because their tour group wants to see the place where the first thirteen victims from Zell Pfarre and the valleys around Eisenkappel, personally sentenced to death by Roland Freisler, the President of the People's Court, were executed.

When I get off the tram at Landsgerichtstrasse, I see the small group waiting for me in front of the court building's enormous entrance. I wave them over. They quickly cross the large intersection, but when the walk signal turns red, Father stops in the middle of the multilane road and can't go forwards or backwards. The passing cars honk and crowd past him. I rush over to help him.

Father is trembling when I take him by the hand. Come, hurry, I say.

I can't, he says with a smile and only wakes from his paralysis when the pedestrian light turns green again. Vienna is not for me, he sighs once he reaches the sidewalk, everything moves too fast. Why didn't he keep walking, Michi wants to know, and Father shrugs. He is holding a plastic jug in his left hand.

What are you carrying around, I ask. Cider, Father answers. He had brought ten liters of cider for the celebration and has been carrying the canister around pointlessly for half the day, but just leaving it somewhere didn't seem like an intelligent thing to do.

I suggest we accompany our relatives to the Ringstrasse and from there I will take Father to the city center and show him St. Stephen's cathedral and the Michaelerplatz, where the Theater Institute is.

We stroll past the Institute building towards the university. With my arm outstretched, I trace the curve of the Ringstrasse and point out the parliament building, city hall, and the Burg, as it's called, saying, look, I often go to this theater. Nice, very nice, Michi says, but Father declares that you'd never get him inside so grand a building, wild horses couldn't drag him in there. You'll have to go into the palatial university building when I get my doctorate, I say. No, Father counters, he'll wait outside for me on his tractor. Laughing, we set up a meeting place near the State Opera.

I continue on with Father. On Heldenplatz he stops under the statue of Archduke Karl and stands up straight, as if he wanted to raise his eyes from the shelter of his brow towards the light. With his old, gray-green suit, he looks like someone who has wandered into the city by mistake. His brown tie has a loud green and orange pattern. The collar of his white shirt is twisted and one of the points is sticking out. I try to straighten it as if in passing, but it pops right back up. Father has cinched up his baggy trousers so tightly with a belt that folds have gathered around his waist. His sunken chest has not filled out a jacket for a long time. His hair is short, but shaggy at the nape. I catch myself blaming Mother for the shortcomings in Father's appearance. How can she allow him to let himself go like this, I think and immediately regret expecting Mother to look after him like a little boy. It would never occur to Father to buy himself anything new. Just trying on clothes in a shop would be too great a hurdle. The saleswomen's glances unnerve and annoy him unbearably. He feels defenseless and thrown back on himself and his pitiful appearance, as he says. Father's forlornness in the city troubles me. You could easily overlook him, I think, but if you talked to him, you would immediately feel responsible for him, you would automatically look out for him, to make sure he didn't go astray.

Under the Michaelerkuppel, the dome at the entrance of the imperial palace, I point out the stairway to the Theater Institute with more than a little pride. I tell Father that I'm studying a regal subject and he asks what regal means. Imperial, I say. Empress of the dung heap, he quips with a smirk. We walk along the Kohlmarkt and the Graben to the cathedral. Father is visibly impressed. He asks when the church was built and listens as I reel off a few dates. Enormous church, he says and sits down in a side aisle before the altar of the Virgin Mary. I make a tour of the cathedral. When I'm done, Father is waiting for me outside. Let's go, he says, he'd like to have something to drink. The crowds on the cathedral square bother him. He looks around for a quieter spot, and on the Graben we find a café counter that doesn't seem to intimidate him. He orders a white wine spritzer and takes off his jacket. After his first sip, he rolls up his sleeves and fumbles for his cigarettes. Do you want one, he asks. I suddenly remember the plastic jug. Where did you leave the jug, I ask. Next to Mary's altar. I thought the Virgin Mary might want a taste of my cider, Father says and grins.

I want a cigarette. Give me one, I say, and Father lights me a cigarette for the first time. Since when do you smoke? he asks. Since just now, I lie and think of the jug in the St. Stephen's cathedral. Father gestures with his hand and the ash from his cigarette, which he had forgotten to tap off, falls on his trousers. I notice a stain on his trousers and rush to convince myself, before I let myself get irritated, that his stained trousers are not important, that I should focus on the essential, on the fact that I'm walking around Vienna with Father for the first time. Father tells me that the Secretary for Women's Issues was very welcoming and gave a challenging speech. She has guts, he says appreciatively, it wouldn't have been possible in Carinthia. I ask if he has taken a look at the book, knowing that he never reads books. He'd even put my volume of poetry in the bookcase unopened. Yes, yes, he says. There's a picture of him in it, but he's not going to read it, even though Leni mentions him. Books don't always tell the truth, he says, they tell made-up stories. He, however, is interested in the truth, in what really happened.

He orders two more spritzers and stands at the counter smiling, one hand resting lightly on his hip, the other raised holding a cigarette, while the waiter serves our drinks. For a moment, everything seems possible.

Father tells me the plum trees are full of fruit and that he hopes he can distill some very good plum brandy this year. He was thinking about getting attractive bottles for the best batches so that he could sell them, but he's still mulling it over. Besides, he bought a few sheep, he says, because he intends to keep only two cows. All the rest doesn't add up, too much work, too complicated. He just can't understand why, despite the long, hard grind, he can barely make ends meet. It will all fall apart, he says and smiles. All of it. He crosses his arms, his cigarette glowing between the fingers of his hand. Then it occurs to him that his brother Tonči can still remember seeing Jurij Tavčman back then on the market place in Eisenkappel, before he was arrested, before he was taken to Klagenfurt and then to Vienna to be beheaded in the Civil Court building. Tavčman had been wearing a white shirt with his collar unbuttoned and had predicted to the people around him that he would be executed. That went straight to the marrow, they knew there was no return, Father tells me.

When I come home next time, I could cut your hair, I say rashly.

But only if I want, Father says looking attentively at the passersby through the window. He is in no rush to rejoin the rest of the family.

Do you like it here in Vienna, he suddenly wants to know. I say yes but am not sure if I should start telling him about it. I merely tell him that I'll probably have to leave the city soon. Aha, Father says. We should probably go, shouldn't we? Let's go, I say and hand him his jacket.

That night Father tells me his head has turned into a furnace. He smelts his headaches like stones to liquefy them, but not with heat, with glacial patience instead. He has an extra attachment on the back of his head, a second skull that slides over the first and is attached to his temples with bandages. I wonder if I should draw Father's attention to his double head, but then he turns his everyday face towards me. Don't say anything that will make him worry, I think, or his head will fall off. He wouldn't survive.

On the second night Father has a choking fit. He says the air has gotten trapped in his brain. He can't get enough oxygen. I lay him on his side on the ground and hold my hand under his temple. In a haze of sleep, I imagine that the pain begins to glitter in Father's corpus callosum and gradually changes color. Pain crystals line the wrinkles of his brain and create an agonizing foam determined to attack every nerve in his body. At fever pitch, the pain finally loses strength and ebbs away. Later, when its glow has hardened, I will extract it from Father's cellular tissue, that is what I think or dream. I will scrape the crystallized blood clots, the copper-colored sponge from my father's brain.

M Y DEPARTURE from Vienna is sudden. Since my scholarship has run out, I decide to finish writing my dissertation in Carinthia. Back home, I store my tableware and the few pieces of furniture I have acquired in my parents' attic in the hope that I'll be able to use them elsewhere soon. The valley's trap snaps shut again.

Now that I'm back in Carinthia, my mother makes her own plans. She thinks it's time for me to take over the responsibilities for the family. She could work as a cleaning woman in Klagenfurt and start a new life, she says. She has endured her marriage long enough, the time comes when enough is enough. As always, she describes Father's episodes in minute detail as if she wanted to explain yet again her reasons for leaving. You've had the chance to study, now you have to be ready to pay the price, she concludes. The minute the two of us are alone, she turns to me, a sorrowful goddess of vengeance. For years I've been dreaming only of snakes, she says, vipers and adders wherever I look. They follow me and creep over me. They've already built nests inside me. I can no longer get rid of the poison my husband has poured over me. To make me give in, Mother pelts me with her despair, her bitterness and rage. Her new plans begin to look like an attack on me. I wake with a start in the middle of the night and fight against emotions that pretend to be adult but are as needy as young children. Shadow-boxing. Spirits from the primordial soup that set upon me. I no longer know what it is I am trying to ward off, I feel threatened, and have no idea what to do with my agitation. How could things have gone so far? Why does Mother see me as an adversary?

When I was a child, my mother was brash, always a bit harried and angry, although she could hide the inner tumult that was connected to my father and grandmother. Occasionally I heard her sobbing, more often singing, and her voice, from near and from afar, sounded like my own, as if the sobs and the songs were coming from me and Mother were speaking with my body. Her feelings were our secret. When I started school, her expressions of emotions dwindled, as did her tears. She withdrew into her work, into her own ideas that culminated in the conviction that one must bear one's fate like a stigma. Once she told me that the Virgin Mary had warned her against marrying my father. She had noticed, while praying, that the statue of the Madonna was crying. From that moment, she suspected she was making a mistake, but it was too late to turn back. Mother seems to revel in the stories of the martyrs and lives of the saints with their stigmata and wounds. The sensuality she tries to repress finds its own means of expression. She has the habit of laughing very loud and inappropriately, of singing almost shrilly in church, and of coughing noisily. I cannot accept her extravagant behavior in public when she demands such discipline and discretion of us at home. On the weekends I spent at home while still in school, I would open her wardrobe and stand in the waves of scent that streamed from her clothing. I felt her underwear and her stockings, examined the embroidered tablecloths, handkerchiefs and pillowcases she kept in a chest like a fairy-tale princess with a hidden treasure. I am avid for her praise, but if I mention it she says that work well done is its own reward and doesn't warrant extra attention. Sometimes, when we are screaming at each other, Mother ends the argument by saying that she doesn't see why she should be more affectionate towards her children when no one in this house is ever kind to her or pays her any attention. Once I have accepted the fact that Father is to blame for Mother's hardness, I stop pestering her. Although we write each other once a month when I'm at university and she always tells me what she is busy with or what is new at home, this does not bring us any closer because Mother envies my freedom, she both admires and condemns it and reproaches me for being too understanding towards Father. She stops asking how I am.

When I move to Vienna, she starts reading literature and puts aside her Catholic horror stories. She reads historical novels, travel writing, books about the Second World War, but also Tolstoy, Flaubert, Lipuš, and Handke. Right now, I'm giving modern literature a try and I find it puzzling, she writes in a letter, but at least I'd like to give it a try. She never had the chance to go to school, but it would have interested her, she writes. She starts writing poetry and gives me her rhymed verses to correct when I come home on vacation. She believes that in life you have to pull yourself together and write stories with endings. It's also important that morality has pride of place because where would things lead if there was no one to show us how things could be.

When Grandmother was alive, Mother was almost never able to talk about herself. She sat next to those telling stories from the past and was never asked for her own. Her family's stories were considered insignificant, nothing very bad happened to her mother during the war, it was said, of course she'd had to raise her children alone as a day laborer, but that was nothing unusual. In the Slovenian convent school where Mother completed a one-year home economics course, they drummed into her head that she must only read chaste, pious books and never pick up the works of depraved writers. Such reading could corrupt a young girl, she was told. She must not read the Slovenian weekly newspaper *Slovenski vestnik*, which the Catholic Church had proscribed because it extolled the partisan tradition. A Slovenian-Carinthian should wear a headscarf whenever possible and not watch any Errol Flynn movies. Very few of the students must have followed these precepts, but my mother wanted to lead a model Catholic life.

Everything seemed to go wrong from the beginning. She remained chaste, certainly, but not long enough. She followed the injunction to marry the first man who approached her, but the reality of marriage fell short of her expectations. Even her children, not long after they were toddlers, developed minds of their own, which left my mother angry and disillusioned. She observed the virtues of temperance and frugality, and not being able to follow the latest fashions made no difference to her. Because there was no money in our household to buy a car and, in any case, she believed a fast vehicle would be too dangerous for Father, she settled for a moped and drove it to church, to do her errands, on outings and visits with her friends. She and her moped became inseparable and sometimes, when I saw her returning from her rides, it seemed to me she was recapturing her lost youth. Her eyes shone, her strong, weather-beaten hands were bursting with energy. She looked like a bold young woman for whom her children were pests and her husband a failure.

Mother has decided to wage one last battle with me because she instinctively feels that I am not on strong footing. She bets everything on the maternal card and loses because, in truth, she never was and never could be vindictive. She abandons her plan to move to Klagenfurt and holds me responsible. I should be aware, she tells me, that it's only for my sake that she's staying in this miserable situation.

Father, on the other hand, shows his sympathy. When I see him in public and he has, as we say, assuaged his thirst and then some, he proclaims, almost shouting, so that everyone can hear, that one's mine, she's a dear one! Since our tractor ride through the frigid winter night, he has turned the Hitler salute into our secret, almost intimate, handshake. If he's in a good mood, he greets me with "Heil Hitler" and takes a perverse glee in the bystanders' reactions. He lets me cut his hair and, as soon as he thinks it's time for another cut, he sets a chair in front of the house, lays a towel over his shoulders, and smiles contentedly when I take his thin hair between my fingers.

His phases of exhaustion are ever more obvious. Ever since he almost lost his left eye in a work accident in the forest, his injuries have been multiplying. He slashes his index finger with a saw, he opens a gash in his leg with an ax. He wants to keep up the frantic and agile pace at which he had always worked and is distressed that he no longer has the necessary strength or stamina. He is diagnosed with emphysema, which he refuses to admit because he does not want to give up cigarettes. Smoking is his elixir of life, he claims. Some days he feels the same as he did back then, in the forest, famished and exhausted after running for days on end, when his companions would give him dried leaves to smoke. That's the only thing that got him back on his feet, he's not going to give it up now. The only concession he's willing to make is agreeing to smoke filtered cigarettes. That will slow the disease a bit, he thinks.

The war invades my nocturnal space.

Huge trucks patrol the access road to our farm. Ambulances, sirens wailing, race between a distant hospital and the invisible battlefield. The house on the high plateau has disappeared. I am homeless now, wandering throughout the land of my childhood, to which I've been banned.

During the day, I cling stubbornly to my poems and my scholarly writings.

At night, I sail to Libya to get Mother where she has gone for a cure. The sea is stormy and dangerous. When we dock our sailboat, I see Mother waiting on a golden throne covered with jewels. She has come down with a fever. Her health is worse than it has ever been. I am very worried about her.

IN THE so-called "commemorative year" of Austria's annexation to the Third Reich fifty years earlier, Austria officially offers the surviving victims of National Socialism a reparations premium of 5,000 schillings.

Father's cousin Peter comes to visit and draws his attention to the sum. Peter tells Father that he must realize he, too, is a victim of the Nazis.

What's that supposed to mean, a victim, Father asks as if someone had tossed him a hot potato he would like to drop as quickly as possible. He's had enough of this circus, he says. He went to Klagenfurt a few times with his mother, back then, after the War, to testify in court against the police officer who had tortured and mistreated him. The officer sat in front of him, and Father was asked if he recognized him. The officer had looked at him, and Father didn't say a thing. He doesn't know why not. He just couldn't bring himself to do it. He thought to himself, the hell with him, I'm not saying anything.

I look at Father, astounded. What good would it have done, he asks to calm me down.

When Father receives his premium, he takes advantage of a moment when we are alone in the kitchen to whisper that he wants to spend the money only on himself. What good was all that suffering! Just to hand the money over to Mother for the household? He wants me to take my brother's car, now that I have a driver's license, and drive him to the dentist in Prevalje so he can get his dentures fixed.

One day in late August, I drive Father to Slovenia. The roads in the southern end of the Jaun Valley are lined with cornfields and swaths of blackened, overripe sunflowers. In the orchards, early apples rot under the trees. Wasps pursue their wild, frenzied dance over the sparse fruit. Father stretches in the passenger seat and looks at the countryside. His eyes prod the pastures and fields, as if he expected the fruit, plants, and vegetation to offer information about the length of autumn or the severity of the coming winter.

We cross the border at Bleiberg and drive to Prevalje via Poljana.

In the dentist office, there are two of his countrymen who also want to take advantage of the less expensive fees. Father says he would much rather have a Slovenian dentist rummaging around in his mouth than a Carinthian one, because Slovenians don't run out of patience as quickly. His dentures haven't fit properly for weeks and have been hurting him. He wants to have them fixed, finally, he can't bear it any longer, he tells me while waiting his turn. When he is called in, I tell him I'll wait for him in a café across the street.

Father shows up after an hour. It was rough going, he says. His bottom dentures have to be redone and it took forever to get a proper dental cast. I think we deserve a good lunch, he says, don't you?

Before leaving Prevalje, he buys ten cartons of Yugoslavian cigarettes in the town's largest store. Ten cartons, you really want to smuggle ten cartons across the border, I ask in surprise. Why not, he says, I have to spend the money on something. He can get the cartons past the customs officers.

Outside Prevalje, we turn onto a gravel road that rises steeply through a small forest. Higher up, we have a beautiful view of the landscape on both sides of the border. Father knows the local inn, he stopped in with his hunting friends once on the way home from Šmartno, where they had been invited on a hunt. We order pork roast and look around the small, low-ceilinged room. A few villagers sit drinking at the next table. Father gives them a nod and says that they serve a good roast pork here. A man at the next table asks if we're from Carinthia. Yes, yes, we're from the land of Carinthia, Father says and orders another beer. The owner joins the next table and Father and I are soon caught up in the local talk, even if we have nothing to add and don't necessarily want to hear it either.

Father waves over the owner and tells her with a grin that he'd like to treat everyone to a round. What are you celebrating, the owner wants to know.

Nothing special, Father says. The round is on me, he calls out to the locals and smirks as if he'd just played a prank on them.

Father is relaxed when we leave the inn. It occurs to him that he could buy some tools at the Slovenian co-op in Bleiburg. The pitchforks and axes at home haven't been in good shape for a long time.

We approach the border. He lights a cigarette. Now we've got to come up with some good lies, he says and coughs. After checking our passports, the Slovenian customs officer waves us through. The Austrian asks if we have anything to declare. Nothing, I tell him, but Father says, a pack of cigarettes and waves the pack under the officer's nose.

Open the trunk, the customs officer says. Now it's serious, I think and feel slightly lightheaded as I get out of the car. When I open the trunk, the customs officer immediately discovers the cartons of cigarettes under the wool blanket and pulls them out one by one. Our smuggling attempt fails. Father, who acknowledges ownership of the cigarettes, is called into the office. He must hand eight cartons over to customs and pay duty taxes on the remaining two. They told me I should be glad I got off so lightly, he says, *porca duš*, he swears as he gets back in the car. That went to hell, blast it, that really went to hell, he says and trembles as he stuffs what is left of the money in his wallet. As if I hadn't suspected, he grumbles, the officers at Lavamünd aren't as strict. At Holmec, they're bored, they don't have anything else to do. After this fiasco, he can do without the Slovenian co-op in Bleiburg, too. He wants to go straight home via Globasnitz.

During the drive home, the afternoon lends the sun a warm golden tone that plunges the Jaun valley into a limpid melancholy. The light has softened all garish tones and heralds the end of summer. I look at the Peca, our local peak, which I'm skirting in a half circle, with astonishment because its north face looks downright soft. On this side, the Peca is a big-bellied mountain, a long sloping pile of sand, overgrown with woods and green meadows. Blocs of limestone rise from its extended back giving the peak a more severe air. Small green domes and cones cluster around the Peca like young animals crowding around their mother. This is where the Alps end, here the steep white flanks lose their provocative hardness. Behind it, the landscape of tangled and intertwined hills extends like an impregnable valley of canyons and wooded domes that have lost none of their reclusive and rebellious character.

After the little village of Globasnitz that huddles up against a wooded slope on the southern edge of the Jaun Valley, we turn onto a narrow gravel road to the Luscha saddle pass that the locals use as a supply road. This single lane road is making me uneasy, and I pray the entire way that no vehicle will come from the opposite direction. Father senses my worry and to reassure me, tells me not to be afraid, he often drove this road on his motorcycle without lights and he always made it home. What should we do with the rest of the day, he mutters. We could stop for a bite at the Riepl, if Flortsch is at home. What do you think?

After we leave the pastures on the Luscha behind and pass the ecumenical church that Flortsch had built by the side of the road and that always rises into view unexpectedly like a rockslide, we see our neighbor Johi Čemer in front of the church. He waves us over.

I stop and get out of the car with Father. Johi laughs. What has dragged you up this way? He's just making his daily rounds, Johi tells us and offers his hand. Father tells him about the dentist and that customs confiscated eight cartons of cigarettes. Goddamn customs, goddamn it, he says and spits.

Grinning, Johi says he's glad he quit. Now that he doesn't have to worry about cigarettes any more, his lungs work like well-oiled pumps, he can go up and down the mountains as often as he'd like without a problem. He cuts the hay by himself, does all the work in the stalls, too. He can't complain. My engine stutters noticeably, Father says, drumming on his chest with the flat of his hand. At some point it's going to seize up and that will be it for me. Not at all, Johi says, you'll be around for a while yet. You're a tough one! Just think about how much you've been through already. Not long ago, he was reminded of the day the police tracked them from bunker to bunker like two strays, do you still remember, Johi asks. That's the last day he saw his father. When the police dragged him down from the forest because they'd beaten him so badly, he could hardly walk, his father came out of the stables and threw his hands in the air from sheer fright. The police wanted my father to tell them if my mother had joined the partisans. Of course he acted as if he didn't know, then he was arrested and sent to Dachau where he died, Johi says. When he came back from the youth camp Moringen at the end of the war, everything was different; the house burned down, the stables cleaned out, half his family murdered. His mother came back sick from the partisans. The first thing we had to do in our new life was forget the old. First, learning the A B Cs of forgetting, that's a hard school, isn't it, Zdravko, Johi asks Father while looking at me.

Did you get money, too, my father asks.

I have a small pension because of the camp, you know that, Johi says.

Yes, of course, Father replies and repeats that he wants to get his dentures fixed with his payment. That will be it for his pocket money from the government, gone like it was nothing, he says.

To steer the conversation away from the past, I ask where the border with Yugoslavia runs. Both men stretch their right arms out and point towards the south. The border runs over that ridge there and continues behind the pasture on the other side, they answer.

In the very last days before the end of the war, he had been all over the area with partisan couriers, Father recalls. They'd been running for days from persecutors who were on their tracks. Fresh snow had fallen in late April and soldiers who were retreating from the partisans in Styria were streaming over the Luscha pass. His group had almost fallen into the hands of a few police officers who had come up from Globasnitz. He knows this area like his back pocket, Father says, but it's covered with trees now and you can't see the high pastures on the Luscha anymore. That's how life is, Zdravko, Johi says, everything gets overgrown. He thinks about life when he's alone. He wanders over the meadows and fields, looks down into the valleys or up at the mountains and is grateful that no one killed him back then. He often wonders what became of those who denounced the locals – the farmers, the women and children, the elderly – and betrayed them to the Nazis. He let the question of nationality drop on the day he and his neighbor were denounced to the police by a spy from Slovenia. The fact that a Slovenian went to the police and told them this or that one was working with the partisans, the fact that someone believed it was right to deliver people – his own people – made him even worse than the Germans who started from the principle that they were a master race and so had the right to rule over others, Johi says. He doesn't understand how you can denounce people just because you think they're all Communists and should be killed or something. No one needs to tell me anything, I don't care if my children speak Slovenian or not, Johi tells us he has stopped worrying about it. It's not my problem, he says with a smile.

Father doesn't answer. He stares at the ground and draws on his cigarette.

Everything was settled after the war and nothing was quite right again, Johi says, that's how he tries to see it. What Hitlerism was he understands perfectly well, and he is glad to have survived it. Sometimes, when he's out walking, he looks at the spruce trees above the scarp. That's where the partisans killed the farmer Keber because he supposedly had something to do with his neighbors' deportation. It's at moments like that that Johi prefers the worst of peacetime to war, because in wartime everyone goes insane and there's never justice in war, not ever, Johi says.

Yes, Father sighs. His father showed the family where Keber had been buried so his body could be dug up and interred in the cemetery. Grandfather was never able to come to terms with Keber's execution.

A lot of things from his time with the partisans weighed on his mind as long as he lived, Father says. He was disillusioned after the war and loathed politics.

But neither your father nor your wife's three uncles who died fighting with the partisans went to war to fight against Keber, they fought for something else, Johi says. I look at him, surprised, because I have never heard him talk like this before and because I am amazed to hear for the first time that three of my mother's uncles died as partisans. Three woodcutters who decided to desert from the Wehrmacht, and no one in our family ever thought it worth including them in the family history, as if my maternal great-uncles vanished into thin air, as if they had cloaked themselves in mist so they wouldn't be recognized or suspected of doing anything, so they could disappear from history without a trace.

Johi announces it's time to check on his animals and gives me a kiss on the cheek. Father and I are to wait for him and then accompany him home. His wife will fix us something to eat.

Father says he'll think about it and offers Johi his hand.

When we are alone, my father starts off towards the spruce trees above the scarp. Once we are up top, he takes a few steps to the right and to the left and circles the few trees that are scattered about the steep meadow. Climb up here, he says, I want to show you something. He comes to a stop and taps the ground with his foot. Right there, that's where they stuffed him. From his jacket pocket he pulls a small candle he probably picked up near the church steps and lights it. When I reach him, we sit on the grass. The sycamore leaves are already changing color, Father says after a while, autumn will be here soon. We look at the valley below and are silent. The votive candle's small flame burns behind the red glass until it imperceptibly fades.

IN MY thoughts, I follow the line of the border as it runs between the Luscha's alpine pastures and Mount Olševa, it rises and falls, a wavy line meant to check those passing from here to there, a law written, engraved in the landscape.

Ever since I can remember, I have moved within the border's magnetic field. Those who want to feel safe should respect the border, we are told. There is no point in retelling old stories because they could put our peace at risk. But is the peace in this region truly ours or do the languages spoken here still wear uniforms? Has peace become visible? Can a Slovenian place name stand next to a German one, a symbol more telling than a dove, a rainbow, a monument?

Because of the border, which, in the eyes of the majority of people in this country can only be a national and a linguistic border, I am forced to explain myself and declare my identity: who I am, to which group I belong, why I write in Slovenian or speak German. These declarations have a shadowy side haunted by specters with names like Loyalty and Treason, Possession and Territory, Mine and Yours. Here, crossing the border is not a natural act, it is a political act.

After I finish my dissertation and my second collection of poems appears, I move to Ljubljana. My Slovenian writer colleagues debate, dream, and talk a democratic Slovenian republic into existence that will make everyone forget the Communist decades. They want to extract the Slovenian Republic from the Federal Republic of Yugoslavia and lead it towards independence.

In the times of political upheaval in Slovenia, it is clear to me that I am observing the crisis as a guest, and I feel like a distant relative visiting her family after a long absence who is surprised to see that they have changed. I realize, all of a sudden, that I only know the political reality of Yugoslavia from literature, from a few personal stories and visits.

During the meetings of the writers' association, I ask myself why I feel so weak, so muted in the fight for the so-called apotheosis of the national, for the national state. Why, although I wish for the Slovenians to have their own state, with all my heart in fact, do I still hold myself at a distance? As a member of an ethnic minority, as it is so ineptly put, I have always been engaged with national questions. Why such reservation? Because the efforts made by the Slovenian speakers of Carinthia to ensure public respect for their language were directed at Austria and represented an encouragement for greater openness throughout Austria. They were not related to promoting democracy in Yugoslavia or in the independent state of Slovenia, which did not yet exist.

I experience my hesitation as a liberty but also as a loss because I don't feel under any threat, even if I understand the political crisis and share the Slovenian writers' goals.

In the past my family engaged with questions of nationality when they felt themselves forced to react because being part of their community put them at risk, reacting according to national lines was a matter of survival. They could either forget their language and their culture and adopt German or they could resist and suffer the disastrous consequences. They decided to join the resistance movement from Slovenia who were organizing the fight. At the time of the greatest catastrophe, they joined forces with the Slovenian segment of the European fight against Fascism. They believed in the future, in the liberation and unity of the Slovenians once they found themselves, as a result of Austria's annexation to Nazi Germany, without protection in a state that wanted to expel and annihilate them. Which Austria should they have believed in? In the one that did not exist at the time, that did not defend itself and joined in with National Socialism, that threatened one part of its citizens and delivered the other to the forces of extermination?

And me, what do I stand for? Is there such a thing as engagement along national lines or is it a chimaera?

In Slovenia, the Communist Party is dissolved and with it the myth on which the Party based its right to single party rule – the myth of the partisans and the liberation front. New light is shed on the historical account of the Communists' seizure of power within the liberation moment and this new illumination reveals ever more dead, those purged during the partisans' battle, post-war massacres of military and political opponents, along with innocent civilians when the partisans returned from the forests and joined the Yugoslav People's Army.

After a public event, a historian asks me how the Slovenian Communists in Carinthia would respond to these revelations. I explain to him that, unlike in Slovenia, the Communists in Austria are not in power. Yes, he says, he knows that but the equation partisan equals Communist must exist in Carinthia, too. That's what those who are against the partisans claim, I answer, the equation is wrong.

I cannot help but think of the partisans in our valleys, who look like scattered forest rebels from the perspective of centralized power in Slovenia. They have nothing in common with the partisan iconography, the oversized imagery of steely warriors storming forward that determined the partisans' image for decades in Yugoslavian and Slovenian public opinion. Our partisans, in contrast, look like erratic boulders left behind by revolutionary history. Since only the Communists' merits could be praised in Yugoslavian and Slovenian post-War historiography, it is obvious that the other partisans – the believers and non-believers, the apolitical and the half-hearted, the disappointed, the skeptics, and the disillusioned – are absent from the general awareness.

I tell the historian that I come from the Carinthian side, where those involved aren't blinded by hero worship. They probably would have liked to indulge in it, so they could forget their war wounds and finally experience some recognition. As soon as the partisans come out of the valleys and enter Carinthian public opinion, they are immediately transformed into tragically distorted figures. The moment they leave the safety of their four walls, they find themselves in enemy territory. They have to fight for their historical victory as if it had never been their due.

At a family gathering, I ask Tonči, who was three years older than my father when he fled to the partisans, how Grandfather, a devout Catholic, dealt with the Communists. Tonči says the partisans never challenged Grandfather's religious faith, all that mattered to them was that they could rely on him as commander of a unit of couriers. It would never have worked otherwise in Carinthia, the majority of the Slovenian speaking community was Catholic. When Grandfather would go with Žavcer to recruit for the partisans at some carefully chosen farms this and that side of the Peca, the farmers said they were glad to see the Slovenian army, finally someone who was on their side! They liked the partisans' uniform, but the red star on the cap, not so much. Many of them would have been willing to fight for the emperor because there were fewer problems in the time of the monarchy, they said. But in late 1943, when a victory over the Nazis appeared ever more likely, many of the farmers and laborers said they would be willing to help. Later, when you could feel it would be only a matter of months until the Third Reich had to surrender and the partisans were considered part of the Allied Forces, the partisans no longer asked for support, they demanded it.

We had to keep lists of how many pigs or cows we took from which farms so that people could be compensated after the war, Tonči says.

Some of the smallholders themselves didn't even have enough to survive. Their provisions had run out. He knows of families who were starving because a large unit of famished partisans was camped not far from their remote holding. How could we have managed without the local population? No partisan group could have survived in Carinthia without their help. Where would they have gotten their supplies or their information, Tonči asks. There was no supply line following the partisans with provisions, no one setting up camp stoves in the bunkers. The food came from the local population, there was no other source. In the so-called "beggar-patrols," you had to be very careful not to take more than was sustainable, Tonči says. How often he had hoped that the packages dropped in by the Allies would contain food as well as weapons and medical supplies, especially food. That's what they needed most urgently. Most often we held in our hands new automatic weapons we didn't know how to use. In the courier base Grandfather led, rosaries were said regularly, even in front of the political commissars, Tonči says. The politicals knew we couldn't go home and that those who prayed presented no danger. The commander of the First Carinthian Unit, Franz Pasterk-Lenart from the Lobnik Valley, went to Father Zechner to ask his counsel before he deserted from the Wehrmacht. He couldn't go back, he said, he could no longer reconcile this war with his views. They prayed through the night in the church and, the following morning, Lenart joined the partisans. When his mortal remains were brought to Eisenkappel from Mežica, the priest said at his graveside that with Lenart, one of the most exemplary Catholics in the area had fallen. For the partisans, undecided young men were a much greater threat than the faithful, Tonči explains. Men who wanted to try out the partisan life but left because they couldn't take the miserable conditions of living on the run, because they had to put up with injustices, harsh punishment, because they found it too dangerous, too arduous, too hard to bear. They often betrayed everything, were tricked by the Gestapo or even were sent by the Gestapo to infiltrate partisan ranks. It cost many lives, brought on disasters, and spread mistrust among the fighters. A good partisan was a partisan out of necessity, Tonči says, someone who had no way out but to hide in the forest, someone under the threat of arrest or the KZ, for whom there was no choice but flight because he had been betrayed as an activist, because he had given aid to the partisans, or had deserted from the Wehrmacht. Deserters from the German army were the best fighters, accustomed to military discipline, they were fighting for their own survival, for their families' survival, and they always had their last bullet in reserve, in case they fell into the Germans' hands. As for the politicals, those who were educated, they were partisans out of conviction and so had political roles, but overall they were a minority, Tonči says.

Father recalls that Tine, whom they called the General, once told him at Kovač's place in Ebriach how Gašper, Županc, and Žavcer had been searching for Communists in Carinthia, but in vain. At one of the partisans' general meetings, they concluded that if there weren't enough Communists, well then, they'd have to create some, so they admitted a few activists and fighters into the Communist Party. There were training courses, a few women activists and fighters even passed the entrance exam, a few others remained candidates. The General remained a candidate until the end of the war. A good fighter, but not suited to the class struggle is what a colonel wrote in his report. After the war, he went back to Carinthia, to his farm, Father says. In Ljubljana, they wanted to make him a functionary. They gave him new clothes and a lot to eat, but he gave it all up, as did a few others he knew well. Jurči, a fellow hunter and partisan from Lepena, described how things went at an illegal political gathering after the war. The partisan functionaries demanded the annexation of southern Carinthia to Yugolavia and called on the masses to vote for revolution. Jurči thought that was a bit much. Did we thrash the Nazis so we could now embrace the Communists, he wondered, that he would never get, no, he couldn't get his head around this all or nothing, Mother of God, it only brings misfortune, Jurči would say.

T H E I M A G E of the unknown partisan from the valleys could be redrawn and freed from the armor that hides his many faces.

A partisan must ally himself to the landscape in which he fights. He has to take on the region's colors and forms, he must become invisible, he must be a mountain and a stream, a spruce tree, a house, a hill, a forest, an owl, a snake. He must camouflage himself with the meadows and wrap himself in a coat of foliage. He melts into the paths, into the air, he can appear now here, now there, he can be everywhere at once. He was spotted in this village yesterday and today his shadow is flitting over a distant mountain he is circling. He must defend his house, his land, his own little homeland. A partisan must move like a fish in water. In the water of men, in the human water the enemy is trying to dry up, because the civilian population, unlike the partisans, remains visible, recognizable. A partisan can engage in civilian activities during the day, but under cover of night he has to run and strike. A partisan does not sleep, he has made night his day, he fights to break the enemy's morale, he flees because flight is his triumph and his success. Fear is his brother, his sister, his name, because fear of death can make him endure anything – hunger, disgust, loneliness. The fiercest despair can save him, false wisdom can destroy him. The water in which he swims can carry him and feed him, with mouthfuls small and large, with fatty and lean meat. Without this water, the partisan would perish, he would be left high and dry, he would choke in the mud. It is the air he breathes, it is his vulnerable body. This body will be caressed and beaten, loved and hated, used and abused, felt and dreaded, cherished and broken. It is his extended arm and his stiff leg, his strong heart and his weak flesh. It is his dearest friend and his best enemy. The partisan will give his body a new form, a new face, he will pull it out of oblivion for all to see. Its determination will give him strength. His body's wounds will spur him on, his injuries will drive him, his despair will embolden him. He will be the shout that escapes his body, he will embody the voice that speaks for him.

As soon as the war is over, the unknown partisan will give back to the landscape all that belongs to it. He will take off his camouflage and will move about amongst humans who have become human once again, who will have regained their former appearances, he will be unrecognizable in his resemblance to them. At night, he will weep for the dead, during the day he will do his work and will glorify peace. He will place peace above all else and will leave triumph to the victorious armies. His sense of honor will grow from the certainty of having repulsed humiliation, of having said no, of having drawn a line between himself and injustice. His fragile hope will lend him a face, a monument will be built in honor of his desire to live.

Or will the partisan push revolution to its bloody end, will he continue the fight after the triumphal procession, will he celebrate victory with a slaughter of revenge, will he turn peace into a perpetual war of suspicion and wipe away the bloodbath with murder a thousandfold? His victor's statue stands abandoned in the field, the safety catch on his weapon released, surrounded by ghosts.

IN SLOVENIA, I stop asking myself if anyone around me is annoyed when I speak in Slovenian as I used to do in Carinthia. If it were not for the anxiety in the air caused by the threat of a possible war, I could get used to the delightful, leisurely pace of the Slovenian language, to its ambling, nimble, playful movement.

After a year, I move back to Carinthia. I am drawn by feelings of belonging and troubled by the political contradictions. I still dream of reviving the moribund conversation between Slovenians on either side of the border and begin to work in Carinthia on founding a cross-border literary and cultural magazine, but the project falls through.

While I'm in Klagenfurt working in theater, the Slovenian language begins to withdraw from my writing. One day I will realize that it has disappeared completely from my notes and sketches, it has moved out of my desk drawers, has packed up its most beautiful clothes and left. Offended and tired of my dallying, the beauty has stormed off, I think to myself the day I notice the change. I will wonder if my thinking has changed with this language's departure, if, along with this language that grew on my lips there wasn't also a chain that grew in my hand with which I could pull the world towards me, and so in losing this language, have I lost my grip on the world? Should I have abandoned that indeterminate, insecure land between languages sooner, that land through which I wandered for a long time, a land that required no absolute decisions like choosing to write solely in one language or another?

Outwardly, everything will remain the same, just as it had been. The Slovenian books will remain on my shelves. I will not forget the language nor will I discard or disown it. Nothing will be displaced in the silence. But something permeable and impalpable will have broken. Only the verses of my poems will have slipped into new attire, will have gone to look around elsewhere, because they wanted to escape the no-man's land behind the border.

My desire to write will slacken. My enthusiastic plans will falter. Words will lie scattered around me, as if I had flung them on the ground in a fit of despair and couldn't bring myself to gather them up again. I will feel like I am sitting on a pile of rubble.

But before things reach that point, I find myself standing on Republic Square in Ljubljana on the evening of June 26th, 1991, watching the new Slovenian flag being raised for the first time in honor of the independent republic. I keep repeating a sentence in my mind, trying to engrave it within me: this is a historic day. But what is it I see in this moment laden with symbols? The historical dimension as an excess of imagination? My joy is muted with worry that the Yugoslav People's Army might occupy the border posts that very night. I return to Austria before midnight. In the morning, the Slovenian border is, in fact, occupied by the military. I feel like I have escaped. After paralyzing days in which Slovenia stands on the brink of war, the Yugoslav People's Army retreats unexpectedly from the new republic.

T H E T H R E A T of war in Slovenia almost makes Father lose his mind. From the early afternoon on, he sits, slightly tipsy, at the kitchen table, grumbling that those people over there in Slovenia have obviously forgotten what war is. He wants me to do him the favor of keeping my distance from all this! Indistinct and long repressed fears take hold of him. For days on end he is overcome with agitation and convinced that everyone has abandoned him.

In a book I learn about post-traumatic stress disorder and am almost relieved to apply the unwieldy medical term to Father. That must be it, I think, this will help me cut through the thicket of personal and political intricacies. On the other hand, can a word change anything about an illness? Is it at all possible to disentangle Father's anxieties, to divide them into nerve cords, cell nuclei, and synapses?

What a strange concept, that the memory of a state of anxiety can span gaps in time and synaptic clefts and reach into the present, causing it to be experienced as alien and unreal, as if the only true reality occurred back then, a long, long time ago and everything happening now is simply a distraction from the essential.

I read about the dwindling of empathy in the now, about the sense of being imprisoned in one's body in whose metabolism the past has become trapped like a germ of memory, a living microbe that takes possession of the individual in certain situations, invades him and cuts him off from the present.

Father is reborn through the recollection of past suffering, if it is, in fact, suffering and not just a drunken dance of shadows. He compulsively reinvents then rejects himself. His state of extreme tension relaxes only when he drinks, when his body descends into a state of stupor and disinhibition, where borders dissolve, when he becomes a soft mass drifting aimlessly in his consciousness. Only then can he breathe and eject all that is tangled, piled up, frozen within him. A human volcano.

Anxiety is the fundamental difference, the divide between him and us. It forms the internal core of his survival and admits no feelings for us. As soon as he feels such emotions, he pushes us away. His life seems to be concentrated and intensified in those moments when alcohol takes away his reserve.

In Father's landscape of branching and deformed anxiety that sometimes appears from the outside as much more vast than it could possible be in reality, in this countryside a word from me cannot venture alone. I cannot assume that the solitary word I send on a journey will reach the core of his anxiety, that his anxiety will approach the word and identify itself. Father's anxiety will not want to call out, this way, word, this is where you must aim. It won't let itself be subjugated to that extent and submit to some designation or other. Father's feelings will destroy any language or words that approach him, just as his rages render me mute, his bellowing always conquers my speech.

Sometimes, when his depression stretches out over several days, I begin to suspect that his native landscape might be provoking these disturbances. He acts as if he does not want to see the familiar meadows and mountainsides, as if he would rather retreat to his house and not set foot outdoors, avoid contact with the proliferating vegetation. Is it the landscape that reminds him of the former battleground now threatening to crush him?

Yet how remarkable it is, too, to fight behind the stable, to fall on the potato field or under the cherry tree, to be discovered in the cellar, how strange to be buried under an elderberry bush or under the old fir tree. How strange it is when war enslaves a landscape.

THE WAR breaks out in Bosnia, in Kosovo, and in Croatia. I hear Father, I hear many neighbors and acquaintances complaining in the first months of the war that they can't bear to watch the news on television, that they aren't able to watch war movies either, that they simply cannot bear such films. The horrifying din of war, the grenades, artillery fire drills into them, they lie sleepless in bed for hours and hours, they toss and turn, they can't help thinking of those poor people, running from their burning houses, it's all too much, do the politicians not understand what it means to be in a war?

The memories of the residents of these valleys begin to revolt, they rise up and take over. After the end of Nazism, they still knew their stories, they told each other what they had lived through, they could recognize themselves in another's suffering. But then the fear sets in that they'd be excluded because of their stories and seen as alien in a country that wanted to hear other stories and dismissed theirs as unimportant. They know their history is not mentioned in Austrian history books, certainly not in Carinthian history books in which the region's history begins with the end of the First World War, is interrupted and takes up again at the end of the Second World War. Those with stories to tell know this and they have learned to stay quiet.

Now, however, they dig up what they remember, pull it out of the sack, let it fall as if casually, in the hope that someone listening will pick it up. There could be someone out there who wants to learn more. It's about time.

Admittedly, no one is asking at all insistently about their past. Those who do ask are circumspect, as if they didn't want to touch old wounds, as if they were afraid of learning too much, perhaps even about their own families. Very quickly, the old fear washes over those about to tell their own stories, the worry that these stories could be used against them, could revive buried antagonisms, could betray friendships, or could make them appear suspicious somehow or other.

And so these almost-storytellers quickly stuff back into the sack what they have let fall and act as if their remarks had slipped out by mistake, a blunder, they won't open their mouths if there are strangers in the room. I am considered a stranger, I know that.

And yet, a few of these silent men and women are waiting only to be asked for their stories to come tumbling out. They don't know where to begin, the force of their memories disconcerts them, they stumble from one person to the next, from year to year, cannot follow the chronology, confuse names and places, assume that everyone knows what they mean. They talk about ghosts, about farms and smallholdings that no longer exist, that were overgrown with brushwood or razed to the ground long ago. They can even recall the stories of others, all the things that could have happened, the things they had feared most.

When the erratic narratives become too much for me, I wonder why these stories crumble to pieces in the tellers' consciousness, with no connection to a larger context, as if each person were left with his or her own war, as if the isolation of the witnesses were part of oblivion's strategy. I start asking questions and searching for connections. What I hear eats away at me. It merges with the childhood stories trapped inside me. I am constantly circling the abyss of history into which everything seems to have sunk.

T H E   W A R seems to have retreated into the forests of our valleys. It has made the fields and meadows, the slopes and hills, the mountainsides and streambeds into its battleground. It has ripped the houses, stables, kitchens, and cellars from their purpose and turned them into bastions. It has taken the landscape into its clutches, sunk its teeth into the earth, it has read the geographical map as a map of war.

The battlefield is no longer visible, ambushes threaten everywhere, what is trusted changes, familiar faces appear in masks. War's territory is camouflaged. Like the battle itself, it has no borders or limits. The slaughter fragments into skirmishes. The field of honor is the farmer's larder.

The enemy fights with bread and water, with clothing and meat, with work and silence. The Gestapo put on the disguise of partisans, the Slovenian language is their cover. The front passes through the most vulnerable point. Fighters are dragged from the forest by the hair on the heads of their wives, their children, and their parents. They are fought against through their families standing in the fields and not in the trenches. They are punished threefold for their resistance and are left to ask themselves, until the ends of their lives, if the fight against the Nazis was worth the cost of engaging in this conflict and delivering up their family members to the Nazis' collective punishment. It is on the farms that the most superb battles are fought and the most summary trials executed. Minor stories to which no one can bear witness, human lives, quickly seized, sooner discarded. No one saw, no one wanted to believe. Things seen could rob you of sleep and speech, but the Gestapo wants people to speak; all bandits seen and recognized must be reported in the right language. The partisans, on the other hand, demand silence, no one must know they had come, and no sooner come, they are gone.

That's how it begins after the first two hundred Slovenian families are evacuated from their farms on Himmler's orders. It begins with bread for the partisans, with soup for those resisting – bread becomes a weapon. Here, the enemy wears aprons, skirts, school uniforms. Without knowing they have become combatants, they wear their hair peacefully braided, have never once held a gun, yet they are *accomplices of these terrorist bandits, one or more times, they have offered the bandits food, shelter, or another form of assistance. They have lost their honor. They have abetted enemies of the Reich and are therefore condemned to death. They are dishonorable for all eternity.*

What remains are the children who must listen as the police harass and beat their mothers, screams in their ears, leaflets in their milk canisters, secret messages in their braids, letters in snowballs, lice in their hair.

What remains are footsteps in the snow that the children wipe away, the stink in the school where they are beaten because they can't speak German. *Carinthians speak German!*, and they all shit their pants when German is beaten into their fingers and heads with slaps and caning. They still greet each other the same way today, hey, shitter, smelly-assed crybaby, you still scared?

History crumbles to pieces: Father to the Wehrmacht, Father deserts, Mother to Ravensbrück, younger brother, older brother to Dachau, to Stein an der Donau, to the Gestapo prison in Klagenfurt, to Mauthausen, Lublin, Moringen, Auschwitz. And Rosa's mother who gives food to a snitch because she believes he is a partisan. When she realizes her mistake, she grabs her three children and escapes into the forest, hides there, runs to find the partisans, children sent to stay with their grandparents, children who watch as other children are led away chained to a grown man, Mimi and her boy, barely ten years old. And children who hug their mother when they stop by at night to get clean clothes, who want to go with her into the enemy forest.

Father fallen in battle, fallen for Hitler. And Stanko who watches as the Vivoda family and Šopar and Breček families are taken away, and Simon who refuses to go, who drinks himself unconscious and is thrown onto the hay cart by the police, so they can get him off his farm. The dead cattle in the Mikej farm meadow with their swollen bellies, their legs sticking up in the air, starting to stink after a few days, the stable burned down, the farmer's family all gone to join the partisans. The fighter shot dead in the snow, buried under branches, the dangling legs and heads of the dead when they are driven off in the hay cart. Herding the cows near freshly dug graves, war, summer, snow.

Didn't recognize her brother's shoes after the police shot and covered him with dirt, Vinzenz, buried next to his sister's stable, she didn't recognize the shoes sticking out of the pit. Only later, weeks later, did my grandmother, my Bica, realize it was her brother who lay under the eaves, he and an unknown partisan behind the house in the meadow, buried in the snow. In the spring, the bloody pile that won't thaw, and Bica who can't get out of bed, she lies in bed dead-tired, like a corpse. She doesn't speak, doesn't eat. The children take care of the animals and cook for their mother. They urge to get up, to finally get out of bed, to finally be as grown up as they are.

The police hunt partisans by day, never at night. The houses surrounded, an entire patrol, twenty, thirty, forty, fifty men against women and children and shadows in the forest. The sounds of combat in the house, in the fields, in front of the stable, farms in flames, the hole in the chest of the dead partisan, mown down by a machine gun next to the front door of the house, Anna's screams as she runs around the house until she collapses, exhausted, until she admits defeat by this war that ambushed her in her kitchen. The green slime that Mirka vomits when she learns her husband has died in Auschwitz. The young girl the SS hung by her legs who is later forced to watch as the partisans threaten her father. The slaps, the aching heads of the children, while the police empty the larder so there will be nothing left for the bandits who are everywhere, in the hay and in the stable, in the storage shed, foodstuffs buried to save them from raids by the police, by the partisans. The fighters, shot and bleeding, in the cellars and bunkers and rooms. No light in the kitchen, the partisans' trembling bodies in the dark, rubbed down with vinegar, rubbed with vinegar all night. Kach's cattle, leaving the barn in quick step, the farmer's wife and her sister ran to the partisans and died fighting, the men, Juri and Johan, arrested with Maria and Anna. More ashes from Ravensbrück, from Lublin, died of, deceased on, the eight names of the dead in front of the empty farm, looted clean, that cannot be revived after the war and finally falls to ruin. Battles near the school, the children huddling on the classroom floor, trembling with fear, two Germans drinking milk at Dimnik's and shot in the field, blood flows from their jackets, milk drips from their bellies. The women from the Vivodas' farm, chased into the forest, deported to Ravensbrück and to Auschwitz. Remained in Auschwitz, Klari. And again cows confiscated in Vellach, the whole family in the bunker, their grandfather with a gunshot wound in the stomach, their father turned gray with the partisans, lost his hair almost over night. Torture in Burggasse in Klagenfurt, others are forced to listen, to get them to betray where the rest are, passersby who spit on the prisoners being taken to the train station or back to the prison. Marija, proud Marija, for whom Mother's skill as a seamstress is no help, the embroidered aprons she receives as gifts at Christmas or Easter. She believes the men who claim they know her brother Johan, the first partisan, Kadrovec the Green, they want to rejoin him, they need her to help them. She helps them, she believes the renegade fighters who claim to know so much, she trusts them completely until the sitting room at the Golob farm fills with neighbors and activists, until she realizes they're surrounded by the Gestapo, who arrest her, and the jails in Klagenfurt and Begunje fill up. A good haul, right into the net, in Zell a list of sympathizers is found, both local and from the surrounding area, punitive action is taken. Marija, the serene beauty of the summer of '42, the unconscious beauty, beaten black and blue, before the Freisler tribunal, not a square inch of her skin unbruised, a silent body to whom chilly April brings death in 1943, the ax decapitates her, her brother follows her in death, in the Vienna Civil Court. The family torn apart, the mother sent to Ravensbrück, the father to Stein an der Donau, all that's left is the rosary from the camp, the beads that glide through fingers are formed from dried chewed bread. The war has shredded all the brothers, too. And Jurij from Lobnik Valley, who, before his decapitation in Vienna, stitched in his handkerchief the words I wait, I believe, I hope, I love – *čakam, verujem, upam, ljubim*. Two partisans in the Bistričniks' sitting room, the house surrounded by the police, the aunt shot dead before the door, behind the house a dead resistance fighter whom they had tortured at the neighbors', the partisans' corpses, naked and disfigured, for whom graves are dug under the spruce trees, on the far side of the fields, at the edge of the forest. The graves in the snow and the putrid corpses. Blood in the lower cellar, brains spattered over the turnips, blood on the shelves, the bellowing farmhand, beaten to death by partisans. The Piskernik girls, whimpering before the secret partisan court sentences them to death, the deserter, Franz, shot by partisans in the Hrevelnik bunker. The three Blajs brothers, Jakob, Filip, and Janez, who treat a wounded partisan, are arrested by the Gestapo, and whose ashes return to the orphaned farm. Escape after arrest, the many varieties of escape.

Johan Hojnik escaped after his arrest, his grandfather, father, and mother, killed by the police, shot dead, he saw the bloodbath with his own eyes, the bodies on the manure pile, burned. Paula fled after her arrest, after her father was tortured to death in the Gestapo prison in Klagenfurt, dead of a ruptured bladder, of kidney failure; fled after her mother gave birth in Aichach, a baby girl, a sweet thing, fled after the police confiscated thirty head of sheep, twelve head of cattle, and two horses, escaped on the way to prison as her brothers Josef and Jakob would later, or rescued at the last minute like Ivanka, Malka, Marija, and all the rest. That's how women become partisans. The children in the orphaned homes waiting for their parents to return, picking lice from their hair, their visits to the prison, their begging, their pleading, their tears. Children who no longer recognize their mothers after they return from the camps, the strange, aged women, the peculiar, silent fathers. Bernarda Hirtl, born in Ravensbrück, survived. Thanks to Tinca, who brought the mother home with her five-month old child. The Peršmans' bodies, left to rot, moved days later to the Rastočniks' place, behind the stable, swarms of flies on the stinking coffins. No one is willing to dig graves for the family, only the parish priest, Father Zechner, digs tirelessly all night with Marta until others begin to mourn and to hope the nightmare will end, that this affliction will come to an end forever. The partisans hounded in the last winter of the war, victory almost within reach, no more *if* or *maybe*, they want to be supported, the saddle must be brought out, the bull butchered, bread baked, the cows milked, dough-nuts filled, laundry cleaned, a dance organized, victory is certain, death is certain, all-pervasive suspicion reigns, each suspects the other, inter-rogations of supposed informers, secret execution squads, shovels and spades, the trigger-happy commander.

The miserable life of a fighter, constant hunger, disgusting raw meat that cannot be cooked because a fire would betray them, no milk, no vegetables, oozing wounds, the cold, the filth. He could only bear it all because he knew he was fighting the destroyers, Tine says, because of the confidence that they were fighting the Nazis, that they were doing something to resist their "total war." Three years a partisan, three years fighting the Nazis, no one can tell him anything on this front. It gives him strength in times of doubt, nothing more, nothing else.

How do the survivors return after the end of the war? Illegally, fleeing from the farthest corners of the continent? Do they emerge from the forests and camps and make the trek home alone or in groups? They approach their plundered, ruined, or burned down homes cautiously. Still fleeing, still feeling they are doing something wrong? Are they the victors or the vanquished? Will they remember the names of the dead or would they rather forget them? Will they find words for their suffering, which should be victorious but instead brings desolation?

They sense that others will come and occupy the space of their experience, others who can tell a more coherent story, while they only have sparse and scattered fragments. They sense that among them, among the survivors and the victors there will still be winners and losers. They sense that they will have to rein in their hope, that it will suffice only to make ends meet, no more than that.

The British will search their homes for weapons and propaganda, because former partisans in their families could threaten the border with demands for an annexation to Yugoslavia.

Yesterday's allies become adversaries. The Slovenian Communists will separate the wheat from the chaff among the fighters, he's one of ours, they'll say, but he is not, this one is a dedicated fighter, that one is not, that one hesitates, doesn't trust us, this one believes. The Austrian Communists will exclude Slovenian Titoists from the Party, the Church will threaten the partisans' families with excommunication and at Mass will tell them to their faces that there is no place for them in church as long as they believe in the partisans. Mobs will attack the first Slovenian cultural events. Regional authorities in Carinthia will open investigations into whether or not the partisans committed murder and who had denounced, arrested, and killed opponents of the partisans of the war, but nothing more, nothing else interests them, there is nothing else they want to expose, investigate, remember. They spread a cloak of silence over the rest. Those are private matters.

Is the plunder divided up in peacetime? In peacetime must one be afraid of losing one's reason, of turning away a friend and embracing an enemy?

The hesitant, the cautious, the wounded, the horrified, the silent, the distraught will all be at a disadvantage. The politics that brought about the war will deny them compassion. Those wounded on many levels will trail behind. So as not to provoke the majority of its citizens, the

Nazi sympathizers and the German-nationals, the new Austrian state will distrust those who fought against National Socialism. Because, it is argued, what is dubious about their resistance is not that it was directed against the Nazis, what is objectionable about it is that it allowed them to form their own opinions about the Slovenian community's role in Carinthia's future, opinions that then had to be respected during the negotiations for the Austrian state treaty, that's all we need, a law giving generous protection to a minority as a countermove to Yugoslavian territorial claims, according to the wishes of the occupying powers! And all the while, Austria had nothing to do with the Nazis, Austria itself was a victim, didn't understand what was happening, didn't join in, it wasn't even a country in that difficult time. No one in this country so gifted in dissimulation ever welcomed the Nazis, no one longed for the Greater German Reich, no one made themselves guilty, no one assisted the Final Solution, they just took part a little bit in the shooting, the assassinations, the gassing, but that doesn't count, nothing counts.

Politics believes the language of war. The politically engaged Slovenians will look at the non-political without comprehension, because they were the ones, after all, who fought for their rights, because they themselves took on the task of being identifiable, of being vulnerable to attack, of being a buffer. They sought refuge in action while those who were beaten down remain silent and refuse to understand why their fight for survival should become a pretext for the victory of an ideology. The revolution: an empty promise.

Properties are only gradually freed from the war's clutches. The meadows and fields slowly become willing to give up their dead, the edges of the forest and its clearings to eject their corpses. The meadows will have incubated the dead that nested in them like strange, blackened caterpillars. The fox will no longer be able to gnaw on the legs of the hastily buried. The strips of land along the forest edge will once again be left undisturbed, the meadows will be nothing more than meadows, the fields simply fields. The sheltering landscape will finally have had enough of those using her to hide, it will expose its mountainsides and stretch its bare slopes towards the sun. The landscape's silence will herald peace for its inhabitants. It will no longer put them to flight, except with rain and cold. The inhabitants will return to the fields and meadows. They will repair the fences and sow seeds, they will replant the shady slopes and thin out the forests. They will regain their foothold on the steep hangs, the dark hollows, the hospitable clearings. They will go back to work in the count's forests and repair their homes. The forests will take a long time to banish their ghosts because in the forests blood will continue to flow from wounds inflicted on the woodsmen by saws and axes, by falling branches, by tree trunks sliding into the valley – gaping wounds from which blood will flow unlike the exploding wounds caused by bullets and hand grenades. The blood, pulsing, spurting from the fighters' veins, to the rhythm of their heartbeat, the pus, the fragrant scent of fresh game, the smell of mushrooms and mold, the forest's coolness, its generosity, the forest can still be benevolent. It can still spread its branches over man and animal, can let exhausted creatures sleep on its branches, it can lay its boughs over the graves of those shot or hunted down and can offer its twigs as a last mouthful. It can keep the peace while roe deer and stags are gutted on the forest floor. The forest cannot weep or moan, the trees only divulge their memory when they are felled. Their memory is kept hidden in their growth rings, in their deformations and burls. The forest grows slowly and with the trees' long breath it grows from the past into the present, but still it grows.

Many survivors will abandon their homes and farms. They will no longer want to cultivate their land because they have been marked by the war. They will starve their memories of the war with silence. They will fear being recognized as the wounded and the beaten because that could deepen their shame. Years later they will be afraid of describing their persecution by the Nazis to the former Sturmbahnführer SA, currently an extreme right politician, psychiatrist, and official advisor to the local government. They will be unwilling to submit to the belated examination of victims by their former enemies. The meaning of it all will be lost with the passage of time. Their experiences will be strewn about like garbage, waiting for the proper context. It will be destroyed.

The others who cannot forget and who will search for meaning in their experiences, will experience defeat. They will not be able to find peace in their own country, knowing that they did what was right. They will be called into question, they will call themselves into question, no one will come to their defense. They will wonder why the Slovenian language always provokes violence. A people welded together and torn apart by suffering. Few will wonder if they betrayed another intentionally or by mistake, out of stupidity or carelessness, out of injured pride or revenge. Many will be consumed with the question of who denounced them, who sent their families into the abyss, and all will sense that suffering cannot be overcome by suspicion and speculation, that it's better to suppress the shadows of war, to thwart them with marriages and family ties. Life must go on somehow.

They will pull themselves together, they will celebrate weddings and come together in new families, they will not be able to put mistrust behind them, after the war they will let themselves be persuaded to demonstrate for more justice, for more bread, and for Josip Broz-Tito. In Eisenkappel, they will clash with German speakers, fists will fly, sticks will be brandished, men and women will come to blows. The people from the valleys will swallow the rejection, they will return to their houses and barns, they will never trust anyone. They will never again let politics near, never let politics threaten or murder them. They will wait until their homeland, their country, which abandoned them in their time of greatest need, finally welcomes them, finally mourns their murdered and their dead, finally recognizes their names and shares their sorrow, finally honors their resistance. They will wait for decades. They will note how slowly the wheels of justice turn in this country, how sedately the government agencies move, how negligently and reluctantly traces of the Nazis are erased, but above all, do not rush, do not be conspicuous, so that everything can recover its old beauty, so that nothing will have been, so that nothing will recall the Nazis.

They will notice that the destruction, although vanquished and subdued, gives rise to strange blooms, reinvents itself, blossoms unnoticed, and cannot give up its fantasies of death. The most insignificant people will succumb to its charms and will shoot or hang or douse themselves with gasoline and set themselves alight. Their families will puzzle over who has sown this despair among them, who has left such darkness inside them. They will bow down before the irrevocable, fathers will beat their sons, the sons will despise their fathers, husbands will forbid their wives to speak.

The properties invaded by the cold will begin to crumble, but those who have left are unable to leave their fear behind. They will dream of small, modest joys, of the opportunity to find work and rest, of earning enough to get by, of marrying, of raising children. They will feel as if they have finally escaped the unhappy times. Only now and then will they be caught short by pictures of parents deceased or killed, by flashes of memory that strike them to the core. They will have a sense of being brushed by ghosts, of needing to close the curtains and sit down, after a time they will rise numbly and open the window to take in the world, to delight in the passersby, in the houses and flower-covered balconies, in the streets or in the stillness of their rooms. They will feel overcome by the present and will store their wounded faces in a box, will pack them away with the faded photographs, and will don their Sunday faces radiating confidence.

FATHER will take up the challenge and will return to his parents' home. With Grandfather's help, he will replace the windows and doors, the roof. He will put the first animals in the orphaned stall. The war will have transformed him. At twelve, he will have the feeling of being on intimate terms with violence and the fear of death. He will wake up screaming at night. He will hear Grandfather's curses, and when the partisan officials stop in to persuade Grandfather to send his boy to school, Father will refuse to go. He will be able to work in the forest with his father. At fifteen, he will cut a gash in his knee with an ax and on his way home, alone, will faint several times and almost bleed to death. He will lie in the hospital for weeks and, immobile in his cast, will be tossed out of bed by a boisterous fellow patient. His parents will give him new clothes. His new suit will not go with his clunky, hobnailed shoes. He will learn how to play the clarinet and will perform for weddings. He'll be the life of the party, as they say, will buy himself a motorcycle and a leather jacket with the first money he earns and will use the motorcycle to go to the Slovenian agricultural school in Föderlach, after all. He will go to school and write papers on crop cultivation and animal husbandry and forestry.

He will perform in plays, he'll stand on the stage in the rectory and mimic an innkeeper wearing a false moustache and a white apron, he'll play a police officer who doesn't threaten him. He doesn't know if he's any good at theater, he will say right after he's brought the house down yet again, after he has slept off a binge.

He will get his hunting license and will no longer go poaching in the local hunting grounds. He will fall in love and want to marry the young Karla. We need a good worker on the farm, Grandmother will say, because it's time to pass it on. On his wedding day, he will feel the cold rise within, the paralysis that had gripped him as a child, the sense of alienation, the fear of being one of two, of three, or of four. He will have the feeling he has married a servant who is incapable of helping him, he won't rejoice as he did on the day of their engagement, won't invite his wife to dance, won't seek her out when she locks herself in the bathroom and weeps. He will want to hurt her, to push her away, from the very beginning, so that everything will stay the way it is, so that his wife will learn despair and her love be put to the test. He will work in the neighbors' woods to earn some extra income, for years he'll spend the cold winters dragging logs with his horse from the Count's forests. He will watch his children playing and not know if he should fear them or cherish them.

He will sit with the neighbors and tell them stories, how he stepped on a wasps' nest, how he fell out of the pear tree, how a splinter of wood hit him in the eye, how his hunting dog caught a badger, how a fox plundered his hen house, how he hid the dead hares from the hunters, how he escaped a horned viper, how a wild sow blocked his path, how lightning struck the fir trees, he will tell them about the wood grouse he hit and the enormous stag he missed. He will plant his fruit trees, as he learned, in places sheltered from the wind and will track the streams of cold air. He will prune the apple trees to help them form beautiful crowns. He will graft new shoots onto cherry and pear trees, he will store the prepared branches, bound in cloth, in the cellar and, in the spring, he will cut and graft them onto the stock. After spreading sealing compound over the clefts and binding them with cloth, Father will talk to the trees and encourage them to accept the scions. He will decide the layout of the fields, haul out the manure, and plow them. He will rub the earth between his fingers to see if it's too moist or too dry, if the soil will crumble or break into clods. He will draw straight furrows with the reversible plow and will call out to those manning the winch to tell them when to turn the motor on or off. He will harrow and sow the seeds, he will reap the grain and bind it in sheaves. Later, he will stop raising grain and will let clover take over his fields, he will sell his horse and buy a tractor, he will check on the gestations of his three cows by touching and palpating them, he and Mother will watch over the calving cows all night, he will spread clean, dry hay on the ground and wait for each calf's front feet, its head, and will go get Pepi if the head does not appear and the calf is turned upside down. He will wipe mucus from the newborn calf's muzzle. He will slaughter two pigs each year, dazing the animals with a stunbolt gun, then cutting their throats and collecting the blood in a pan so it can be taken to the kitchen. He will scrape the pigs' skin, will hoist them up by their hind legs, cut off their heads, slit open their stomachs, pull out the entrails, hang the intestines and the serous membrane on a hook, saw the animal in two, and pat the animal from top to bottom, praising it all the while. He will carry the intestines to the stream in a wheelbarrow, where they will be washed clean, scraped with a piece of wood until they are translucent, the light-colored tripe then placed in the white bucket, a viscous rope. He will take the animal turned meat to an unheated room and will cut it into pieces. He will pat the layer of fat, the shoulders, the back, he will caress its stomach, what a fine animal, what good meat. He will add his special seasoning to the cut and ground meat, hoping his sausage will be good this year, that his ham will delight the palette. He will distill his plum schnapps, day and night he will feed the fire heating the still full of mash, he will control the cooling, will taste the distillate, will keep his eye trained on the fire for the second round, so that the middle step, the very heart of his passion for distilling schnapps, will proceed slowly. He will carve the number of liters into the stillhouse wall with a knife. He will build wooden fences and gates, he will mow the grass and bring in the hay. He will repair his tools, replace the handles of his pitchforks, cut the wooden tines for the rake with a spokeshave, on his carpenter's bench he will sand planks and baseboards, spread glue on the edges, he will sharpen his scythes. He will build a house.

His work done, he will cross the courtyard and sit down on the front doorstep or will nod off at the kitchen table. He will feel worthless and deprived of speech. His headaches and stomachaches will turn him into a groaning body that gets in its own way and would like to get rid of itself.

He will watch his children, he won't push them to work, won't issue a single order, now and then he will ask them to do something, he will leave the commands to his wife, he will delight in their efforts, will resign himself to their stubbornness, he won't take them seriously, will court their affection, and will believe them lost because of their youth. He will lose confidence and be happy when anyone is friendly towards him, he won't forget any act of kindness, will be astonished by it, and will be touched by any show of helpfulness and respect.

He will believe in death because death, like violence, can change everything. He will want to throw his life out of the window, as he will put it, let's throw ourselves out the window, clear out, let's laugh, drink, work ourselves to death. What could possibly happen when he climbs up on his tractor, dead drunk, and drives away, when he tries to pull logs through an impassable section of the mountainside with a cable attached to his tractor and the front wheels lift, so what if he uses the circular saw with only one good eye? When will they finally feel sorry for him, when will they appreciate all he does?

If only he didn't suffer from this inertia which takes more effort every year to overcome. He can't move, he doesn't know how to beat the resistance within, the torpor that holds him captive. How do you withstand the deterioration you bring on yourself, the withering of the body?

As soon as his strength begins to wane, withered branches start to appear on the fruit trees, their crowns thicken, the new shoots wither, the number of animals in the stable dwindles, the fields he had been leasing are reclaimed by the owner. As soon as he gives up his work in the forests, the farmers' felling strips turn into clear cut slopes, on which the logging seems more like pillaging.

He will give up hunting, unable to keep up with the young ones or hit the prey having only one good eye. His bee colonies become infested with mites, the floors of the bee-houses are littered with legs of bees, bits of wax, mutilated insects. He will take the bees one by one and will scrape the mite larvae from their crumpled wings, an abdomen will detach from a thorax.

One summer day, he will finally lay his resolve as a farmer to rest. I will spend that Sunday with him.

HIS favorite cow was about to calve. He and Mother could not agree when the animal should be brought down from the summer pastures and housed in the stable.

On that Sunday morning, he wants to check on her but can't find her. He calls and paces up and down the pasture, he notices that the fence has been torn down near a steep, dangerous drop, the grass and bushes are matted down, he calls to me to come with him. We have to go down, he says, the cow might have fallen into the gulch when the labor pains set in. We slide down the steep slope, holding onto the hazel bushes and rampant goat's beard, and find the cow lying in the stream, its legs folded underneath it, the calf protruding half way out of its vagina, cold and lifeless, drowned on its way into life, the mucus washed away by the cold water, its slippery coat ashen, drenched. Father groans and pulls the dead calf out of the cow. How long has she been lying in the water, he laments, how long. The animal tries to stand up and looks at us pitifully. Father wraps his arm around the cow's neck. Stand up, stand up, he begs the animal and it rears up, but its feet and fetlocks collapse. She has a fever, Father says, we have to get Pepi and pull her from the water.

When Pepi arrives with his tractor and realizes he and Father won't be able to pull the cow from the streambed alone, more neighbors are called to help. Father stands with his shoes in the stream, soaked to his knees and shivering. I lay my forehead on the cow's face and see faint white steam rising from its trembling back. Its eyes emit such a profound creaturely sorrow, the men will not look at the animal because the sight will remind them of something they cannot bear at this moment.

I stumble home and return to the scene of the accident with rubber boots for Father. In the meantime, the men have tried to get the cow onto its feet, but its injuries from the fall are too serious. Pepi says they will have to shoot her, there's nothing else they can do. Father blows his nose into his handkerchief. He's weeping. Go get your gun, let's get it over with quickly, he asks of Pepi and lays his hand on the cow's curly forehead.

Pepi gets his rifle and when he's standing in the water he says to Father that calving cows cannot die, he really doesn't want to do this, only out of friendship will he take care of it, though it's unbearable.

I turn away, I don't want to see any more.

Right after, they haul the dying cow out of the water with the tractor and drag it to the street, the dead calf and afterbirth are placed beside it, and a tarpaulin is spread over this misery.

The men go home.

Father says he doesn't want to do this anymore, he will never forgive Mother for leaving the cow in the pasture so long, even Pepi had wept when he had to shoot the cow.

It's already dark when Mother arrives home. She gets off her moped and hurries into the kitchen. She saw the dead cow and the calf on the side of the road and stopped, she says, panting, she called the cow's name and the animal lifted its head and looked at her, Good Lord, she saw a ghost, Mother continues, her heart shrank, how could this happen!

As my parents' argument swells, I leave the house.

I drive slowly down the access road.

The property has plunged into darkness. The forest seems to be slipping into the depths, the rushing of the stream is interspersed with tiny needles that prick my ears. When I pass the covered cow, I stop but do not get out of the car.

At night I dream that the valleys and slopes are turned inward towards the mountain's core, like the lining of a coat. The darkness that surrounded me on the way to town persists in the mountains. Daylight is concentrated in small suns, which, as I am aware, occasionally bathe everything in a glittering light and then retreat. They hang in the firmament like weightless yellow balls. I'm in a hurry to get home because something terrible has happened. I know that mother is in the sitting room and could help me. I want to find her and yank open the door. A horrifying creature lunges at me, half-girl, half-lizard. I fling it against the side of the house, against the cliffs, against the mountain. I call for Mother, but she remains distant. When I can no longer move my feet, I start to hover and float into the void.

MY parents decide to sell their last cow. Father comes down with pneumonia and does not leave the house for two weeks. It has all hit him to the marrow, Mother says. They have decided to stop raising animals, they have to stick to the most essential, to what they can still manage, she says.

Father's lungs are slowly deteriorating and his weight dwindles along with his breath. After he has recovered from the bout of pneumonia, his upper body resembles a beetle's carapace, from which protrudes a head drawn in between his shoulders and two arms and two legs similar to an insect's slender limbs. Father's fragile rib cage presses against his crooked spine like a wicker basket. His steps grow shorter and slower. The lines in his face are rough furrows. Bones are Father's most striking feature, his knobby knees, his thin, sinewy forearms, his exhausted fingers. The distances he is still able to cover grow shorter and his outings less frequent. He hesitates for a long time before gathering his strength to go into the forest to chop firewood, repair a fence, or drive the sheep that have replaced the cows into their pens. Before long he needs to stop and rest in the middle of the courtyard when he goes to get his hard cider from the cellar or to check on his ailing bee colonies and he has to double over because he's lost his breath. We try to persuade him to carry the portable oxygen tank, to which he is hooked up in the evening, since it would make it easier for him to walk, but he refuses to give in to his weakness, as if it were beneath his dignity. Sometimes, when he feels ill, he holds on to one of the plum trees that border the courtyard.

In the penultimate year of his life, Father receives a payment from the newly founded Austrian National Fund for Victims of National Socialism, a symbolic reparation. Most of all, he is pleased that his suffering has been recognized. He wants to use the money to fix the tractor, he says. If he puts it off much longer, the tractor will die before he does.

In the spring, he makes his last careful attempts to prune the apple tree and remove the branches broken under the weight of the snow. He is like a wizened child who would like to spend the entire day up in a tree, but has to climb down the ladder so as not to risk a fall. In early summer, he must admit defeat and stay in bed. He is hooked up to a breathing device. Without oxygen he can just barely manage to go to the toilet or take a bath. Mother and my brother have moved his bed to the sitting room so he can take part in daily life and visitors can comfortably sit with him and not have the feeling they are in a sick room. Medications pile up on the side table Mother has placed next to his bed. Father abhors being taken care of by Mother, but Mother has decided she will nurse him. Whether or not he wants her to, whether or not she wants to, she believes it is her duty to endure the closeness necessitated by his illness.

Father suffers a great deal. His face is slightly swollen from the medication, his hands, in contrast, have become softer and more delicate. When he sits up in bed, he looks at us like someone who is smiling as he drowns, holding his head above water in the certainty that he will soon go under. He doesn't want to sign over his property, he's at a loss, he says in response to my urging, he sees no future for his holding and doesn't want to think about the decline of his farm. It's up to us to work out an agreement after his death.

He begins to take an interest in my work and asks questions, what it is I do in the theater, what does a dramaturge do, he asks if I earn enough money, if the public in Carinthia likes our work. Once he informs me that he watched a production of *Nabucco* on television. A broadcast from the National Opera, Father says, the National Opera in Vienna! In one scene, photographs of murdered Viennese Jews were held up on signs. He thought that was a good idea, just think, Viennese Jews, he says.

When we sit around the old farm table on Sundays and spoon up our noodle soup, he looks at us, shakes his head and says with feigned seriousness, you're all half-wits, a bunch of half-wits! Our soup spoons pause in the air for a moment. I can't help but guffaw, which particularly pleases him, all the more since it makes Mother grimace.

Father only becomes lively when his cousins visit. He even lets his careless relatives persuade him to play the accordion, which completely exhausts him. But what won't we do to cheat illness a bit, he tells himself, even if all that's left of him after the exuberant celebration is a pained grin which he forces himself to maintain with great effort. He can no longer play cards, but he likes to watch his sons and neighbors play. On weekends he asks Bertl, his successor in hunting, to tell him what's new in the hunting ground, what animals have been seen leaving the forest to graze, or what they plan to do to contain the game browsing.

One day Father's cousin Kati comes to visit. She is preparing a song recital with Mother. The women created a duo to present their own poems set to music, Marian songs, and partisan songs.

Like Kati, Mother has begun setting her poems to music and dreams of publishing them in a book. I'd like to have my own book someday, she says, pushing a few of her texts or poems across the table for me to read.

When I ask Father how he's doing that day, he says, how do you think I'm doing? I've been listening to those two women practicing next to me for two hours. It's not exactly uplifting.

With your voices, you're going to scare away the audience, he sneers. After such howling, the crowd will have thinned out. Enough out of you, button your lip, Kati tells him. Shall we sing something for you?

Yes, Father says impishly, he'd like to hear Katrca's song again. The women stand at the foot of his bed and start singing: *Pihljaj vetrič mi hladan doli na Koroško plan, tam, kjer dom moj prazen zdaj stoji, hiti tja oj vetrič ti! Ne bom njegovega več vinca pil, v njegovi senci se ne bom hladil, njegove njive ne bom več oral, le nesi zadnji mu pozdrav! Ko boš izpolnil mojo mi željo, takrat, o vetrič, mene večne bo. Življenje svoje sem že dokončal. Bom v tuji zemlji mirno spal.* Oh, dear cool breeze, blow towards the fields of Carinthia, where my house stands empty, alas, hurry, dear breeze. Never again will I drink wine, never again will the shadow of my house cool me, never again will I plow my field. Carry my final greeting with you! As soon as you have granted me my final wish, dear wind, I will be no more. I will have ended my life and will lie at peace in foreign ground.

Father is satisfied. After sitting down, Kati says she always gets tears in her eyes when she sings that song because it makes her think of Katrca and of her dead mother, Urša, who was Katrca's sister. Before Katrca died, she had sent the poem from the Ravensbrück concentration camp with the request that Urša set it to music so it wouldn't be forgotten. Her mother composed a melody for the poem, Kati explains. She set many poems to music, mostly her own. And yet her mother couldn't even write, she was illiterate. She composed the poems in her head while working in the fields all day and then dictated them to her husband in the evening. That's how her plays, stories, and poems came to be. Her mother was the real poet in the family, a better poet than she herself is, Kati says, that much she has to admit, though she has written a lot recently.

Our family is a poet's nest, it's enough to make you lose your mind, Father says giving Mother and me a mischievous look. In our family it's like the annual fair, one poet after another, you can barely escape all the poems. Besides, he wrote a poem himself, when he was twelve years old, with the partisans. He can remember one stanza, Father says: *Ko pasel sem jaz kravce, je prišel policist, v oreh me je obesil in mislil, da sem list.* As I was taking the cows to pasture, a policeman came and hung me from the walnut tree. He thought I was foliage. Father sits on his bed and grins.

IN late autumn, Father's body is caught in a vice of pain that squeezes him mercilessly. His struggle to live frays our nerves. We can hardly bear the thought of his suffering and we start to resent the family doctor who stops by regularly for not being able to alleviate his pain. Father absolutely refuses to go to the hospital, he wants to die at home, that is his express wish, he tells us. By now he can barely move, can hardly sit up anymore. He must relieve himself lying down. He's not happy about it, but now and then he has to groan loudly, he says, the pain is too great. Every touch is torture and our helpless hands that want to soothe him are a punishment.

Relatives and neighbors come to visit, saying they want to chat with him. They bring wine because Father once said that he'd like to drink a glass or two every day. It's necessary, he claims. More than anything, he'd like to drink a whole bottle of plum schnapps, if he were certain he could handle it.

I very much want Father to be able to die at peace, but he is far from reconciled to what's coming. I even imagine that he's asking for help when he looks at me. One day he says, in my room there's a notebook of Mici's in my night table drawer. Take it. It's for you. I stop myself from asking if the thought that he might have betrayed Mici when the police were beating her up has been tormenting him. He has never spoken of Mici, but he kept the notebook. Why do I not ask? Does his agitation have something to do with Mother, with whom he has had a marriage filled with rancor and strife? Would he like to reconcile with her and does he lack the energy to do so? Is his fear a last rebellion against the loss of life that he experiences as a pitiful remnant within or is there something unspoken, something older that's choking him? I will never know.

On January 3rd, on his birthday, we will drink a glass of wine with Father.

Three days later, his face will turn pale and bloodless. He will tell me that yesterday, on his name day, his cousins had come to visit. They had laughed and sung, it was a circus, he says. The celebration wore him out so completely, he'll probably die. In the meantime, I should go and look at how many bottles of wine were given as gifts. I go to the backroom and count the bottles. Thirty-three, I say. Well, I'll have to live a long while yet, Father says with a forced smile.

The next morning, my brother calls to tell me Father is dead. He passed away in the early morning hours.

When I arrive home, Father is laid out on the sickbed in his black suit. Mother washed and dressed his body. She stands up from the sick bed when I enter the room and she gestures towards him with her hand. Here he is, she says, weeping. He has finished with it all.

The community gives us permission to lay Father out at home. A last exception.

When the casket is delivered, Pepi comes and pauses on the doorstep to recite an ancient farewell prayer, which he is now the last to know. Pepi helps my brother set up the trestles for the bier under the south-facing windows in the sitting room. Father is laid in the casket and lifted onto the bier. I comb his hair for the last time. Touching his head, it feels like I am caressing a stone. Mother interlaces Father's fingers and places a cross in his folded hands.

The casket with the corpse is bathed in a white, winter morning light. The sitting room is like a wide ship drifting slowly on the open sea: the glittering light, the muted sounds of daily life, the whispering in the kitchen, the silent weeping, the sunlight reflected on the snow, the brownish violet spots on Father's forearms, the white of the shroud, the crocheted lace border, the open door, the whining of the dog on its chain outside that has caught the scent of death, the unhurried movements, the open tenderness, long desired and no longer willing to be masked.

The room is not yet filled with mourners, with flowers or wreaths or candles, we still have time to draw the deceased near in order to release him again. No one knows when he or she will take leave of the deceased, but they each engage in this hidden act. I use the pauses between prayers and the hours in which only one or two mourners linger in the room to observe Father's lifeless form, his milky yellow skin, his sunken eyes. He seems to have frozen in his last moment and to have been seized with fear. He looks as if he were holding in his last breath, as if he had frozen this breath, put it aside, retaining it for later, for some other time.

Over the next two days, people stream into the house to say goodbye to Father. We are busy serving the visitors, who in turn help us keep our countenance.

On the evening before the burial, Mother sits next to me by the casket. She places her hand on my thigh without a word and leans her shoulder against mine, a sisterly gesture. Has she returned to me as a sister, I wonder, and I try to give her a hug. It's all fine, I say when she stands up and returns to the kitchen.

The day of Father's funeral, the pallbearers come at an early hour. They are the hunters from Lepena. We share some soup near the deceased whose casket has been closed. Pepi recites the ancient prayer again. The coffin is lifted out through the living room window and is laid on the doorstep. The deceased is encouraged to take leave of his home and his family. With slow steps, they carry him across the courtyard and again he's encouraged to bid farewell to his fields, pastures, and slopes.

As the gravediggers lower Father into the pit after Mass and the coffin is laid in the ground, I believe I hear an exhalation that comes either from me or from the casket. An exhalation emitted straight from a small, dark throat and echoing far and wide. Shocked, I look into the grave. Is it my breath or Father's, is it my relief that I finally have his loss behind me or is it Father's blocked, conserved, gagging breath now drawing in air, finally released from any restraints and floating away?

So be it, so be it, I think on the drive back to the city.

I DREAM that the region I am fleeing is frozen. The sky is a glacier in which the valley appears like a mirage. Fissures of light streak through the frozen surface like crystalline borders. A frozen carapace of air has enclosed the valley beneath it and is constricting it. Crabs, snails, jellyfish, leeches, worms, and mottled amphibians crawl across the surface of the ice. The water that has lain like a coat of crystal over the hills, the trees, and the properties, that nestled, supple and light, protectively against everything, now begins to move. In the next moment, at the slightest breath of wind, I think, it will evaporate, blow away, scatter, and drain away. Nothing can remain the way it is.

Later I hear a rushing sound growing ever louder coming from the valley and suddenly I see the water beginning to rise. I say to my brother, come on, we have to go, we have to leave the house! We hurry to the forest, above the slope with the old plum trees, as we did when Father chased us with his shotgun. We watch the house fill with water, we hear the orebodies collapse deep within the massive mountain. The mineral deposits are used up, nothing more will be extracted, the tunnels are flooded. Then the water drains away and we return to our home. Water stains and smears of dirt line the walls, the flood has left its mark. The windows are closed and the panes of glass intact. I am amazed that the windows could withstand the mass of water and tell my brother, we have to clean up, we have to clean it all up!

AFTER Father's funeral, my mind sinks into a stupor.

Standing by his grave, I return to the familiar silence, to the leaving of things unsaid that had always characterized our conversations.

At home we sit across from one another, each of the siblings bearing the weight of their own father, each one with a father figure hanging around their neck and we stare at each other, tired from carrying our father's weight, exhausted by the stories and the memories that always sound like reproaches when we recount them to each other, you have no idea what Father and I, and so on. And this, too, the various echoes and feelings, the different acts of rebellion, grief mixed with disappointment.

Mother has reached a nadir in her state of exhaustion that has lasted months, if not years, and she wanders through the house high-strung and irritable. She believes she has gotten through the worst, that she has reached an ending. She feels responsible for everything and is convinced that we, who have witnessed her efforts, don't appreciate them enough. She accompanied Father to his death. His last glance was directed at her, she says and shivers with horror at the thought of all that cannot be solved or expressed.

And I, child of my child-father, ridiculous, simply ridiculous to chain myself and my life to the past, to old suffering because of him, to jeopardize my life, and would like to leave it all untouched, to push away all that is repressed, all that obligates and burdens me. It should all be left undisturbed for a time, I decide, to age on its own.

But I am not left in peace. In forgetful Carinthia, I learn how to be unable to forget. The ground on which I stand must have an invisible underside that is saturated with what has been, from which I seem to grow and onto which I am always thrown back. Again and again, the region falls prey to a kind of vertigo in which it claims a version of history that is nothing more than a phantom justification through which it believes itself on the right side. All those crushed under the wheels of National Socialism are excluded from this self-image.

Now and then I flinch in my thoughts, it's all still present, I think, all of it. It's all festering inside me and around me, visible or invisible, audible or inaudible, as if I were a micro-organism, a spark of consciousness, a wheel that becomes a chain or bouncing ball, a field that blooms or disintegrates. I seem caught in the middle of an antagonism that Nazism and the resistance against it have created in the inhabitants of the region, an antagonism as absolute as pain. Only those who suffer this antagonism can feel it.

IN Father's night table drawer, next to his long unused clarinet, I find Mici's blue songbook and stored underneath it, my grandmother's stained, red camp notebook.

Stunned, I sit down on the bed. The small legacy weighs heavy in my hand. The exuberant Mici wrote Slovenian songs, poems, and letters in verse to her lover and to her aunts Katrca, Urša, Leni, Malka, and Angela in her small notebook, turning language into an exhilarating rush of sound, an uninterrupted song. It's the only thing left of her.

I start reading Grandmother's camp notebook, which I'd often held in my hands as a child.

Memories of Grandmother's room come flooding back, memories of the very particular milky light that transformed the incomprehensible things she was telling me into brief moments of intimacy that circled in the air like fine particles of dust and by the next night lay upon the objects in the room as if nothing had ever disturbed them.

At first Grandmother wrote in a firm hand, her words are awkward, not intended to be written down, but to be spoken. Although she can barely write – her sentences are neither grammatically nor syntactically correct – she must have been convinced her story had to be set down.

Je bilo u tork opoldne 12 Oktober je locitev od hise in od temalih Sinov Tonček in Zdravko. Toje bilo hudo zamene ker jas nisem kriva nic. It was midday on Tuesday, the 12th of October, the separation from my home and my two little boys, Tonček and Zdravko. It was hard for me because I'm not guilty, Grandmother writes.

She was held in the Eisenkappel jail for two hours, then taken to Klagenfurt, and after three weeks, at six in the morning on November 2nd, from Klagenfurt to Maribor. It was wonderful, *čudovito*, she writes, how children spat at us on the street and screamed terrible things. In Maribor, they were given a dinner of potatoes and turnips.

At three in the morning there was good coffee and good bread. We were allowed to take a slice of bread, a bit of soft cheese, and a spoonful of jam as provisions for the trip to Vienna. In Vienna, *Ven*, Grandmother writes, she had to sleep on a cement floor. The food was terrible, there was only potato soup, and no spoons, she had to fish out the pieces of potato with her fingers. After ten days, they went on to Prague, *Prak*, she writes, there they were plagued with bedbugs, the food was bad, there was no dinner, in the mornings just a bit of coffee, then on and on without food or water to Berlin. They were left for a night and a day with nothing to eat. It was good she was sick at the time, her throat hurt too much to swallow. Then they went on to Ravensbrück, there it was very strange, she writes, humans are not animals!

She has no words to describe all the unhappy things to come, she writes. She needs only three small pages for one and a half years in the concentration camp, then she writes *rajža*, the journey, on April 28th and means the beginning of the odyssey that would bring her back to Lepena months later. On May 14th, Mirow, the first place name before Wesenberg and Rheinsberg, written in a feverish script that betrays her excitement. She writes phonetically the names of the places where she stops on her way home or simply passes through. The longer her trip home lasts, the more disjointed the names become. She notes them down in the moving cattle car, later in the train compartment. The places of survival seem bombed out, just as the cities Grandmother had talked about must have looked. August 15th, Dresden, *Tresten*, Grandmother writes. After a few, barely legible names, Bratislava appears, spelled correctly, then Budapest, on August 24th, *Subotica*, we have been in the best of moods, she writes. There was much meat to eat and a lot of schnapps, spent the 25th in the baths and danced and celebrated all weekend. Later she writes *Belkad*, meaning Belgrade, beautiful city, Grandmother declares, on August 30th, a sad morning in the Zagreb train station, then *Vellenje* and *Slovenkrac* for Slovenian Gradec, then *Hrevelje* for the Hrevelnik property in Lepena. She closes the account of her travels with the half sentence, at home was the fear yes or no, *doma toje blo strah jabol ne*.

– 279 –

I place the photographs she left me on my desk. In her younger years, Grandmother's feelings burst out impetuously. She looks into the camera with the self-assurance of a wealthy farmer's daughter. The high spirits she controls with difficulty and her pride are almost tangible. In the 1920s, she wears bright-colored dresses and patterned shirts with collars completely trimmed with lace. After several miscarriages, she looks more serious and more plump. As a married woman, she wears dark dresses and cotton tights or an elegant suit with a leather bag, leather gloves and custom-made shoes on special occasions. In the summer, she tries to cover her thin hair with straw hats and to keep her severe face in the shadows, as she once told me. I was still proud, she'd said, but already aged from work, from the drudgery.

After the war, the glow of Grandmother's eyes is directed inward. Her smile looks tired, exhausted, never lively anymore. Her posture has lost its earlier confidence. The straw hats have been replaced by kerchiefs she ties precisely under her chin so the tips stick out stiffly from her neck. She is more than a little proud of her elegant scarves of gleaming viscose or silk. She has lost a great deal of weight and, since she is always cold, she wears a wool vest or a sweater under her clothes. On wedding pictures, with her angular face and her prominent, hooked nose amidst the happy group, she looks like a remnant of the past that refuses to fit in to the present. Her silhouette gives the impression that she has been expelled from life several times, but then was brought back after all and took up her life again, if not out of joy, then at least out of submissiveness, not from deep conviction, but from a sense of duty.

At home, Grandmother wears a cotton scarf tied at the nape, old clothes, wool tights, and patterned skirts that she replaces with black satin skirts and more elegant blouses only on Sundays and holidays. Earlier, I used to think I had to represent something, but later I felt like I'd been crossed out, she says. The photographs show Father's metamorphosis from a child to an adolescent. How his face changed after Grandmother's arrest and the police interrogation, how the childish aspect withdrew and turned into something bitter, hard, and obstinate, how the wound took root in Father and occupied his body like a parasite.

One day, I tell Tonči about Grandmother's camp book and my aimless wandering through the family's past. He is pleased to hear about it and brings me a file folder, mentioning that he believes Grandmother's papers belong with me.

Among the old bills and letters in the folder I find Grandmother's report card from the year 1914 which notes that she was excused from 256 half-days of lessons and had 23 unexcused absences. How many days did she even go to school? I find the ruling of the Klagenfurt Civil Court from December 1947 on the restitution of property confiscated by the German Reich to the legal owners, to my grandfather Michael, and beneath it Grandmother's Ravensbrück spoon and her *Certificate of Residence*, issued to her on the day of her forty-first birthday, September 6th, 1945, on her return from the concentration camp. There are also the letters from friends she had made in the camp, Grandmother's request for a victim's pension, the notification from the regional government of Carinthia informing her that the Carinthian Commission had denied her request on the grounds that the medical examination obtained could not establish damage to her health at the levels required to qualify; then Grandmother's appeal in response to the communication, formulated by someone who knew how to write, listing the conditions she suffers as a result of her incarceration in the camp, nervous disorders, shortness of breath, painful swelling of the legs and joints, leaving her unable to work for days at a time, debilitating headaches, severe menstrual cramps – she had already had to list all of these for the police department functionary who had drawn up the deposition, she notes, and I can imagine the situation in which Grandmother must describe her suffering to an indifferent official who doesn't understand Slovenian; the response from the Ministry of Social Affairs in Vienna, late May, 1951, that she has been granted a victim's pension; Grandmother's letter of November 6th, 1951, addressed to the office of Carinthian regional government, inquiring why her victim's pension is not being disbursed, a communication from November, 1953, addressed to the Carinthian regional government, asking why her officially awarded imprisonment compensation has not been paid, the answer from the Carinthian government that notice of compensation payment is effective beginning only in October 1953 and will not be sent to the National Ministry for Social Affairs for payment prior to that date, then, completely unexpectedly, the house blessing handwritten by my great-grandmother, a blessing so powerful it can protect those who dwell in the house from storms, from thunder and lightning, from hail and from fire, from curses, slander, and from the plague, but not from all the rest.

The protective barrier I tried to build between me and my family breaks down once again. For a moment, I'm afraid of being overrun by the past, of being crushed beneath its weight. I decide to put all these fragments – memories and family stories, what is present and what is absent – into written form, to reinvent myself from memory, to write myself a body composed of air and intuition, of scents and odors, of voices and sounds, out of things past and dreamt, out of mere traces.

I could recover what is irretrievable and establish that it has returned in a new form, that it has transformed itself and me. I could reassemble what has fallen or been torn apart to let what's underneath shine through. I could surround what has been with an invisible body that seals and subjugates it.

I DECIDE to go to Ravensbrück, to visit the camp I have so often crossed in my mind that I believe I know it. I want to walk through Grandmother's story one last time in order to take my leave of this familiar place.

On the day Grandmother was admitted to the concentration camp, I walk down the Street of Nations in Fürstenberg an der Havel, which leads to the camp.

The autumn landscape around me is unwelcoming, it seems to belong to the past and yet it's of the present, only of the present. I think how Grandmother's eyes might have scanned this landscape on the evening of November 13th. Did she have time to look around at her journey's destination, to take in the Brandenburgian, yellow-brown and gray autumn, the birch trees' yellow leaves hanging from the branches like colorful pennants?

After walking for a long time, the lake, Schwedtsee, flashes to my right, with its bare, motionless surface. The *Kommandantur* building suddenly appears before me.

The first view through the camp gate, the emptiness, the central square cleared of barracks, the black gravel, the rust-red foliage, the clean camp streets, a single poplar-lined boulevard.

The *Appellplatz*, the roll call square, looks smaller than I'd imagined, you can almost take it in with a single glance. As a child, when Grandmother would tell me about the camp, I pictured a large open space that extended to the horizon, a world of prisoners and dead bodies.

I circle the empty, level area of the service buildings. The bathhouses for the admittance procedure, now a patch of grass, the prisoners' kitchen, the *Appellplatz*, now covered with gravel, the place where the barracks stood, today just a lawn, blocks five to seven written on the plaque, block six, for political prisoners, a specter from Grandmother's story, stood in the center, behind a linden tree that was not there then. The Jewish block, eleven, next to block twelve, in the foreground was the infirmary, behind it the industrial buildings, the sewing shop. Neither visible nor accessible is the Siemens compound for *regular employment*, the men's camp, the tented area for those waiting for the gas chamber. What has been preserved is the brick-work trinity of death, the building containing the cells, now a museum, where Katrca's verses are displayed above the names of the Yugoslavian women who died in Ravensbrück, the crematorium and field of graves, the gas chambers marked with a memorial stone.

I could still hear Grandmother's breathing when she spoke. *Čudno, čudno*, all that can happen to people, she said.

In the archives, I find the list of the convoy that arrived the evening of November 13th, 1943, with my grandmother's name and prisoner number, the names of her neighbors, of Paula Maloveršnik, of the farming families Pegrin and Kach, of Maria and Anna Rotter, of Polish women, Jewish women, a Czech woman. I find the list from November 30th, 1943, the day when Mici was brought to Ravensbrück. She was brought with 64 women via Leipzig in *a special preventive detention convoy to Fürstenberg due to overcrowding of the Leipzig prison*. With her were women from Ličkov, Dnipropetrovsk, Krowno, Krasnodar, Kursk, Glauchau, Karlsbad, Wurzen, Kaliningrad, Prague, Ebensee, Vienna, Pörtschach, from Ebriach, from Lepena, from Koprein and Waidisch, Magdalena Kölich, the woman from the Mozgan farm, Maria Paul and her daughter Amalia Paul, Johanna Grubelnik from Ebriach. I find Malka assigned to block sixteen with the Polish women.

In Ravensbrück, the women from our valleys met women from all over Europe, from the Carinthian margins to a center of the war, where the lives of European women crossed, they were taken from remote Carinthia to a hot spot of death. What did the women from the valleys have in common with women from Poland and Czechoslovakia, and Jews from Italy, Romania, and Hungary, with women from France, Belgium, Russia and Ukraine, with Gypsies, with women from Croatia and Latvia, with Austrians and ethnic Germans in Eastern European countries, with women from Norway, Serbia, and Slovenia, from Holland and Denmark? What did they have to say to each other on leaving this place where they had grasped the magnitude of the war? I want to believe that the women of this camp had more in common than history written along national lines could ever dare conceive.

I leave the grounds of the camp. No sense of relief sets in as the gate of the *Kommandantur* swings shut behind me, I give no sigh, feel no consolation. It is the place that was at work inside Grandmother. She lived in its magnetic field and used it as a point of orientation. It defined her and held her feelings in its sway. And now the phantom fades behind me, a vanishing apparition, a fragile surface disintegrating at the edges, underneath which history turns dark, in which Grandmother's stories resound like echoes from a long lost time.

The angel of history will have flown over me. His wings will have thrown a shadow over the camp. I couldn't make out his horrified expression in the half-light, I just believed for a moment that I had heard the beat of wings, a gust of wind in his wings, in which are entangled the storms of what is to come.

For a moment I feel like a child who has been running to escape time, time that advances behind me like a silent glacier, that slides inexorably over all that has been, that buries, that crushes and grinds up all that seems inalterable. With each step, I move further into the present, I bump into myself, I can hear my voice, a voice I recognize, a voice that has not surfaced from the Babel of sentences for a long time, a voice that was keeping hidden.

The angel of oblivion must have forgotten to wipe the traces of the past from my memory. He led me through a sea in which vestiges and fragments were floating. He made my sentences collide against the drifting shards and debris, so they would be wounded, so they would become sharper. He finally removed the picture of the cherubs from above my bed. I will never meet this angel. He will remain formless. He will disappear into books. He will be a story.

AFTER many years, Grandmother returns to me in a dream. I was not expecting her and I feel I have been caught red-handed. She sits on the forest path behind our house and has woven the wool she'd spun into funnel-shaped canopies that look like dendrites and she is using them to catch voices. She tells me a few voices have already fallen into her net. You just have to be patient and not give up hope. The woven funnels are bigger than she is. I go up to her. She signals with her hand to let me know I shouldn't make any noise. Not so loud, she says, or you can't hear anything.